The Torch

Michael Huckabee

Writers Club Press
San Jose New York Lincoln Shanghai

The Torch

All Rights Reserved © 2000 by Michael Huckabee

No part of this book may be reproduced or transmitted in any form or by any means, graphic, electronic, or mechanical, including photocopying, recording, taping, or by any information storage or retrieval system, without the permission in writing from the publisher.

Published by Writers Club Press
an imprint of iUniverse.com, Inc.

For information address:
iUniverse.com, Inc.
620 North 48th Street
Suite 201
Lincoln, NE 68504-3467
www.iuniverse.com

Scripture taken from the *HOLY BIBLE, NEW INTERNATIONAL VERSION.* NIV. Copyright 1973, 1978, 1984 by International Bible Society. Used by permission of Zondervan Publishing House. All rights reserved. "My Jesus, I Love Thee" lyrics, public domain.

ISBN: 0-595-09625-5

Printed in the United States of America

For those who—when it's hard—still believe.

My thanks to those who shared the Russia experience: Mike Boldt, Grant Gustafson, Mike Leigh, Pastor Kevin Lund, Kelly McElvain, the late Doug Mills and his wife, Joyce, Pastor David Oldham, Traci Porter, Kevin Ray, and Gary Yost. And thanks to Rick Burke and Gary Adams for making it happen.

Also, I appreciate the support and friendship of those who saw this manuscript in development: Laurie Horn, Pastor Jeff McKearney, the late Bernie Palmer and his wife, Marge, Jean Huckabee, Cindy Hall, Michelle Brown, Bonnie Adams, Paul and Margaret Hensley, Marcia Claesson, Cheryl Rooney and Denise Lockard.

My greatest love goes to those who never stopped believing: Nancy, Tyler, Tanner, Bailey, and Emily.

Chapter 1

Flames chased the smoke rolling out of the fifth floor apartment window. Hot strikes of color bit into the cool night air without a witness. All of Bolshoigorsk slept, including the Slava Gdansk family.

The fire began near the front door and raced to the cramped kitchen, igniting greasy remains of fried potatoes and fish broth. Flames crept up tattered wallpaper, eating through the plaster wall to reach Slava and his bride of five years, Oksana, sleeping in the tiny bedroom's twin bed.

Across the hall, a fiery trail led to the larger bare-walled living room where a daybed cradled two boys—one two years old and the other almost five. The blaze swept to the boys' doorway, angry colors whirling in a crimson tornado about to touch down across the threshold.

A flare leaped into the room, erupting as it reached fresh air and combustible furniture. In seconds, sparks teased the blanket hanging to the floor of the boys' bed. Igniting the corner of a sheet, doom slithered toward its unknowing victims.

In their sleep the boys squiggled away from the glowing light, coughing on the dark smoke that replaced their air. The dull roar of the fire lulled their slumber.

It was time for Brael to get these people moving.

With supernatural speed he soared to the kitchen, the combustion ignoring the rush of his pure white gown. Through the inferno storming the wall to the bedroom he eyed a cupboard of glass cups and plates. Brael tore it from the wall, dishes shattering on the fiery floor.

* * * * *

What was that? Slava's mind groped in a sleepy delirium. *It's so stuffy.*

Throwing off the top blanket, he roused enough to realize he was gasping for air.

Choking in the dark, he glimpsed the dusty orange hues stealing around the doorway to his room.

"Fire!" he screamed in horror. "Oksana!" His wife stirred, then jolted awake. "Fire! I'll get the boys!"

Darting to the living room, he found his sons surrounded by lapping tongues of the blaze.

"Fire, Vladislav, fire!" he shouted to his oldest. The only response was a weak cough, the thin air robbing consciousness. Slava grabbed curtains from the far side of the room to flog the bed. "Wake up, Vlad! Fire, Andrei!"

Smoky fumes tightened around Slava's lungs. He exhaled heavily to make room for air, but the effort strangled him more. Scooping up his sons in the curtains, he heard weak, frightened cries mix with their coughs. "You must wake up!"

Tasting greasy charcoal smoke, Slava rushed through the flames huddling at the hall. His wife was at the door of their bedroom, hands over her mouth in a silent scream. She was but a shadow, the bright consuming flames thundering behind her.

"Here, take Andrei!" He handed her the whimpering two year-old. Adjusting his grip on Vladislav, he followed his wife out the burned hole of the front door.

In the hall, Oksana shrieked. Sparks turned into small flares on the curtain wrapped around her youngest.

"Keep moving. I'll get them!" Slava slapped the smoking covers as he pushed his family down the five flights of stairs to the outside air.

"Take them to Gallo's!" Slava yelled to his wife. "Have her call for help!" He dashed back into the complex. *Get these people out of here!*

At each stairwell he beat on doors so hard his fists throbbed. Shouts were replaced by uncontrollable coughing, his chest heaving for clean air. At the third floor, smoke was sneaking down the stairs. *Must get to the top!*

Clawing through murky clouds he reached the fifth floor. Just off the stairwell, his apartment was swallowed in the holocaust. Black fog filled the hall.

Furiously pounding on walls and doors of the neighboring flats, his choked consciousness waned. He lost his bearings in the blinding smoke, banging into walls deliriously.

Too late, too late.

He collapsed to the floor, the smoke smothering him into the floorboards. Holding his breath, he craved a wisp of air. His exhausted lungs forced a sputtered cough.

I'm going to die.

* * * * *

Halfway around the world, another fire was being set. Hot coals of emotions stoked this blaze.

"Dad won't care anyway!" Hillary slammed the door behind her. Stomping down the front steps, she ran to the gravel road in front of her house.

At the door, her mother was afraid to yell for fear the neighbors would hear. Gossip circulated about the frequent battles the Wells' family faced with a physician father who was never home and a mother who could not play the double role to their only daughter.

The chilly spring night caused Hillary's skin to tighten with goose bumps. Darkness closed in with a slight breeze making the evergreens and elms sway, their moonlit shadows pointing huge fingers at her. A faint whistling in the tree tops sounded like mocking laughter, twisting the sixteen-year-old's depression inward. She stormed down the road, tripping over loose gravel. Cursing, she broke into a jagged run.

I can't even walk right.

"Shut up!" she yelled at herself. Looking back at her house, the only light came from the kitchen window. She knew her mother would be reaching under the sink even now. Reaching for a bottle.

I drive her to drink.

"Stop it! Stop it!" Tears coursed down her cheeks as she staggered and slowed a half mile toward the county road. Barking dogs in the distance interrupted the lonely solitude. She shivered in the darkness.

It's no use. Despair hounded her.

"It isn't worth it!" she muttered. "It just isn't worth it!"

She was a pretty girl once. Cute blonde curls and giggles melted the hearts of strangers and relations alike. Life was fun then, but faked. People were so easy to please. It was all a waste. So what if she wasn't adorable now? Who needs friends?

The county road stretched through five miles of cornfields into Windwood. She stepped onto the black pavement, oblivious to any traffic. There was none, yet.

"Please, car—come hard and fast," she prayed. Her eyes pooled with tears.

After pigtails and toothless smiles faded, school performance became the standard. 'Surely she'll be smart, her dad's a doctor.' No one told her it was wrong to be average. She found out the hard way. Her parents' disappointment hurt worse than a beating.

No friends. No dad. An alcoholic mother. Neglect turned to discouragement. She scarred over on the outside, covering deep, raw wounds. Lethal wounds, left untreated.

* * * * *

Kison flew invisibly alongside Hillary. His reassurance and comfort fell on a deaf soul. Too often he had to bandage these emotions, coercing her to choose life.

Tonight was different. He did not plead against death this time. His instructions were to hold back.

It would begin with that white Subaru hatchback in the distance.

* * * * *

Hillary faintly heard the car above the roar of her own self-doubt.
I screw up everything.
"Please come fast, please don't see me!" she pleaded, fleeing her hopelessness. Pity and ugliness joined defeat as her emotions simmered. *They'll never miss me. I'm better off gone.*
She breathed fast, the brisk night air burning her lungs. Moving along the edge of the road, she felt the car approach behind her. With angry eyes steadfast to the ground, hatred began a slow boil under cover.
This is right. This will end the pain.
She loathed the feeling the depression had broke open. Worth destroyed, everything turned against her. She was trapped. Seething anger fueled overwhelming futility. There was only one way out.
Timing it just right, she could jump.
I'm going to do it this time.
The car's diesel rumbling was clearly audible. Hillary saw the headlight beams in her peripheral vision as she tramped along the shoulder. With emotions raging, her only control was escape. Forever.
The car began to pull wide around her, but no matter—she could hurdle the distance. Two more seconds.
Suddenly the car screeched! Hillary leaped into its path, but the brakes slammed hard, too early. Her eyes fastened on the frightened lady behind the wheel.
Why did she brake now!
The driver's gaze quickly left hers and looked toward the ground. A brown furry blur scurried across the road just beyond the car's lights.
The driver braked for a cat.
Nauseated by the stench of burnt rubber and her erupting anxiety, Hillary stumbled. Her ribs banged against the car hood. She yelled an obscenity, more out of discouragement than from pain.

The driver of the car jumped out. "Are you okay?"

Hillary hid her sobbing, bowed low at the front of the car.

"Are you hurt?" The driver stepped closer.

"I'm fine!" Hillary stood with her back to the woman.

"If it hadn't been for that cat, I might have hit you."

Turning to face the woman, Hillary narrowed her gaze. Black rings of smeared mascara surrounded her fiery red eyes, making her appearance frightening.

The thirty-ish blonde driver, hands held down and open, took a step toward her. "I am so sorry."

Hillary heard warm sincerity in the voice, a compassion she had not known for some time. For a moment, she wondered why this caring woman was so concerned when no one else was. Her own wrath and worthlessness consumed her again. She turned away, covering her face with her hands.

"Please, go away." She broke into tears.

"My name is Sarah, Sarah Townsend," the driver said softly, taking another step. "I'd really like to help you."

Hillary felt Sarah's hand lightly touch her shoulder. She let it stay without a word.

"I'm not about to leave you here alone. Come back to my car. Let's just sit for a minute."

A lengthy moment passed. Hillary leaned against the car but didn't turn.

"C'mon," said the gentle voice. "Just sit in my car."

Hillary remained imprisoned. The dead weight of her own body hung lifelessly on her frame. There was nothing left.

"Let me go."

"I can't do that."

Hillary's voice was monotone and surreal. "Let me go."

"Just slip over to my car. It's okay."

Hillary felt the hand gently tug her shoulder. Turning, she couldn't recognize her own effort. Still trapped, she allowed herself to be led to the car.

"You're freezing. Let me grab a blanket." Sarah reached into the backseat and unfolded a plaid flannel cover. As she closed the passenger door, Hillary put her head back and closed her eyes.

Sarah walked around the car and got in the driver's side. She reached the heat controls and made sure the vents pointed to her passenger.

"Could I ask what your name is?" Sarah began.

Hillary remained silent. Her eyes cracked open for a moment, a deadpan stare beyond the windshield.

"Are you sure you're not hurt?"

There's nothing to say. Let me go.

"You want to go somewhere? I'll take you there."

Not where I want to go. Hillary turned her head away. *I'm gone.*

Sarah leaned back and flipped on her emergency flashers. A semi-truck raced by, making the hatchback heave.

Silence played with Hillary's mind. *Whose life am I going to ruin now?*

Vultures of desperation and blame circled her defenseless emotions.

I can't even do a simple suicide.

She tightened her eyelids and rocked her head to shake out the voice.

I'm hopeless. Can't waste this lady's time.

She felt the warm air from the car heater hit her feet. It felt good.

Am I doomed?

The voice seemed quieter, a little distant. Hillary slightly opened her eyes to see Sarah, head leaned back. Her eyes were shut but her lips were moving, as if she was speaking.

It's over, I think. The sound was a far away whisper.

Hillary couldn't keep her eyes open. The warmth of the blanket and heater lulled her to rest.

It's safe here. The voice is gone. This lady's praying. I just want to forget it all.

She didn't even stir when the car started down the road.

After a few miles of country road and searching prayer, Sarah drove to the only business in town open at this late hour. She pulled into the Windwood Dairy Queen.

Chapter 2

"Slava!" Oksana's yell was accompanied by a puff of frozen air. "Slava!"

A pinkish hue crossed the horizon. The crisp air nipped at Oksana's bare arms, but she didn't notice.

He had to be around here, but where? People clustered in groups around the building, unknowing and uncaring of her frantic search. The police weren't letting anyone into the building, saying the top floor could collapse. "Everyone's out. Everyone's accounted for," they told her.

Then where's my husband?

She twice ran the dirt path around the block, yelling his name, peeking at every shadow resembling a body. No Slava. An old stump made her think she'd found him asleep, exhausted from his efforts. Angrily kicking it, she nursed a throbbing bruise on her toe.

Firemen in dull crimson coats congregated around two trucks, reeling in hoses. She limped over to them.

"Did any of you see my husband?"

The men ignored her, locker room laughing and bragging on about the fire. She grabbed the stiff blackened rubber sleeve of a man a foot taller than her. He turned, his grizzled face swiped with sweaty streaks of charcoal. The rank smell of smoke and body odor filled the air.

"Did you see a man in there, thin, my height, black hair?"

"What? No, lady. Everyone's out. Not a soul in there."

Someone mumbled something and they all broke out in disgusting laughter. Oksana suddenly felt the cold frost and shivered, rubbing her arms.

"My husband was the first one to notice the fire. He went back in to help his neighbors."

"What floor did you live on?" another fireman asked.

"Fifth, the top floor."

The crew fell silent.

"None of us could get to the fifth floor," the man said. "It wasn't safe. We contained the fire on that floor from outside."

Oksana's heart dropped. "And you're all leaving?"

"All our men are accounted for," the first fireman barked. "We were told everyone was out. Some guy said the fifth floor was clear."

Oksana looked to the sky, forcing tears away. "Who told you? What did he look like?"

"The old man—over there."

Oksana looked across the muddied lawn. Pavel Alotov. He lived down the hall. She hobbled a bee line for him.

"Mr. Alotov?" As he looked her way, she unconsciously fingered her stringy hair, fighting for composure.

"Did you see Slava inside?" she asked.

"Ah, Mrs. Gdansk! How are your children, safe, yes?"

"Yes, yes, they're fine. Slava had me take them over to a friend's. But he went back into the flat to knock on your door. Did you see him?" Her emotions were rising.

"Was that who was yelling and pounding? It was the noise that woke me up. Don't know if I would have stirred if it was not for him. Where is he?"

Unable to speak, Oksana held a pleading gaze with Mr. Alotov.

Please tell me you saw him. Tell me he helped you down the stairs. Tell me he's outside. Tell me he's safe.

A policeman interrupted to speak to Alotov. Oksana turned her back to hide the gush of tears about to break. *He's got to be here.*

She walked away from the crowds, rounding the block a third time. Openly weeping, her cheeks glistened with tears reflecting the morning's dawn.

"Oh, God. Oh, Slava. You cannot be gone. You cannot."

As she turned the farthest corner of the building, she saw a shadow of someone walking toward her. Coming closer, it was a fireman carrying something. Something large. Her blurred eyes blinked.

The fireman wore a shiny gold coat, clean of soot and dirt. And he carried a body. A man. Suddenly her tears were dry.

"Is this who you're looking for, lady?" The voice was deep and gentle.

"Slava?" she asked, hesitant.

The fireman carefully laid the body down. In the early dawn, his coat was unusually bright. Was it just the reflection of the sun's rays? Oksana couldn't clearly see the figure on the ground until the fireman stepped away.

A breeze blew past with an unusual scent of fresh mint leaves. The man motioned for Oksana to come closer. "He's breathing better now. He'll be fine."

The body's head turned slowly, black locks cascading above the most beautiful dark brown eyes.

"Slava!"

* * * * *

Intense joy filled the sanctuary with a visible glow that brightened every color. Even the old wooden banisters lining the platform shined with a highly polished grain.

But the joy was in the people.

Two hundred sang with single voice, their features radiant, eyes directed upward, as if all were seeing a most grand sight.

There was power in the air, and if eyes could see, the angelic movements across the room would only be a blur. They were ecstatic, heaven's charges finding a haven they could join to fulfill their highest joy. Multitudes were singing with the people. Many flitted from the rafters to the congregation and back. Small groups of angels hovered over individuals who were particularly contrite, healing convicted hearts. A blind woman on the sixth pew shouted with joy, experiencing sight for the first time. Angels around her shot up like fiery rockets, adding their glorious praise for her healing.

Entering the room, one would have sensed that this was not of the earthly world. The flight and song of the heavenlies were not seen or heard by men, but the enormous joy pressed upon the soul. The force came in waves, raising with a high anthem, lowering with a solemn melody.

After an exhausting exultation, the music tamed, the sounds softened. The people were seated, and a peace settled. Many of the angels took seats among the people, though most were perched around the balcony and ceilings. The brightness of the moment had not dimmed, but it changed to a warm camp fire glow. The room was stuffy, heat generated from the sheer energy of anticipation.

It was time for prayer before the Holy of Holies.

The Song Leader stood and spontaneously began a soft, melodious prayer. "Lord, we stand in Your holy place," he chanted. "To You we bring our worship and praise. For You alone are holy, and You alone are worthy, and You alone are King."

As he prayed, others blended in with their voices. Some were in harmony, some in counterpoint, as in the warm-up of a great symphony. The music rose with occasional shouts of adoration or appeal:

"God, forgive!"

"Lord, we praise You!"

"You are the Most High God!"

"Lord, please heal!"

"My Lord, my Lord, my Lord!"

"To You alone!"

The sounds swelled with triumph and conviction. Victories claimed, battles waged, mercies sought, love adored, all with a harmonious fervor that wished to see no end. The angels were again in motion, extending the communion of the people with God. Some flew in perfect circles above the gathering, others in staircase fashion ascended the heavens, creating glorious choreographs of worship, all supported by the prayers from below.

At last the music softened and the sanctuary grew silent. The only interruption was an occasional soft cry of a love overwhelmed. The gathering had offered their praise. Now it was time to hear the One they had come to adore.

The angelic movements had stopped, each hovering directly over his charge. Angels' heads were lifted skyward, arms upraised, as was the position of many in the pews. The quietness was intense, almost frightening, as was the Voice they were seeking. But each person heard, each felt, each knew, that they stood in the presence of the living God!

* * * * *

"John! Honey, wake up!"

The woman nudged the wheel of her chair into her husband's ribs as he laid sprawled out on the living room floor. "You're dreaming again. Wake up."

"Wha—what?" he groggily responded.

"It's almost time for work, John. You've got to get going."

"Oh, God," he muttered. "What a worship! What a vision!"

"Honey, snap out of it!" She leaned over the side of her wheelchair and rubbed his shoulder. "You're still asleep!"

Melinda knew this dream all to well. Her husband would start praying and then slip into this comatose sleep of ethereal visions. Only cold showers and hot coffee would completely orient him again. This morning there was no time.

"Melinda." He was coming out of it. "It came again."
"You don't have time, John, c'mon."
"Give me a second, Mel. It was all so real."
"The same one?"
"Yes. The angels, the worship, the prayers—identical."
"Any idea what it means this time?"
"I don't know. Maybe some sort of confirmation. I'm not sure."

He rose from the floor, his eyes red, his cheeks marked by the sculptured pile of the carpeting. His tall dangling frame stretched high and his first steps were slow. He leaned over to the attractive brunette in her wheelchair, her diminutive size overshadowed by the black and chrome surrounding her. He slipped his arm under her thinned legs and scooped her out of the chair.

"I love you." he said before kissing her cheek.

She threw her arms around his neck and kissed his lips in return. "You have to get going."

"This dreaming keeps getting in the way. Am I crazy? Is God trying to tell me something?"

"You're crazy." She kissed him long.

Perplexed for over a year, John Camelson still had no answers. At first it seemed completely bizarre. He was a salesman for a local lumber and hardware store; what did a worship dream have to do with him? He chocked it up to too many late night tacos.

But it came back, tacos or not. Over and over again, almost daily, like a recurring dream. He couldn't believe it meant anything, but why would he keep having it?

Then, a year ago, he was asked to be a song leader in his church. No big deal, just pick out the hymns. Considering the vision, he had to accept.

A few months later, the Russia trip came up. He was asked to lead a church planting team from his congregation. The mission board wanted someone with experience in leading worship. John and Melinda thought about it only briefly. He had to go.

It was too coincidental, being drawn into avenues of worship alongside the peculiar vision.

All the while, the vision visited him unchanged. John questioned all the more its purpose.

* * * * *

Maliel stood at John's side. He heard John's thoughts as plainly as if they were spoken, and he would respond to him as if in conversation. It was Maliel who convinced John of the integrity of this worship vision. He helped him look at the faces in the crowd, helped him see the actions of the angels, and described to him the awesome Glory experienced in such worship.

Yet, the vision's purpose remained as unknown as Maliel's constant presence. As a guardian angel, he knew it was not the right time.

* * * * *

"I'm just sure this six-and-a-half will work," the heavy set lady piped at the young man as she forced her swollen foot deeper into the pump. "Just get that shoe horn around my heel."

Tony squatted on the short stool in front of the lady, perspiration beading on his forehead as he rocked the sweaty, odorous foot into the ruby red pump that was two sizes too small.

"Ma'am, I'm sorry, but I'm afraid we're going to hurt your foot to force it any further." His true concern was actually more for the health of the shoe. This foot had obviously taken a lot of squeezing in the past.

"You're not trying hard enough, young man!" she barked. "I always wear a six-and-a-half pump. I know it will work."

She had to have this shoe because of the multicolored, full-length skirt that matched it "superbly, simply superbly," she earlier touted. After Tony displayed six other styles that fit, she still had to have this pair. The way the woman belted her paisley dress, she was used to squeezing into more petite sizes.

Desperate moves were required. This woman was not about to leave. Tony was supposed to have left the store forty-five minutes ago.

"Okay, Ma'am, hold on." Tony turned his back to the lady. Lifting her foot under his arm forced her to lean back. Like a blacksmith shoeing a horse, he used both hands to bear down on the shoe; one working the toes, the other twisting the heel. With her leg stretched taut, the force shoved the lady firmly into the back of the chair.

Tight-lipped and red-faced, her foot forcibly shrank to fill the slender shoe. She let out a muffled chirp as the shoe finally slid over her heel.

"There!" He stood heaving like he had just completed the final leg-tie of calf-roping in record time. "How does that feel?"

* * * * *

Dashing away, Tony arrived at the church ten minutes late. The Russia group was inside a classroom praying. He stood outside the door and composed himself.

When John Camelson approached him two weeks ago about speaking to the group, he was dumbfounded.

"Tony, you have the clearest ability to evangelize as anyone," John had said. "I truly think you have a gift. If you won't go to Russia with us, please at least share with us how you do it."

He shivered as he recalled how close he had come to joining the Russia team. Several people encouraged him to go, but his summer was dedicated to making money for his third year of pre-med studies. He couldn't fathom being gone for two weeks, spending a couple thousand, and returning to face his college bills. "God can take care of that," he was told, but he didn't believe God should be tested.

Besides, if he went to Russia, everyone would be looking to him to go "save someone." That wasn't how it worked. People would be disillusioned with God if he was unable to make something happen.

They'd be disappointed in him, too.

It was four weeks before the Russia team would depart. The group of six men and women were completing their weekly training on cross-cultural ministry. Tony was excited for them, only a twinge of regret that he was not going.

"Tony?"

His thoughts were interrupted when John opened the door. "We didn't know you were out here."

"Sorry I'm late. Had one tough customer at work."

"That's okay. I knew you'd be here. Are you ready?"

"No, but that won't make any difference to you, I suppose." Tony smiled and grabbed a shoe box that he had brought with him.

"Not in the least, Tony. It just means you'll have to rely more on God. What's in the box?"

"Oh, just some things to help make a point."

The group was seated around a large rectangular table, notebooks spread out with small discipleship booklets and Bibles scattered here and there. John offered Tony a chair, sitting down in his own to join the others. They exchanged greetings as Tony was well acquainted with each person. There were the Hensleys, a retired couple in the church forever; Mr. Jonas, his junior high math teacher; Howard Matson, the church youth pastor; and Sarah Townsend. He winked at Sarah subtly when he caught her eye. She guardedly but warmly smiled back.

John motioned for Tony to go ahead. He stood, cleared his throat, and feigned more confidence than he felt.

"It is a privilege to be able to speak with you as a part of your training. I know you've been heavily studying witnessing techniques, cultural issues, language barriers, and so on, and I hope what I share with you today will help you further prepare for your trip." He moved the shoe box directly in front of him and placed his hands on the lid.

"Inside this box is something I have found extremely valuable. It will help you in witnessing successfully to the Russians. I understand that a good deal of your time will be spent walking the streets and approaching people with the Gospel. This type of street evangelism can be challenging, and at times most discouraging. Besides the frustration of being rejected or arguing over distracting side issues, it can really be exhausting work to your body, and in particular to your feet." He fingered the lid to the box.

"From my experience fitting shoes the last two summers, I believe that one of the most important tools you can have is a pair of good-fitting shoes." He opened the box and hauled out a pair of light brown loafers.

As he held up the shoes, the group looked on in confusion. Except Sarah. She sneaked a smile.

"Notice the high arch support and the soft but strong insole," Tony continued. "These features are critical to your success in avoiding those ugly blisters and swollen ankles that often occur with heavy street evangelism."

Sarah couldn't hold it and let her giggles spring loose. Mr. and Mrs. Hensley still looked confused, but everyone else caught on. Snickers turned into laughs.

Tony pretended to persist. "Now be sure you have double-stitching at every seam for that wear-and-tear of jumping mud puddles and dodging thrown tomatoes."

Even the Hensley's were laughing now. Sarah threw one of the booklets at Tony. John caught his breath to speak. "Tony, please—that's enough!"

"But John, I have much more to say. We've got leather uppers, heel support, waterproofing," Tony continued sarcastically.

John played out his role. "Tony, we wanted you to talk about evangelism, not shoes!"

"Oohhh," Tony drawled. "But you said you wanted me to share because of my background. I just assumed you meant from my experience as a shoe salesman. This is how you can put your best foot forward when sharing the gospel!" Tony again raised the pair of shoes for emphasis. He let himself break into a smile.

"You see, when I was asked to speak about witnessing, I couldn't imagine why on earth you would think I'd have anything to say. I'm just a college kid, trying to make it into medical school. Some say I have a gift—I don't think so. God changes lives. I have no secret recipe for you.

"I'm surprised myself at some of the things I say to people. I don't know where the words come from. I'm not really doing anything, other than trying to stay out of God's way." Tony smirked, bringing understanding smiles from the rest of the group.

"All that being said, I'd still like to share with you a story from Scripture. It's how Christ evangelized. Let's use Him as the model." Tony cracked his Bible and related a story of the woman at the well.

Chapter 3

Slava jerked sideways as he grabbed the seat back ahead of him. He bumped shoulders with the man beside him as the bus veered left, then right. Before settling back, he bounced off the seat like a rubber ball. Coming down hard against the thin cushion, metal springs broke his fall. The bus driver dodged one pothole, but landed squarely in this one.

Slava rode three hours on the bus to Nizhnekamsk every two months to meet with seven other pastors. The leader of this group, Gregori Hatir, was a fine dynamic pastor of a tightly organized house church. This man helped provide a network of support between the Moscow Bible School and the outreach pastors in this area of the Commonwealth of Independent States.

Unless someone had been able to get an open phone line to Hatir, this would be the first he would know of the fire. Although a week had gone by, the horror was still fresh, leaping through flames to find his boys, not knowing if they would be alive or dead. His last recollection was collapsing to the floor of the hall. Oksana told him about the fireman. She was convinced it was an angel. He couldn't remember.

He shuddered with anguish as he remembered huddling with Oksana and his boys the next day, looking over the charred remains of his flat and belongings.

A widow from the church who lived in the apartment building next door offered her flat as a temporary home. Though the apartment was crowded, the woman's gracious hospitality surrounded his family with comfort and love. Several families heard of the fire and offered clothing and other help for Slava and his family.

Now, as he arrived at an old warehouse where the Nizhnekamsk church met, he looked forward to sharing with his pastor friends. These meetings were a great source of encouragement.

Inside, the gray cement walls made the room cavernous. On the south wall a red banner with Lenin's face hung high, a remnant of the former USSR. The men sat in metal chairs around a table on the north end, talking excitedly, oblivious to his arrival. He pulled out a folding chair and sat down before he realized they were buzzing about the fire.

"How did you hear about the fire?" he interrupted.

"Do you mean the fire in Bugluma, or the one in Brother Nikolai's home in Chistopol?" Gregori Hatir asked

"I mean the fire in my flat a week ago!"

Talk erupted like a cloudburst. Slava's home was not the only one torched. In the same week, pastors from two other towns suffered the same. Pastor Nikolai's youngest daughter was still hospitalized with burn injuries.

"Brothers, these fires were not accidents." Hatir looked around the table, his lean jaw set firm. "Who would persecute you or your church?"

Nikolai spoke first. "The government church has been hounding us since we started meeting a year ago. Their bishop has called me with threats about God striking us, but I never put any stock in it, until now. I had no thought of them harming my family." He trembled, and a brother beside him took his shoulder. "Would they really do something like this?"

"We must be careful not to make any accusations unless we're sure," Hatir cautioned. "But think carefully about how the fires could have started. Raphael, how about you?"

Pastor Raphael was from Bugluma, just thirty minutes from Bolshoigorsk. "If I had to accuse someone, I would consider someone in our city government. They've spread rumors about our church; such things as that we take children from other homes and brainwash them, or that we want to cause riots. But I had no suspicion of the fire being arson."

Slava was shaken. "The firemen said it was probably electrical. I have no enemies. Our government has not opposed us, and no one seems offended by our meetings."

"We have to be on our guard," Hatir said. "We don't want any more of this."

"But what should our brothers do who have already suffered?" asked a pastor from Kazan. "Shouldn't we try to find out who's responsible?"

"We must be able to support our conclusions," Hatir said. "If government or religious leaders are behind these fires, they would take great pleasure in blaming us for the hysteria we would create if we could not defend our claims."

"Then what can we do?" asked Nikolai.

Pastor Breznikov, in his fifties amongst all the other younger men spoke. "I suggest that Brother Slava be asked to inquire in his community about the possibility of arson. He seems to have the best rapport with the local government, and his humility would allow him to speak to the authorities with respect and not accusation."

Everyone uttered agreement.

"Slava, can you speak to your town leaders about this?" Hatir asked. "Can you explore the cause of your fire without creating undue suspicion?"

"I could raise the issue with our deputy mayor at least, and go from there."

"Let's take a moment to pray," Hatir said.

He was followed by several others sincerely asking for wisdom.

*****

Sarah woke with a start at the sound of the clock radio. Rather than her usual irritation at the rudeness of the alarm, this morning she felt surprisingly rested. There was a new sense of excitement that she couldn't explain. *I feel like a kid waking up on her sixth birthday.*

She showered and dressed, picking out a bright yellow blouse to wear with her jeans. Sitting with her Bible, she turned to a chapter in Romans. Twenty minutes into it, the words seemed especially fresh. She started on her prayer list, but after a moment of silence, she paused. *God, what is it? What's making my heart tremble?* It was an overwhelming feeling; not undesirable, yet unexplainable.

"God, please take all of me," she spoke out loud. "I want to be filled completely by You today. Lord, thank You for this joy I feel—oh, Lord, my heart bursts for joy in You." Her eyes welled up. "God, what is this? I have not sensed You here like this for a long time. Oh God, thank You. Take me, use me; take this joy. Make me a beacon for You."

Time seemed of no matter right now. This was the work of the Glory.

A little over an hour passed. Sarah had to get going with the day. Her desire was to linger, to wait on God longer. It was a sweet presence this morning. But the day beckoned to her.

She dialed Melinda Camelson's.

"Hi, Melinda. Sorry to bother you."

"That's no problem, Sarah. What's up?"

"I need to ask if you could help me. I met a girl who is really hurting. It seemed like the Lord brought us together and she needs help, but I'm not sure what to do. Could I run some thoughts by you sometime today?"

"Any time that works for you." She paused. "By the way, how is your support coming?"

"It's all in, Mel. Can you believe it? All twenty-three hundred is in. Isn't God the greatest?"

"Sarah, that's wonderful! Let's celebrate with a cup of coffee. How about three o'clock? Katie Ann will be napping then."

"Wonderful, Mel. The girl's name is Hillary Wells. Do you know her?"

"No, I don't believe I do, unless she's Dr. Wells' daughter. I think he has a teenager. I've never met her, but I'd be glad to visit with you about it."

"Thanks, Mel, I really appreciate it. You know, I have such a sense of energy this morning, like the world is just spinning so fast around me. I'm so excited about what is to come!"

"You sound like you're just shy of heaven. Everything is falling into place so well for you. I can't wait to hear all about it."

"At three o'clock then. I'll be there. Goodbye, Mel."

Sarah hung up the phone and went to her next task—a letter to her parents. She tried to write monthly, but almost two had slipped by. As the only daughter of retired farmers living two states away, her single lifestyle kept the family wondering. Sarah was twenty-six, not yet married, not yet interested. 'I've got too much life in me, and I can't confine it to one man yet, Mom,' she would say.

"Dear Mom and Daddy," she began writing. She loved them dearly and knew they were always praying for her, and for her future husband.

"My mission support is raised!" she wrote. "I can't believe it! In six weeks, I'll be on my way to Russia! My last day of work at the hospital is Monday. Some are surprised that I'm going. I hope God will use me."

She went on to write about her friends at work, the recent damp weather, and the singles volleyball tourney, until she filled the page front and back. She started to say goodbye.

"Mom and Daddy, please don't worry about me. God is so close to me now, and especially today I feel His arms of love around me. You both take care. I love you, Sarah."

As she walked out to her mailbox, a red coupe shot into her apartment drive. She turned with a smile.

"Hey, Sarah, is today our lucky day?"

The young man's sandy-haired head bobbed out the window of the car. Tony Barton consistently proposed to Sarah at every encounter. He was serious, but knew she wasn't, and he was never in a hurry to accept the rejection.

"Nope, it's too sunny for a wedding today, Tony," she called sarcastically from the porch. She knew she was fortunate to have a man like him after her, and she always enjoyed time spent with him. He was just short of obnoxiously funny, and considered a hunk by the town's standard.

Someday, she told herself, maybe someday.

"Well then, how about lunch? I'm done at the shoe shop around one o'clock. Can I come by then? The Burger House has a special just for you: a Russian burger basted with Vodka, Siberian fries and Lenin's lemonade."

"How did they know my favorites?" she responded with a cute smile. This lunch company did sound fun on a day like today. "Lunch would be great, Tony—but let me meet you there, okay? I've got some errands to run."

"She said 'yes', she said 'yes' everybody! Did you hear it?" he yelled to the empty streets. "Today, lunch—tomorrow, my bride! See you at one then."

* * * * *

An angel beside Tony nodded to his compatriot standing beside Sarah. Fortas was stroking Tony's shoulders, as if in preparation for a strenuous sport. Both heralds knew this one would have the hardest struggle with what would happen today.

* * * * *

Sarah's final errand before lunch was a delivery to a delightful widow who lived in a farm house three miles south of town. The woman had given a generous gift to Sarah's mission support, putting her over the top. Sarah had a plate of fresh baked cinnamon rolls to celebrate the event. Mrs. Davis was eighty-years-old, spry as those thirty years younger. Her inimitable spirit sustained her and many others who befriended her. This visit would be a highlight of the morning.

"Sarah, how sweet of you!" Mrs. Davis exclaimed at the door. After a big hug Sarah tried to express her thanks for the money gift.

"Now none of it, deary," Mrs. Davis cut her off. "That's the Lord's money and He told me to give it to you. He's the One to thank."

"But Grandma Davis, I feel so blessed. You couldn't imagine how happy I am. Your gift completed my support. I can finally go to Russia!"

"Oh my! The Lord be praised and praised forever!"

Grandma Davis' face shone like a candle's flame. Her radiance filled the room with an endearing reverence. Sarah was solemn as she realized the elder woman was silently praying right at this moment, a thanksgiving prayer.

The widow prayed out loud, "Lord, You know every need. Thank you for showing me where You wanted Your hand extended. Lord, take Sarah into Your hands." She grasped Sarah's shoulders. "Take this young girl, Father, and keep her safe in Your arms. Prepare her for Your will, give her strength and show her Your reward. Bring those who will miss her into Your fold of faith. Lord Jesus, I hear cries of those who don't want her to leave. Oh, Father, prepare our hearts. Lord, minister to us. May we know You, Father. May we know Your will. Father, keep us together. Help us understand."

Grandma Davis' voice softened, and Sarah felt the arthritic hands shake slightly as they held her shoulders. With eyes closed Sarah tensed during the fervent prayer. God was here and the groanings of His Spirit were being aired. She felt like crying, felt a sadness that she couldn't comprehend.

It was quiet now, Grandma's lips moving slightly, tears trickling down her cheeks. Her grasp of Sarah's shoulders loosened and they fell into an embrace, both weeping.

Sarah spoke first. "Oh Grandma Davis, this shouldn't be so sad. I wanted to celebrate with you."

"You don't know of the celebration you have today. This is a time to rejoice. But deary, your joy will be our sorrow for a while."

"But Grandma Davis, the time will go fast. I'll be back before you know it."

"My dear, I'm not sure of what God has made known to me, but I may get to visit you before you come to visit me."

"What do you mean?"

Grandma Davis occasionally had a word from God. She often seemed to know more than she let on.

"Would you really come to Russia, to see me?" Sarah asked.

"My child, I would love to visit you, wherever you are. Let's just look forward to the future together. Now, tell me all about your plans. When do you leave?"

They continued their chat another thirty minutes, sitting side by side on the davenport. When Sarah stood to leave, she was again led into prayer with the old saint.

Sarah never tired of praying with this woman, but this was richer than she could ever remember. They hugged goodbye, and she lingered in the motherly grasp.

Seeing tears in Grandma's eyes again, Sarah left quickly to escape the uncomfortable farewell. Grandma stood on the porch waving as Sarah drove away.

It was a straight stretch down the country road. Far beyond the farm house, Sarah could still make out the figure of Grandma Davis waving. Her final thought was what a special moment heaven would have when Grandma Davis hit the doors. God's irony showed true in the next moment.

*****

Tony was seated at The Burger House, knowing something was wrong. Fortas made him uneasy. "It's not good, Tony."

The words were not clear, but the message took hold.

Where could she be?

It was half past one. Sarah wouldn't be this late without calling. He stepped outside, looking down the road for her car.

John was just passing by The Burger House when he saw Tony step outside. He pulled over, and Tony approached his car.

"Hi, John. You here for lunch?"

"I just happened to see you, uh, as I drove by." John spoke carefully. Too carefully. As they walked back into the restaurant, he asked, "How are you, Tony?"

Something was wrong.

"Alright, I guess. I was waiting here to have lunch with Sarah and she's late. Have you seen her?"

"Tony, you won't believe it." John sat in a booth across from him and wiped his eyes. His words chilled the air, numbing his friend. "Sarah was in a car accident this morning. She, uh, she didn't make it, Tony."

Tony's face flushed white. "What?"

He knew it was true. The ominous feelings were confirmed.

John's voice broke. "She had just been at Grandma Davis. Apparently she lost control of her car on the country road. The police said she didn't stand a chance. Oh, Tony, I am so sorry."

John touched Tony's arm, but he flinched and drew away.

He was pale and speechless. No tears, no questions. Only a dull and listless face that would not meet eyes. Suddenly he dashed from the table and out the door.

"Tony!" John called out without a response. "Tony!"

Before John could reach the door, the red coupe roared away.

Chapter 4

"Lord, please take care of Tony," John tried to pray aloud. "Go with him wherever he is, comfort him. Help us all to know You are in control, Lord." He choked, tasting tears at his lips. "Oh, Jesus, it can't be right! Why did she have to die?"

John left the Burger House, driving back home to be with Melinda. Just a short while ago, their quiet Saturday lunch had been interrupted by the phone call about Sarah's death. Before they could react to their own shock, the doorbell rang. At the door, three of Sarah's girlfriends stood in tears, asking for Melinda.

John figured a drive might do him some good. Had he known he would be the one to tell Tony, he never would have left the house.

He pulled into his driveway and sat in the car, head over the steering wheel, weeping. It didn't make any sense.

When he finally entered the house, Melinda's emotions seemed under control, probably for the sake of the younger girls. He leaned over from behind her wheelchair and hugged her with his cheek against hers.

She whispered, "I'm so glad you're home. I'm not sure I could hold myself together much longer."

"I ran into Tony downtown."

She lifted her head away, her sad eyes questioning his.

"He hadn't heard yet," John said quietly. "I had to tell him."

"Oh, John," Melinda whispered. "How did he take it?"

John's eyes filled again, his lower lip quivering. "Not good."

His embrace tightened, and he felt her body shudder. Trying to speak again, he stopped before his words fell out as tears. He realized he was trembling, too.

The girls moved for the front door and Melinda broke away from John with enough composure to speak. "I'm sorry, girls."

"We need to go anyway, Mrs. C," one of them said. "You've been a big help."

"We'll just go for a drive—the fresh air will do us good," another one said.

"Please come back anytime," Melinda offered. "And, again I am so sorry."

John was amazed his wife could keep her tears at bay as she yelled out the door to them, "Let's keep praying for Sarah's family, okay?"

She closed the door and turned, her face sunken. She wheeled to John, and he knelt just as she collapsed forward into his arms.

"Oh, God!" she wailed. "Oh, my God!" Her pent up mourning burst in a torrent.

Holding her trembling body, John's own tears were exhausted. He moved her to the couch and sat with her, her cool damp cheek against his. Words were ill fit. Stroking her hair, his heart broke with hers.

* * * * *

Across town, Tony sat on the front steps where he had earlier made the lunch date with the girl of his dreams. Hunched over, his hair was tousled from his fingers repeatedly raking through it. His eyes were glassy, an unfocused stare gazing down the empty street.

Every moment of his last time with Sarah replayed before him. She looked beautiful to him, the sun accenting her blonde locks just this morning. She was so carefree and excited about life. Her mood was always contagious to him. Even the short time with her this morning was enough to keep him charged all day. It had been a gorgeous morning; a million dollars couldn't have replaced his joy.

He knew Sarah was opening up. They were falling in love. Her quips always put marriage aside, but he could sense she hoped for a future together just as much as he did.

His thoughts were abruptly quenched with a flashback of the scene of her death.

When he left John at the restaurant, he drove the only country road she could have been on; the one out to Grandma Davis. He raced to prove it could not have been Sarah—there had to have been a mistake.

The red and blue lights of a single police cruiser flashed near a ravine two miles out of town. As he came closer, the mangled shell of a white hatchback laid upside down in a flattened area of a wheat field. The broken windshield formed a shattered frame around the dark cavity where only Sarah could have been.

He slowed his speed coming upon the wreck, the truth of the moment setting in. Sarah had died. He slowly shook his head—now not in disbelief, but in shock.

"Hey, mister! No gawking now," the policeman yelled to him. The officer approached his car, but Tony was in no condition to talk. He reared a three-point turn and sped back to town.

Now he remembered every conversation they shared together, right on this porch. It was a favorite conclusion to their evenings together, especially Sunday evenings after church. They discussed sermons, hard spiritual questions, directions for their lives. Anything was fair game. And they would laugh—oh, how sweet a sound was Sarah's laugh. Points of light would sparkle in her eyes as her giggles turned into infectious heaves of joy.

They prayed on this porch many times as well. He remembered the first time. He embarrassingly asked her to pray with him at the end of their evening together. Not wanting to make her feel uncomfortable, he had planned a nicely generic prayer. He knew enough to avoid asking God for anything that might be too personal in front of her.

As they bowed together, however, she started praying first. She prayed for his life and his walk with God. Then she openly prayed for their friendship, and boldly asked God to lead them in their relationship together. When she was finished, he hardly knew what to pray, and stuttered over a few token thank-yous that sounded rehearsed.

He sighed a relieved 'amen,' and she told him how much she appreciated a man who would pray with her.

That was the first moment he realized he wanted this woman for his wife.

How he now longed to see her drive up and jump out of her hatchback with that tremendous smile, oblivious to any hint of an accident. He was jerked back to reality as the scene of the wreck flashed like a strobe before him. Anger raised inside, replacing his longing for her.

Why, God? Is this justice? Is this the response of a loving God to His children? His tight fists painfully smacked his knees.

A soft voice interrupted his grieving. "Excuse me, is this Sarah Townsend's apartment?"

A young teenage girl with deep mascara about her eyes stood holding an envelope.

The shock of seeing anyone made Tony respond abruptly. "Whatever."

Hillary gawked for a moment. "So, do you know if she's home?"

Unable to voice Sarah's death, it was easier to just say, "No, she's not here."

"Well, that's okay. I just wanted to leave this letter for her." She climbed the steps beside Tony. "I'll just slip it into the screen door."

"Uh, that won't work." He couldn't say it. "She's not—she's not coming home anymore."

Hillary turned to face Tony's back. "What do you mean?"

He paused, searching for what to say. All he found was rage. "She's gone! She died, all right? She rolled her car in a ditch this morning and it's all over!" He shouted the cruel words as much to himself as to the stranger.

Hillary stared into the wet eyes of this man, his tears evidence of the truth. "No. It couldn't be."

"Believe it. I saw the wreck myself. No more Sarah!"

He saw her quiver, but he couldn't care less.

The envelope in her hands dropped to the porch floor, and she ran down the sidewalk.

Tony watched without pity, completely consumed in his own remorse. He openly cried for the first time.

*****

Fortas had to let Tony wrestle his acceptance of this fate. Any success in comforting him was negligible. For the moment, this grief needed time.

His assignment had already been accomplished, for Hillary's letter had been directed to fall at the side of his troubled charge.

After a lengthy time, Tony reached down and picked up the envelope.

*****

Though Slava's ride back to Bolshoigorsk was bumpy, he was delighted with the encouragement he received at the meeting. The news from Pastor Hatir was especially exciting. Bolshoigorsk was one of three churches to be the hosts of an American mission team! He couldn't wait to share the news with Oksana and the church. A group of six Americans would be traveling to Russia next month, living in their homes, helping lead church meetings, and evangelizing their community.

Every Christian in Russia dreamed of meeting a real American Christian. It was thrilling to think of what it must be like to live in a country that had always trusted in God, where religious freedom was encouraged, and where the Bible was readily available.

Slava had heard the stories about Americans. They were so wise and so willing to offer their knowledge. Americans would talk nonstop with fascinating tales. And they laughed so much!

They were known for always bringing large supplies of literature to churches. The sight of stacks of New Testaments, or even just Gospel booklets, seemed miraculous.

But their great wealth was most intriguing. Slava could not believe the stories he had heard about Americans living in separate houses with three bedrooms or more, that every American family drove their own car, or that an average American salary was fifty to one hundred times his own! He'd heard that Americans would bring fine gifts from their country. One friend had told how each member of their church received a ballpoint pen and separate note pads of colored paper. Such generosity from these Americans!

It was a tremendous privilege to know Bolshoigorsk had been selected as a host for the American team. Surely the church would flourish, making an enormous impact on the community. Their visit would help finally establish the church.

He broke into a run when the bus dropped him off a block from the apartment building where his family stayed. Dashing up two flights, he burst into the room.

"You'll never believe who is coming to Bolshoigorsk!" he shouted.

His family and the widow were all sitting in the meager living room. They looked up in surprise, but the adult faces were subdued.

"What are the glum looks for? I have some great news!"

"And I have some bad news for you, Slava," his wife said. She handed him a folded sheet of paper. "Your boss brought this by while you were gone."

"What is it?" Slava opened the sheet. There were just two typed lines and a signature:

Slava Gdansk is hereby immediately terminated from his employment with the Bolshoigorsk Oil Refinery.

Igor Chulstarisk

Slava stared like a deer facing headlights. "Terminated? Why would they do this? I have been no problem to them!"

He had worked in the refinery for eight years, providing his only gainful employment. The church could not salary a pastor, so this job was his only financial support. As a faithful employee, he did any job Mr. Chulstarisk assigned, working extra hours when asked.

"What reason could they have for this?" Oksana asked. "Do you have any idea?"

"None." He was dumbfounded. "Did Mr. Chulstarisk say anything more?"

"Just that he could not be reached until Monday. That was before I knew what the letter said. I had just assumed it was a change in your work schedule. I opened it just before you came home."

"I can't believe it. I've got to borrow a phone and call Alexander. He might know something."

"That's the strangest part, Slava. Mr. Chulstarisk told me to be sure you didn't talk to anyone about the letter. He said to tell you to wait until Monday and speak with him only. That's why I opened the note myself. I knew something wasn't right."

"This is crazy! They take my job, but I can't talk about it!"

He knew he had to follow the orders. The refinery was the town's major industry, with much political clout. The warning was truly a threat.

A couple of years ago, an oil man was fired and complained loudly to the city government that he had been treated unfairly. The next thing Slava heard was that the man was arrested for instigating a drunken brawl, and was sent to prison in Nizhnekamsk. Perhaps it was not so unusual, except that Slava personally knew the meek man never drank alcohol. The man would no more start a fight as squash an ant.

Slava had tried to visit him a couple times during his trips to Nizhnekamsk, but the prison authorities always refused, saying the man was confined with orders to have no visitors. Letters to him were useless, as guards pilfered any gifts and threw away the rest.

"What should we do?" Oksana asked.

Slava tried to calm down. "We pray and we trust God. I must believe this is in His plan."

Slava was not convincing and his wife needed reassurance. He mumbled the next words half-heartedly. "Maybe that is why God has chosen Bolshoigorsk for a visit from a team of American Christians."

Gina, the widow, had stayed quiet. Now she lit up. "What American Christians?"

With little enthusiasm, he told about their church hosting the mission visitors.

Grabbing Slava, Oksana hugged him. "God has not abandoned us."

Gina put her arms around both of them. "This is most wonderful news, Slava."

"It's so hard to know what we should do," Slava limply hugged the ladies back.

Chapter 5

"Please, Slava, come to bed." Oksana stood at the doorway to the kitchen.

"I've got to get this sermon together."

"But it's almost three o'clock."

No response. He sat under a bare bulb's dim light at the small kitchen table, his Bible and wadded up brown paper balls before him.

"You can't keep this up. It's killing you." She gently rubbed his shoulders.

"I used to have no trouble like this. They would always fall together." His face was long and tired. "I've exhausted all my notes. What can I do?"

"Three meetings a week are just too much. Let alone your full-time job." Her voice died as she realized the slap of her last words.

"I guess I'll have more time for church now that I'm fired," he said sharply.

"Oh, Slava, I'm sorry. Come to bed. Please."

"I've got to have something by morning. I'll be there soon." Patting her hand on his shoulder, he flipped through his Scriptures.

Oksana left quietly. This scene was becoming all too familiar.

* * * * *

When she was out of sight, Slava threw down his pencil stub. "Bolshoigorsk deserves better," he muttered.

Bolshoigorsk, nestled in the foothills at the southern end of the Ural Mountains, was a beautiful Russian community of seventy thousand in the oil-rich land of the Commonwealth of Independent States. Through most of the twentieth century, it was a common Soviet city of absolute loyalty to the Kremlin and absolute disbelief in God. With the fall of communism, a shining beacon of spiritual hope had shed its grace into the town. Beginning with an obscure Romanian evangelist holding a week of meetings in Bolshoigorsk, the first evidence of a Christian church was fashioned.

A handful of believers who acknowledged Christ as their Lord during those meetings searched among themselves for a leader. The mantle calmly fell on Slava without discord when he shared of his inward desire to enter the pastoral ministry. Leaving his wife and two young sons for six months, he attended the Moscow Bible School six hundred miles away. The training provided a scriptural foundation to begin the first non-government church in Bolshoigorsk since belief in God was denied a generation ago.

Slava returned to his family and newly born congregation three months ago with fresh energy and a newfound trust in God. Rallying around his leadership, the church grew to twenty or so strong believers, all yearning to glean every grain of understanding that Slava had only just learned himself.

Now, Slava asked God to open His Word so that he could continue to feed this ravenous flock who had already quickly consumed all the spiritual food he had.

Why did scriptural applications escape him? How was he to lead a service of worship without a hint of direction?

He drowsily leaned forward onto the table, finally resting on the open Bible as sleep overcame him. The long trip to Nizhnekamsk, learning of the other fires, the excitement of the Americans' visit, the apparent loss of his job, all emotionally took their toll on the struggling pastor.

* * * * *

Within the hour, angels woke Oksana from her sleep. Seeing the empty place beside her, she knew what had happened.

She helped Slava from the table and pointed him to their room. As she paused to close his Bible, only the angels heard her. "Is this truly what God has called us to?"

The angels had no desire to defend God. Slava's inability to gain insight was not their fault. In fact, at this predawn moment God was directing Brael to comfort and encourage Slava and his wife. The pastoral couple were being shaped by the Glory in a masterful way.

* * * * *

The Bolshoigorsk church came together at 8:30 a.m. at Aunt Gallo's flat. Although related to no one in the church, everyone called her "aunt" as a term of respect. She offered her small one-bedroom apartment as the regular meeting place, with her living room serving as the sanctuary. Seating was provided by "pews" of two-by-twelve planks supported by a few folding chairs. The planks were arranged in five short rows and covered with towels and blankets.

When Slava and Oksana arrived, twelve people were already seated. As was customary, they greeted each other with a hug. Oksana sat toward the back and watched Slava take a seat in the front of the room. The others courteously left him alone. His countenance clearly showed he was deep in thought.

His thoughts had been distant all morning. Oksana knew he was running over several passages he had studied the past week, skimming mental notes for something to say to these people. Oksana's solitary prayer this morning: "Lord, use Slava."

She quietly shared with several that yesterday had been a troublesome day, inwardly aching over the desire to tell them about the termination, but knowing she could not. Without prying, friends asked questions about the fire damage and how the family was getting along.

Oksana tried to respond politely to the caring concern of the small group, but she kept an eye on Slava, silently continuing to pray for him.

Her unspoken prayers were being answered at this very moment.

* * * * *

Brael filtered the continual flow of ideas that raced through Slava, preparing to sift out a verse that was soon to hit home.

"Proverbs sixteen:twenty-five," Brael whispered to Slava's mind.

Immediately Slava opened his Bible to the verse. Drawing his shoulders back, he looked up to the heavens and sighed. He flipped to a New Testament parable. A slight but confident smile drew across his face as he received the message to be shared with this people of Bolshoigorsk this morning.

A lively song was started by Natasha and Elmira in the front row, two eighteen-year-olds who became Christians four months ago. With fervor, the congregation of thirty-some sang the chorus several times. It seemed natural, even common, for the heavens to be praised by these lowly but godly people.

The angels loved it.

Brael was among nearly one hundred in the heavenly host present at this worship. He moved in choreographed circles with others, casting himself right through the congregation. The angelic voices were raised in grand harmony combined with the rest. The throne room of heaven was open and God was blessing His people as they made His praise glorious.

The congregation turned to their hymn books, ratty castaways from a long-ago failed church, but now treasured antiques filled with lyrics of many time-honored Russian hymns. To the tune of 'How Great Thou Art' they sang all seven verses acapella in heartfelt worship. Many eyes welled with tears as the song moved through the strains of God's grace poured out to man.

The angels sang as well, centered over the people. Each human soul's praise was magnified by three or four angels carrying the same exaltation.

More hymns followed in Russian tongue with the same enthusiastic sound of worship, as if the people could never tire. The minoric melodies flooded the heavens with adoration and praise, hearts and voices joined together with angelic communion to give honor to their Lord.

The people remained standing after the final chorus was sung. In the awesome presence of their Lord, each one listened intently. After such intimate worship, there seemed a unique freedom to understand greater truths of God. It was desirable to wait.

Yes! Yes! There it was!

An indescribable sound—a faint chorus of singers, certainly not human. Several people not lost in worship caught eyes with each other to excitedly say, 'Can you hear it?' But not a word was spoken. Who would dare interrupt such a sweet melody? This had to be the holiest of ground, to actually hear the angels sing. Yes, that must be it!

What could sound so beautifully melodious, a full harmony beyond comprehension? The people stood in awe, listening to the refrain of the angels in their highest praise. The music ministered comfort for the hurting, consolation for the grieving, and exhortation for the discouraged. Each one in the congregation felt the entire chorale resounding particularly for their special need.

After a lengthy fifteen minutes, the voiced tones softened to a distant chiming and then disappeared. Such angelic concerts occurred more frequently in these services, although each time felt fresh as the first. It was an incredible encouragement to each believer to have such comfort and joy to share.

Slava broke the silence by quietly announcing, "Let's pray together to thank God for His wonderful presence with us."

He began a quiet word of praise and thanksgiving, the people around him initiating their own prayers. Everyone wanted to tell God something about the mystery they were all privileged to witness.

When the prayer time came to a close, the group was seated. They looked to Slava for the Word from God.

Oksana watched her husband. She had seen it countless times, but it always amazed her.

Slava stood before his congregation, an uncharacteristic smile forming across his face. He looked like a young boy with a secret that all wanted to hear. A long pause effectively caught everyone's attention. He began to preach.

Oksana marveled as the people absorbed every word. She prayed for her husband throughout each sermon, but her loving prayers intensified this time. They were being answered before her eyes.

Slava's message was deliberate and smooth, as if rehearsed for weeks. He spoke with an urgent passion, communicating Scripture with every ounce of his soul. Though it was unlike him to do so in normal conversation, he now used forceful pointing gestures and broad sweeps of his arms to express this nugget of wisdom he had received from the riches of God's storehouse.

Paying little attention to the sermon, Oksana was focused in her praying. With every ebb and flow of his speech, she would pray that his words were being used by God. If he was speaking loudly and boldly, she would pray for Slava himself, that God would give him the understanding he needed at that moment. If he was speaking more softly, Oksana prayed for the people around her, that they would receive the message with open souls, honest before God.

Although she gave up her opportunity to receive her husband's teaching during these times, she knew her prayers were much more important to the work of God. Occasionally she would ask Slava how he felt his sermon had been received, and he would always reply, 'If I know you're praying, I know it is being received in the way God planned.'

Now lost in prayer, the time flew by. Oksana was shocked by a big hug from Mrs. Slenadensk next to her.

"Isn't it wonderful news?"

"What?"

"The Americans! The Americans!"

"Oh, yes! It is wonderful!" Slava was done preaching. He had just announced the American mission team's visit.

"And who would be able to help house members of the team during their two week visit?"

Every hand rose enthusiastically.

"You are a very hospitable congregation. I know you will treat the Americans well, because you have treated my family so kindly since our fire. Your gifts of money, food, and clothing have been such a grand expression of your love."

The words brought Oksana out of the prayer closet, flooded with emotions of recent events.

Slava walked to the back of the room to stand with his wife before continuing. "You cannot know how much your generosity has meant to us."

Oksana leaned into Slava, wondering if he would dare tell the church about his termination. No, he couldn't. With moist eyes, she tried to fight off the hounding questions the next few days would hold.

This is our worship now, she told herself. *Control yourself.*

Yet everywhere before her, she saw the dear faces of the congregation. Many had deprived themselves of food or savings just to help her family in the fire. She could not ask for more.

Burying her head into her husband, she could not hold back the tears.

The congregation felt sympathy for what they believed were tears of overwhelmed gratitude. No one understood that, more so, Oksana cried from the lonely pain of uncertainty.

Chapter 6

Everyone knew it would be a large funeral. The community was typically faithful here. Denominations crossed over without any sense of compromise. At least on these occasions, men and women of varying spiritual color came under one roof to share things of the heavenlies.

The angels knew this. Though a sad moment in the lives of those who would come, the angels were free to rejoice in Sarah's heavenly entrance, and do so in a grand way.

Here was comfort, rest, and peace.

Here was a great opportunity to split the fleshly souls, separating complex worldly issues from the basic dilemma of life and death.

Here, also, was a great challenge to a body of people questioning the wisdom of God. The congregation dealt with the untimely death of a delightful and God-fearing young woman. The sanctuary would soon hear the heartache of these people. The cry would be one unified shout: 'Why?'

John heard the question loudly. He was the one to stand before the full house and offer the answer.

Sarah's parents had requested that John deliver the funeral address. Though he was not a schooled pastor, John had been highly respected by Sarah as the church's worship leader. She had sung in many choirs under John's baton. Also, John and Melinda had been Sarah's parents-away-from-home over the years she had lived in Windwood.

When John was approached to speak at the funeral, he had reluctantly agreed. Now he felt overwhelmed by his own inadequacy, struggling to explain something that he did not, and could not, understand.

In the late night hours of the funeral's eve, he sat in a middle pew of the empty sanctuary. The lights were off except for two small spots illuminating the wooden cross above the pulpit.

God, I don't understand it. Why would You take Sarah? Why would her life—so soon to reach a mission field, so surely guided by You—why must her life end? God, how can this show an unbelieving world that You are Lord? That You are faithful? His thoughts began to sink. *That You are a loving God?*

His prayer was quiet, vacant. The questions posed were out in the open. So were his tears.

John heard no answer.

No voice boomed, "This is why—"

No strikes of lightning. No resurrections.

Just a profound silence that fell upon a man in a middle pew of a dimly lit sanctuary this night.

But angels were all over the place.

Maliel encouraged John, with the help of three ministering angels, to be honest with God, to get those tough questions out. John had to own up to his doubts before God. Then the Lord would minister. With this, the Lord's Spirit went right to work.

The Holy Spirit! Such a wondrous sight! Not an angelic form, no body or flesh here. But a person in every other sense. This vibrant, emotional power came completely unseen, even by the angels. Still, they knew He was there.

Angels encircled John. One ring of cherubim flew parallel to the ground around him, shoulder-high. Another ring flew five feet over his head. A heavenly barrier was created for the work, impenetrable by man or spirit.

The Holy Spirit rose up in John. He felt the presence grow as a seed sprouting within him. Tight muscles of tension and despair were suddenly calmed by an inner comfort. Softly he sang to the words of a verse:

"I know that You can do all things,

No plan of Yours can be thwarted

Surely I spoke of things I did not understand,

Things too wonderful for me to know."

The words came slowly, thoughtfully. John began to sing them again, still a quiet melody. Tears filled his eyes.

God, is this Your truth?

The Holy Spirit called the ministering angels close. They flew in a tight double ring around John, linked hand in hand.

Strengthened, John sang the words boldly. Repeating the song, it took hold of his heart and soul as well as his mind.

"I know that You can do all things,

No plan of Yours can be thwarted.

Surely I spoke of things I did not understand,

Things too wonderful for me to know."

A confidence welled-up from within. God, I don't have to know why.

There was comfort. It was knowledge the world could not accept, but by the power of the Holy Spirit John found peace.

He could trust God.

He thumbed through the back of his Bible, looking at the small concordance.

"'Wonderful,' let's see." Of the twenty or so references to the word 'wonderful', John found the one he needed. "Job forty-two, verse three."

Oh, God! This is from the book of Job! The man who suffered so greatly.

Flipping to chapter forty-two, he found the verses exactly as he had sung them. His heart was full to overflowing. God had laid these verses on his heart. His mind had been touched by the Lord.

Skimming through the pages, his eyes caught a pencil-lined verse in chapter thirteen.

"Wow, Lord, look at this!" he said as if talking to a friend rather than the Author Himself. *This is it, Lord. I see a glimpse of Your plan. Lord, thank You! Thank You for Your Word. I know what I can say tomorrow. Oh, Lord, bless Your name!*

It was the Glory, minutely revealed. Revelation from God had been given to man. At least two hundred angels broadened their flight. The heavenlies were ready to rejoice, for here was a man who understood afresh the work of God. Singing praises, celestial choirs shouted, "Worthy are You, oh Lord. Worthy are You to be praised!"

John could not hear a sound, but he knew in his heart it was time to worship. Pangs like hunger drew him to join the angelic chorus. Moving to the piano at the front of the sanctuary, he began to unknowingly sing with angels. The Lord had just become much bigger than he ever had understood before.

He knew what the funeral service would hold tomorrow.

* * * * *

Kison was patient but nervous as he spoke to Hillary's soul. He had never seen her this distraught. Holding back tears, she stood at the bathroom mirror. Not the kind of grieving he had expected. Not even anger. Hillary just matter-of-factly seemed to accept that there was no more use for life. Sarah's death meant only one thing: the world had given up on her.

"You can't let it get you down," Kison spoke to ears that wouldn't hear. "Come on, you have to see what is down the road for you."

She reached into the back of the medicine cabinet.

Kison prayed, "Lord, give me wisdom."

Sitting on the edge of the bathtub, Hillary gazed into a pill bottle.

Kison raised his voice, "Hillary, drop the bottle. Just drop the bottle." He pulled on her fingers but her grasp only tightened.

Expressionless, she moved with purpose. Pouring a glass of water, she shook at least ten of the pink pills into her hand. In moments, she swallowed three handfuls of two different prescriptions. Finding the living room couch, she stretched out, still clutching one of the empty bottles.

As his charge lapsed into the drug-induced delirium, Kison kept praying. The Lord, he knew, would be faithful. But how?

Twenty minutes passed. Mortal sleep slipped into a fatal rest.

Then Kison's prayers were interrupted. The front door creaked opened. "Thank God!"

* * * * *

The Windwood Hospital Emergency Room doors banged open, the force of a large man's back ramming through them. He turned to face the gurney with Hillary's limp body in his arms. A nurse running to his side helped lay her on the table.

"I knew I could get her here faster if I just brought her myself," he said out of breath. "It looks like at least twenty-four Darvocettes and fifteen of those fifty milligram Stelazines."

The nurse immediately called on the in-room phone for assistance. She raced back with an IV set-up and began working with Hillary's arm. The obvious questions were put aside.

Dr. Wells was thankful the ER nurse on duty was Sheila. She'd helped him through some tight traumas in the past.

"Look, Sheila, call Dr. Bingham up here, will you?" He hoped she didn't notice his trembling. "Her respirations are very shaky. Her heart rate is irregular—I'm not very good at this. I've got to call her mother."

"Yes, Dr. Wells. I'll get him up here right away."

Two nurses appeared at the door, shocked to see Dr. Wells with a stethoscope laid on his daughter's chest. Sheila asked one to call Dr. Bingham for the emergency, and the other to call the poison control center.

In seconds, electrodes on Hillary's chest monitored the sluggish heart rate. A mixture of fluids raced into arm veins via the thin IV tube. A larger tube was being lubricated for insertion down her nose. Dr.

Bingham, along with the three nurses, a respiratory therapist and the laboratory technician, brought care to Hillary's body.

"She's more bradycardic, Dr. Bingham," Sheila noted from the monitor.

"Have an amp of atropine ready," Dr. Bingham said as Hillary's heart rate ran irregularly in the forties.

"Endotracheal tube is in place." Ron, the respiratory therapist leaned over Hillary's head. He quickly connected the Ambu-bag and squeezed oxygen into the tube that entered Hillary's mouth. "Somebody check her lung sounds, please."

A few puffs from the bagged oxygen were heard by a nurse listening to each lung field. "Sounds good to me," she told Ron.

"What's her oxygen saturation?" asked Dr. Bingham.

"Seventy-six percent, but we'll get that up now." Ron gave two-second compressions to the black football breathing air into Hillary.

* * * * *

Kison spent his time invisibly above the table in prayer. Other angels were following their charges closely, preventing any errors and maintaining clear consciences. The room was filled with a light more intense then the overhead beam of the operating lens. This place was hallowed ground, solidly guarded against any interruption of thought, any suggestion of doubt, any slip of the hand.

* * * * *

Dr. Bingham saw more irregular rhythms on the monitor, extra beats from the heart trying to compensate for the slow contractions now dropping down to thirty beats per minute.

"Better give that atropine," he called out, but was forced to retract the order in the next second as Hillary's heart beat turned fatal.

"She's in V-fib!" he shouted, grabbing the two paddles connected to the monitor. The heart tripped into uncontrollable shallow spasms unable to sustain life.

"Everyone clear!" He placed the paddles over her chest. "Two hundred joules charged, right?"

"Two hundred joules," Sheila concurred.

"One—two—three—CLEAR!" Pressing the red button on the paddle sent a riveting force of electricity across Hillary's chest. Her body jolted limply.

All eyes watched the monitor as it jumped off the screen and returned to show—

"She's still in fib! Give me three hundred joules!" Bingham shouted.

"Three hundred joules charged."

Bingham replaced the paddles on Hillary's chest and began the count again. "One—everybody pray—three—CLEAR!"

The shock again forced Hillary's body to flop up and down on the gurney. All eyes were glued to the monitor.

"We've got a sinus rhythm," Sheila declared as everyone saw the welcome wave form on the monitor.

"OK, get some Lidocaine going, fifty milligrams now and start the drip," Dr. Bingham said, eyes never leaving the monitor.

"Thank God," he muttered quietly as Hillary's heart showed a stronger rhythm. "Let's get that lavage going and wash that trash out of her stomach before it poisons her more. Thank God."

* * * * *

Kison passed the same thanksgiving heavenward. The angels kept stern observation of all the work going on over Hillary, but somehow, everyone sensed they were out of trouble. It was apparently ordained: Hillary's life was to be restored.

Chapter 7

Slava woke at five o'clock Monday morning wishing this could be an ordinary day. There was no way.

He planned to report to the refinery at his usual starting time of six o'clock and meet with Mr. Chulstarisk. Hopeful that he would be able to stay and work his shift, he also knew it would be a miracle. In any event, whenever he left the refinery he needed to meet the deputy mayor about the fire in his flat.

No, this would not be an ordinary day.

He quietly slipped on the same clothes he had worn all day yesterday, a light blue pullover sweater and tan trousers with a couple stains on the legs. They were nicer than his work clothes. Oksana had told him to try to look a little dressed up.

He tiptoed down the hall past Gina's room, into the living room where his two boys slept on heavy blankets over the wood floor. Stepping over both of them to get to a small table and window, he sat down to open his Bible for a half-hour of reading and prayer.

Maybe a little more prayer than reading today.

Glancing out the window, he noticed the chilly day was overcast. *The weather feels like I do, blue and uncertain.* A grin curled his lips at his weak attempt to cheer himself.

"Father?"

Slava turned to see which of his sons had whispered his name. Vladislav, the five year-old, sat up on his elbows and gleamed a wide-awake smile.

"Can I get up?"

"No, Vladislav. It is still early. I'm just reading my Bible. You should go back to sleep." He was asking the impossible.

"Father?"

"Yes, Vlad?"

"Aren't you going to work today?"

Slava wondered how he knew to even ask such a question. The boys knew nothing about the termination.

"What do you mean?"

"You don't have your work clothes on."

"Yes, I'm going to work. I just have a meeting with my boss, so I thought I'd wear my nice clothes today." Rubbing the stain on his trousers, he began to wonder if Oksana's idea about his dress was such a good one.

"What kind of meeting, Father?"

"Son, it's not important now. Try to lie down and go back to sleep. Let Father read his Bible."

"Yes, Father." Vladislav obediently snuggled back into his blankets, seemingly satisfied.

Slava looked at his watch. Time was escaping. He reviewed his memory verses and spent ten minutes in prayer. *I'm trusting You for every moment of today. Please hear me* .

A community bus carried most of the workers out to the refinery, a fifteen minute trip from town. Most men kept to themselves and simply did their job. When Slava got on, stares pricked him as he moved past the men dressed in roughened t-shirts and pants. As usual, bus talk was quiet. No one spoke to him as he grabbed an overhead rail, standing toward the rear.

He knew everyone questioned his attire. *I'm going to regret these clothes.*

Staring out the window, he tried not to notice the attention he was receiving. Darker clouds of rain were moving in. He prayed the bus would speed along.

At the next to the last stop, Alexander stepped on and worked his way through the bus to stand beside Slava. He was the only other man on Slava's rig that did not share in the coarse talk and drinking. Though not close, they shared an occasional work break, and Slava enjoyed his company.

Alexander looked Slava over and slightly grinned. "Very nice for the refinery."

Shrugging his shoulders, Slava avoided Alexander's eyes. "Just have a meeting with Mr. Chulstarisk."

Alexander looked expectantly, waiting for Slava to add more. When Slava remained silent, looking away, he turned away also.

Anger rose in Slava. He wished he could ask the whole bus if anyone else was fired. By all appearances everyone was ready for work. Why was he picked out? *Why can't I talk to anybody about it?* He wanted to scream.

Soon enough, the bus reached the refinery and the men filed off through the narrow iron gate to the time clock. A drizzly rain started to fall. Drops added to the stares pounding him as he moved away from the rank and toward a small one-story building.

"Slava Gdansk here to see Mr. Chulstarisk," he said to the young lady at the front desk. He tried to read her expression, see if she knew anything about him. *Does she feel sorry for me? Does she know what I'm here for?*

"Have a seat, Mr. Gdansk. I'll let Mr. Chulstarisk know you are here." If she knew what was going on, she kept it hidden.

In the eternity of five minutes, Slava tried to pray, but every thought was interrupted.

Why me?—It's not fair!—What can I say?—How will I care for my family?

"Gdansk, step in, please." Mr. Chulstarisk appeared at his office door and coolly called to Slava. He was tall, broad shoulders with a wider belly. A bushy untrimmed beard hid most of his jowls. The open collar and rolled up white shirt sleeves gave Slava the impression he had been here for hours. Mr. Chulstarisk was never known for his warmth, but Slava thought under these circumstances he might have some slight benefit of compassion. It did not appear to be so.

"Be seated," Chulstarisk pointed to a metal folding chair across from a wooden desk. The office walls were empty, adding to the room's claustrophobic size. A bare bulb under a suspended reflector lit the room, casting shadows into the corners where cardboard boxes of files were stacked.

Chulstarisk sat down at his desk, finding a resting place for his elbows by haphazardly clearing a stack of papers in front of him. Leaning forward, he met Slava's eyes directly.

"Have you spoken to anyone else about the letter I gave your wife, Gdansk?" This was not a question—it was a demand.

"No, Mr. Chulstarisk. My wife read it, and so did the widow we're staying with, before I even saw it myself. But none of us have mentioned it to anyone."

"Good, Gdansk. You will find it best to keep it that way." He paused, enjoying his power position. While Slava felt confident of his own faultlessness, he let his boss direct this moment.

Chulstarisk continued, "How long did you think you could fool us, cheating on your time card?" He pitched forward in his chair as if about to reach out and grab Slava.

"Cheating? What are you talking about?"

"Oh, come now, Gdansk! We have caught you and your pal, George."

"George? George who? I don't know any George!"

"Stop it, Gdansk! He confessed the whole works. You'd trade off leaving the fields early, and the other one would clock your time card out. He told us everything. You're both finished here!"

"This is crazy!" Slava could not believe his ears. He had no idea who this George could be, nor why anyone would make such an outlandish accusation.

"You're just lucky we didn't haul you to the police, Gdansk! We have witnesses who saw you leave early, and George's confession has exposed the whole scam. The other managers wanted to see you hang for this, but I thought we should try to salvage your reputation—for your family at least. No sense in having them suffer for your foolishness."

Dumbfounded, Slava sat back in his chair without a response.

"I trust you see why it is best you keep quiet, Gdansk." Chulstarisk lowered his voice slightly. "We will try not to let this get out from our office, and I would suggest you not mention it to anyone. If it becomes public, we'll have you run out of town—though that's not far enough for me."

He had returned to threatening. Through the veil of toughness, Slava saw him almost pleading.

"Don't make us do that, Gdansk. If not for yourself, think of your family."

Chulstarisk did not deserve the satisfaction of any further acknowledgment.

"You may go now. I don't plan to see you around this refinery ever again. And remember, if we hear any disgruntled charges coming from you, it'll be your end. Understand?"

Slava stood up and walked to the door. Turning back on the threshold, he eyed his boss. "I am innocent." Before Chulstarisk could respond, he left.

"Good day, Mr. Gdansk," the office secretary said cheerfully as he left through the front door.

Slava turned and surprised himself with a smile to the woman. While his countenance remained collected, inwardly his mind was racing.

Lord, what is going on? What was Mr. Chulstarisk talking about? Who could make such accusations?

The drizzle had turned into a light rain under dark clouds as Slava walked out the iron gates toward town. It was a two-hour trek on foot, his only way home. But the rain was easily ignored. He was consumed with justifying himself in the face of these charges.

Lord, someone at work has created this lie and told Mr. Chulstarisk all about it. No, it would have to be a group of people, if there are other witnesses. And this guy named George lost his job over it too, except he has to be lying as well—about me, at least. Why would anyone make up such a story? Why would anyone want to ruin my life?

* * * * *

Brael tried to help by entering into Slava's one-sided conversation. "And why are you not supposed to tell anyone why you're fired?"

I cannot talk to anyone about it, or else they will arrest me, Slava thought.

Brael responded in thought. "Yes, but why would they be so afraid to have you talk about it?"

Mr. Chulstarisk said he wanted to protect my family, but that's a weak reason. Chulstarisk didn't know me from the other workers until today. Why would he care about my family?

He responded to his own question. *There must be more to it. Could it be he doesn't want me to talk to anyone about it, because he knows it's a lie? Because he knows I could prove my innocence?*

Brael tried to move Slava to consider the bigger picture. "So why would Chulstarisk want to take your job and frame you with a fraudulent reputation?"

Why, indeed. Why would anyone see me as someone they needed out of their way?

Brael let Slava ponder these thoughts as God brought the rain showers. Right now his charge didn't need answers. He needed faith.

Slava's thoughts met a dead end. He had hoped the walk into town would clear his mind and bring some order to this nonsense. Instead, he found himself perplexed with more questions. Wiping the rain from his face, his own tears of frustration mixed with the droplets.

My Lord, I am so confused! What am I to do? Something's terribly wrong. Please change Mr. Chulstarisk's decision. He's got to realize there's been a horrible mistake. Oh, Lord, I don't know what You would have me do.

Facing his own unemployment cluttered his desperate thoughts as he trudged along the wet road's shoulder. *Lord, I need You to be with my wife and children. How will I provide for them?*

His cries joined the steady rain, helplessness consuming him. *Lord, how can I be the husband and father You want me to be? Oh, my God—what shall I do?*

Brael remained silent. This was where Slava would build another stone into his wall of faithfulness. He needed to completely depend on God. God was worthy to be trusted. He needed to realize this on his own.

Slowed by self-defeat and the muddy path, Slava silently cried, facing his future alone with his God. *There's no where else for me to turn, Lord. You've got to move in my life. I don't know. Oh, Lord, I don't think there is anything else I can do.*

Through wet eyes he looked ahead to see the city of Bolshoigorsk.

More than once he had come this way to pray over the city, asking God to bless it. To save it. Now his prayers were for his own life.

The apathy of God seemed to abound.

Are you there, God? Do You care? Do You have any thought about me? About my family? About these children of Yours in Bolshoigorsk?

He turned aside and went to his knees, hands across his face to hold the gush of tears. Downcast eyes met puddles before him, dotted by ripples of rain drops.

Catching his breath, a sparkle of light reflected in the water.

Looking up, he saw a beam of sunlight shoot through the dark granite clouds directly into the city.

It was a natural event, not uncommon at all. Of course, the sun will shine after the rain falls. It happens all the time. But he could not help but wonder. Would God shape this moment, just for him?

Slava's sea of emotions began to calm. It was so obvious. A small ray of light darted out from the clouds, its beam broadening as it hit the city. Light, warmth and cheer shined in an otherwise dark corner of town.

Now another ray broke through, and another. Each one broadening the target, expanding the sunshine's strike across Bolshoigorsk.

Slava rose. In his hopelessness he was finding the only Hope he could believe. The essence of the man God chose to pioneer the Bolshoigorsk church was renewed.

Lord, forgive me. Forgive me that I have not trusted You. You gave me confidence while I sat before Mr. Chulstarisk, and I trust You for the same now. You protected me and my family in the fire, and I know You can protect me now. You cared for me as we lost all our belongings, and I know You will care for me now.

Basking in the sunshine, Slava received the forgiveness of his Lord. A breeze blew past him with a crisp after-the-rain scent. Beams of sunlight highlighted the entire town now, a marker of what God desired. Slava regained his vision. God was moving.

The fire! Somebody torched my home, Now somebody's torched my job.

Quickening his pace, he reasoned through the common thread of the fire and his firing. On the outskirts of town, he broke into a run to reach home and change his sopping clothes.

He had a meeting with the deputy mayor.

* * * * *

In minutes Slava was at his borrowed flat. He told Oksana he could not discuss the refinery meeting but that everything was going to be fine. Oksana tottered, spun by a whirlwind as Slava blew out the door in dry clothes shouting, "I should be home in two or three hours. I'll explain it all then."

He had a fifteen minute walk to the city building, an older three-story complex marked with four large concrete pillars on each side of the main double doors. Once a stately building, the chipped paint and broken light globes gave evidence of the depressed civic and economic toll of the past generation.

Here were the offices of most Bolshoigorsk government officials, excluding the police station two blocks down. The deputy mayor, Renat Dontestansk, had befriended Slava several years ago when Slava was more involved in drinking than ministry. At that time, Renat was a street repairman, and together they had spent many an evening discussing life over a bottle of vodka. Both were single and knew their limits, enough commonalities between them to bridge a friendship. Their lives took separate roads in recent years, but Slava had hoped for an opportunity to meet up with Renat again. This business seemed heaven-sent.

"Good morning," Slava said at the counter of the front receptionist. "Could I speak with the deputy mayor?"

Appointments were unusual in Bolshoigorsk. City officials were haphazardly available on a drop-in basis.

"Yes, Mr. Dontestansk is available," the receptionist responded. "May I tell him who is here?"

"I am Slava Gdansk."

"Thank you, Mr. Gdansk. Please have a seat. It will be just a few moments."

"Thank you." Slava moved to the empty lobby, taking a seat in one of several old wooden lounge chairs. Sitting on the only cushion without a rip, he nodded to the armed guard in uniform at the inside entrance. The guard ignored him.

Moments passed into ten minutes before a suited man approached Slava. "Mr. Gdansk?"

"Yes?" Slava got up, not recognizing the man.

"I am afraid Mr. Dontestansk is in a meeting with another citizen and is unable to meet with you."

"Oh. I had understood from the receptionist that he was not busy."

"No, unfortunately he is occupied and will be for the rest of the morning. I hope you understand."

"Well—yes, of course." Slava was disappointed. Some action was needed to start the fire investigation. "I would be glad to wait for him, even if I could have ten minutes of his time."

"That would be impossible, Mr. Gdansk. I am afraid I must ask you to leave."

The uniformed guard showed up two steps behind the suit.

"Fine, fine. I understand," Slava responded politely. There was much more opposition here than necessary.

He made his way out the door, walking back to his flat. *So, I am even off limits to the city now. Lord, I'm ready for your next plan.*

He walked through a residential area of three-story flats lining both sides of the street, patiently sorting through any other possible contacts he could seek out.

Suddenly from the dark alley between two flats, he heard his name called.

"Slava?"

Squinting into the dark shadows between the buildings, he stepped toward the alley.

"Yes?"

"Slava, it's me, Renat," the dark voice responded.

Slava found his old friend dressed in a business suit.

"Renat! What are you doing here?"

"It's good to see you, my friend," Renat said quietly with a sheepish smile. "I'm sorry to have to hunt for you like this."

"I don't understand. Why couldn't you see me at your office?"

"Slava, you are bad news. They say you have built an organization under the guise of a church to try to control the city. Rumor has it you're stealing money from the refinery to finance the take-over. I know you, Slava. I know it cannot be true."

"Thanks, Renat."

"But I cannot speak to you. If you come to us we are to have you arrested. I prevented it this morning by arguing that they had no charges against you yet. It will only be a matter of time."

"Who are 'they', Renat? Who is against me and our church?"

"It is better that you do not know, Slava. Just stop what you are doing in your church. Move out of town if you must. It is for your own safety."

"Renat, I cannot do that. You wouldn't either. Why are you so scared about this?"

"Slava, it's bigger than you realize. It's not just your church. It's the whole town, probably the whole province. I've already said more than I should. Please, get undercover for a while."

"I'll do some praying about it, Renat."

"Do more than that. I must go before I am missed."

Before Slava could say goodbye, Renat was racing down the back alley into the darkness.

Even though it was a sunny walk home, Slava moved quickly, staying far away from any other darkened alleys. No more surprises today.

Chapter 8

The Windwood Community Church sanctuary was filled fifteen minutes before the funeral was to begin. The early attendance of the people gave evidence of the yearning. Linking emotional arms, the community was here to face the agonizing questions of why Sarah Townsend died.

As each person entered, their guardian angel was told by heralds at the doorway to pose the questions of the hour. There was no need to dwell on the sadness of the moment. Each angel suggested to their beloved that they contemplate what God was doing. Why would Sarah be called to die? Is this any way for a loving God to act? What about her place on the mission field? What about those of us who love Sarah so much and miss her so deeply? Why would our God allow us to suffer with this loss? Is He really in control?

A private room off the sanctuary was reserved for Sarah's family. The room also served for choir robing and the over-fifty Sunday School class, but today the wardrobe closets were closed and folding chairs scattered about the room were filled by small huddles of people.

Entering the room, John first noticed Sarah's parents, Ed and Cleora, seated in the center. Aunts, uncles and cousins were pacing, sitting or standing around a handful of stiffly dressed young children. Amidst the unsettled and awkward feelings here, there was little to say.

John found the senior pastor, Charles McMahon, and with him circulated to different relatives. Hand clasps, hugs and condolences were received with small talk. The room's atmosphere became less stuffy as occupations, weather reports, road trips, and family relations were explained. Words of comfort came easy to John. Though he knew little about these people, he cared. Angels were at work in this arena, encouraging the relatives' acceptance of John as a man of God. He needed credibility to convincingly bring a word of hope over the next hour.

"Mrs. Townsend, hello," John said, reaching a hand to the grieving mother's shoulder. "How did you sleep last night?"

"Actually, a little better than I thought I would," Cleora responded. She had appreciated John's short but comforting visits over the last couple of days. The special stories he had shared of his own friendship with Sarah meant much.

"The sleeping pills from that Dr. Wells were a big help," Ed Townsend said. "Thanks for putting us in touch with him."

"Yes, thank you," Cleora added. "By the way, have you heard how his daughter is doing?"

John marveled at the small town chatter. Dr. Wells' daughter's suicide attempt was even known by these out-of-town visitors. "I've heard downtown that she's better, but I don't really know, Mrs. Townsend."

"Yes, well, that was certainly sad," Cleora responded, momentarily oblivious to the circumstances of her own grief.

Pastor McMahon stepped over to the Townsends and John. "Mr. and Mrs. Townsend, I'd like to briefly run through our service arrangements with you again."

"Yes, fine," Ed said.

"The service order will be the same as we discussed last evening, except John has requested that the congregation sing one hymn after his message."

"That would be fine. What song is it?" Ed asked.

"One I know meant a lot to Sarah recently," John offered. "'My Jesus, I Love Thee.'"

Cleora nodded with a forced smile of approval. The anticipation of this moment, the funeral of her only daughter, was taking its toll. Sarah's parents had shown remarkable strength in the wake of the tragedy.

Since their arrival two days ago, John had twice visited their hotel suite at the Windwood Inn. Each time he was treated with great kindness by this grieving couple, surpassing his own offerings of sympathy and love.

Their generosity, however, did not replace their sadness. John would never forget the wailing cry of Sarah's father the first night he was with them. While sharing a story of Sarah's first puppy when she was a little girl, Mr. Townsend lost control. He ran into the bedroom and closed the door, but the howl vibrated John's soul. Mrs. Townsend left to be with him, leaving John alone in their small outer room.

Despite bright floral arrangements and a multitude of fresh-baked breads and cakes that local friends had sent, the pervasive anguish in the hotel room that night seemed overwhelming. The incredible loss deeply tore at these parents' hearts. Their bleeding flowed in unrestrained mourning resounding within those small walls.

John sat alone in the room, amazed at this family's response. A funeral away from the hometown of the family had to be difficult. While Sarah's parents agonized over her death, they still wanted Sarah's church and community family here to share in the bereavement, before they returned to their home two states away for a second memorial service and burial.

"This is where Sarah was most able to touch lives for her Savior," Sarah's mother had told him earlier that night. "God doesn't want us to leave with her before she can have a moment to share her last thoughts with the special people of Windwood. That's why we wanted you to lead the service, John. You know best what Sarah would have wanted to say to her dear friends here, and you will know what Jesus wants these people to hear as well."

Now, moments before the funeral was to begin, John was able to look confidently at the Townsends and agree. God had a special message for Windwood. He was anxious to see it unfold.

The closed cherry wood coffin in the front of the sanctuary was adorned with sprays of carnations, chrysanthemums, and roses. The bright yellows and reds reflected off the coffin's brass trim, making a beautiful monument to the once bubbly, energetic life it held. Easels surrounding the platform held more floral arrangements with wide ribbons bearing scripted names such as 'my dear sister,' 'our beloved niece,' and several bearing 'our best friend.'

John sat on the platform with Pastor McMahon and two soloists, the latter both cousins of Sarah's. The sanctuary was completely filled, ushers racing to set up folding chairs in the back of the church. It was definitely the largest funeral Windwood Community Church had seen for a long time.

The organ played sacred hymns as Sarah's family entered and sat in the first two rows in front of John. At least twenty or so were here for this special service, which impressed John since surely they would all attend the service in Sarah's hometown two days from now.

Pastor McMahon squeezed John's knee and whispered, "I'll be praying for you." He stepped to the pulpit and warmly greeted the great crowd. After introducing those on the platform, he had everyone rise to sing all four verses of 'It Is Well With My Soul.'

John's thoughts were clear as he sang the first verse, but clouds of tears began to blur his focus as he broke into the chorus. Gazing across the coffin to the family, and past them to the many friends gathered for one reason, the pity he felt was overpowering.

Sarah would never have wanted this to be so sad.

It was John's last earth-borne thought. He sat down after the final chorus, his musings focused elsewhere. The two solos and the obituary reading proceeded, but John was unaware. He was being angelically primed.

* * * * *

Though the congregation sat quietly, a flutter of heavenly activity covered the room. A beehive was tame compared to thousands of angels ministering to those assembled here.

At every perimeter point of the sanctuary, large winged angels hovered with gleaming swords, cherubim guarding the holy service. Floating over the platform, a congregate of angels lifted their hands to heaven in praise of their King. The remaining angels were either personal guardians or additional comforters assisting the four hundred or so people who questioned the wisdom of God.

The Holy Spirit's presence was in the hearts of believers who unknowingly sat strategically across the sanctuary. These Christians clung to their faith without necessarily understanding God's ways. Their prayers were dry kindling for the blazing work of the angels.

John moved to the pulpit now, sharing his memories of Sarah and her relationship with Jesus Christ. The words conveyed only part of the message the congregation was hearing.

Angels gently but busily shot arrows of truth into the souls of the people. Ricocheting declarations would dart past the minds of the congregation: Jesus Christ died for you; all things work together for good; God is in control; I came to bring you life; where, oh death, is thy sting; for God so loved the world; for He cares for you.

Working feverishly, the angels confronted doubting human emotions with great truths of God. Reconciliation was not the goal, as the angels stirred up, more than resolved, concerns of the questioning grievers.

From the pulpit, John began to relate his own questions of God in the wake of Sarah's death, intensifying the faithless accusations laid against the Lord. The agony of the flesh was livid. John's voice echoed the altercation of man versus God. Sarah's death was not right, fair or justified.

The angels suddenly froze while John announced the key words that would drive the congregation home to their Savior.

"But then I found God's reply."

It was quiet enough to hear the ruffle of an angel's wing. The people were rapt to John. This was the moment, this was the precise desire on the hearts of the bereaved. *Please tell us, what does God have to say in the midst of this utter tragedy!*

John opened his Bible to the book of Job, chapter forty-one. Briefly setting the stage, he reminded everyone of the place Job held in God's realm, a faithful man enduring the loss of family, health, and wealth to fulfill God's pre-eminent will.

The angels turned to their charges and again went to work, more calmly addressing their beloved with the anticipation of God's response.

The congregation faced the elemental dilemma—is God really in control?

"Let's ask Job, everyone." As a lawyer leading a jury, John interrogated the witness.

"Job?" he boomed, addressing the air. "Was God unfair to you? Was what He did to you right and justified?"

The question lingered across the sanctuary.

"Listen to Job's response. Hear what he says in the Bible: 'I know that God can do all things; no plan of His can be thwarted. Surely I earlier spoke of things I did not understand, things too wonderful for me to know.'"

Angel wings began waving again, pockets of Spirit-led inspiration taking hold. Tears stopped flowing. Each person was able to step apart from their emotions for the moment. Provoked by angels, they saw a glimmer of God's hope.

The angels nurtured the ripening harvest of praise as people saw a hint of the intent of God—not to harm the children He loved, but to proceed with a plan that His children could not comprehend.

John continued, "And look how Job defends his faith in God in the midst of his struggles in chapter thirteen: Job says, 'though He slay me, yet will I hope in Him.'

He closed his Scriptures. "No further questions, Job, you may step down. Next, let us turn our questions to a more recent witness of God's more unpopular actions. Can we for a moment imagine that we could ask Sarah herself of God's purpose?

"Let's ask her, in the way that each of us know her. Let's ask Sarah, 'Was God unfair? Was what He has done right and justified?' What would Sarah's response be?"

The Holy Spirit washed over the congregation like a great wave, ripples of angels floating in His wake. Enlightenment settled across the sanctuary sea, as the throng of souls felt a sense of peace. John offered the response Sarah would have, but everyone knew the words already.

"Sarah would be delighted to continue in God's will, right? Whether it be crippling disease, a situational disaster or this present death, she would never doubt. If God be the Guide, Sarah would willingly go anywhere. No one would dispute that. Her hope would always remain in God."

Angels performed little work here. The Spirit brought conviction and comfort in the mighty tide that washed away doubt and faithlessness.

The congregation understood. They did not need to know exactly why God would do what He does. God's master plan could not be thwarted. They could rest with that.

In a blur of time, the auditorium was filled with the sounds of the final hymn. It was robust singing for a funeral, not the sound of a dirge. The third and fourth verses gave a final testimony of Sarah's faithfulness. A lasting mark was made on the congregation as they sang:

"I'll love Thee in life, I will love Thee in death,

And praise Thee as long as Thou lendest me breath;

And say when the death-dew lies cold on my brow;

If ever I loved Thee, my Jesus 'tis now.

In mansions of glory and endless delight,

I'll ever adore Thee in heaven so bright;

I'll sing with the glittering crown on my brow;

If ever I loved Thee, my Jesus, 'tis now."

The people were ready to release Sarah's life to God's domain, and do so with acceptance and confidence in God's design.

* * * * *

John stood close to Melinda's side, meeting attenders after the service. Tears, handshakes, and hugs of comfort were shared. Straining to see Tony, John could not find him in the crowd.

He hardly remembered a thing. After being lost in mournful thoughts during the opening hymn, John's mind was blank until he found himself boastfully singing during the final hymn. Many people were blessed, but he hardly knew what had happened.

"So, Melinda, tell me about the service," he said as he wheeled her out the door of the darkened church at last. "What did you think? I can hardly remember any of it. I was lost in my thoughts, I guess."

"John, you did fine, but it wasn't really you," she paused wistfully. "Something special happened in that service. I think you could have whistled 'Dixie', and God would have been able to move this crowd closer to Him."

During the car ride home, they quietly reflected on their perceptions of the funeral. It was still hard to understand why Sarah was called home, but her death was somehow more easily accepted. Against the background of a vastly incomprehensible God Who had just moved mightily in their presence to minister love and comfort, they knew they could trust His motives.

* * * * *

Actually, Tony was not at the funeral.

He still could not handle the grief, much less talk to anyone about it.

Anger at God, at life, and at Sarah was uncontrollable. He feared he would blow up again. The remorse he felt for the young girl he had yelled at at Sarah's apartment only more deeply drove him into his despair.

Knowing he should be at Sarah's funeral, he angrily ignored his conscience and drove his red coupe out of town.

His speed carried him quickly to a dirt road two miles past the city limits. Skidding ninety degrees to make the turn, he recklessly sped down the country road. Tony's tight forearms caused the steering wheel to veer right, then left. The loose gravel created a gut-wrenching carnival ride.

"Why did you have to die, Sarah? Why?"

Though shouted, the words did little to vent his anger. The roar of the coupe combined with the guttural rush of thrown gravel, forming a deafening absence of any answer.

* * * * *

Fortas stayed with Tony, but his counsel was of no use. He needed help. Consulting the heavens, he immediately had two intervention angels.

An intense light flashed. The two guest angels' golden faces and bright white gowns suddenly appeared just to the side of the speeding car. Tony screamed loud and braked hard. The car skidded in a half circle, about-face on the road. He peered out in search of the apparitions, but they were gone.

Fortas seized the opportunity as Tony's mind was shocked open.

"Tony, there's no reason for you to drive like that!" The words thundered clearly in his head. "You've got to get a hold of yourself!"

Tony conceded, but he could not escape saying, "What did I just see? Didn't I just see two people, or bodies, or beings—right out there?"

Fortas left the questions unanswered. Drawing attention to angels too often led to ungodly mysticism. Fortas' purpose was still ahead.

"Tony, why are you driving like a madman? Don't you see how your anger is dangerous? This has got to stop!"

I have to control myself, Tony agreed. *It's silly of me to drive like this. I can't let my anger get away from me. This was a close one. Whatever was out there, if it was real, I could have hurt someone.*

"Why don't you get out of the car," Fortas directed. "Get some air. Look around. What did you see, anyway?"

Believing the thoughts to be his own, Tony got out and looked across the road. It was mid-afternoon, the spring sunshine beaming across the emerald wheat fields to either side of him. A slight breeze tickled his ear, and he turned in its direction as if the wind had tapped him on the shoulder.

There it was. Its position unchanged, metal twisted and ripped as if it had been forced through a fan blade. Sarah's white hatchback was not the ominous tomb of the other day. Today it was a piece of junk, ready to be slung into the compress.

Why hasn't this thing been towed away?

He walked down across the shallow gully and into the wheat field several paces until he reached the rear. It was eerie, seeing what had held the evaporation of a life. Tony felt like he was intruding in a forbidden zone. A fleeting thought shot through him, a fear that he might be seen by someone. He shook it off as silliness and walked far around to the driver's side.

In a glance he saw a movement of a hand. Someone's hand. His heart leaped into his throat.

Someone else is here!

"Oh my! Excuse me!" The old lady jumped back from the door.

"Mrs. Davis!" Tony caught his breath. "What are you doing here?"

"Oh, Tony, my dear lad. You really gave my heart a skip!" She was catching her breath as well. "I walked down here from my house. It may sound a bit odd, but I just wasn't up for Sarah's funeral today, so many people and all. I thought I might spend a little time here, thinking about her."

Tony understood better than he let on. He nodded his head and waited to hear more. There were many stories about this peculiar lady and her occasionally supernatural ways.

"I think there's something special about the place where God takes his child back to Himself, don't you?" she asked. "Sometimes it's hospital beds, or bedrooms, or maybe automobiles," she gestured in front of her. "You can hardly help but imagine the presence of angels rejoicing at the homecoming of God's special ones."

"Did you see any angels out here, Mrs. Davis?"

"Oh no, Tony. I don't mean I can see them."

Tony sighed, disappointed.

"But you can tell they're out there, can't you?"

This time she waited, eyes pinned on Tony as if she knew.

"Well—yes, maybe," he replied.

"So this is where Sarah was the moment she saw her life turn fully glorified. What a moment, to be in the presence of Jesus, face to face. It's almost like there's a window to heaven right here. Sometimes I think I can get a little glimmer through the curtains before the window closes again." She gazed into the blue sky, viewing the entryway of heaven itself. "In any event, it's a very hallowed place, wouldn't you say?"

He wished she would stop asking him to agree with her. This was way beyond him.

"It's hard to figure out God sometimes, isn't it?" she continued. "The timing of His actions, I mean. It doesn't seem to make sense." Her words picked at him. "But sometimes we have to imagine what it would be like in the shoes of the one who has suffered."

Tony raised his head to look into Grandma Davis' sapphire eyes. They beamed at him with an honest radiancy.

"Like Jesus, for example. Everyone can feel horrible about the death He had to suffer, but no one who believes in Him would call it wrong or a mistake. That's because we know what Jesus was thinking about it. He told us it would happen, He knew He had to suffer it, and He was willing to do it—out of His love for us. Who am I to suggest there was a better plan?

"Well, now I try to put myself in Sarah's shoes," Grandma Davis looked up to the heavens. "I think she would say, if we could see her now, that she's happier than she could ever be. No more worldly worries, no more pain, enjoying the Savior she has served so faithfully. So who am I to want to interrupt that?"

Tony had to take his eyes off Grandma Davis as they began to moisten. "She meant so much to me."

Grandma Davis reached out her hand to his. "I know she did."

He looked up with wet eyes. Somehow she really did know.

"And for that, your pain will be there to reckon with. You miss her, Tony. There's nothing wrong with that. Yet, we have to give God room to move, trusting beyond understanding. We must ask Him what role He wants us to play as He executes His plan for the world He loves. Your grieving may be just the path He has chosen for you, to enter new circumstances of His design."

Tony thought of the strange young girl he angrily scared away on Sarah's steps. "Yes, but what if our own stupid actions screw up His plan?"

"Do you really think you could mess up God's plan, Tony?"

She held a glowing smile. He couldn't help but meekly smile back. "No, I guess I can't."

She took Tony's arm, and they began to walk away.

"Now you listen to me, Tony. I think I can tell you that God's plan for you, right now, is to take me back to my house down this road. His plan for me, I believe, is to serve you some iced tea and brownies. Are you willing to follow God's plan?" Her smile beamed with her soft sarcasm.

"It sounds like a great plan to me."

Chapter 9

Tony was reluctant to face John after the funeral, but he had to.

His convictions were firmly held two days after seeing Grandma Davis. He had to act. There wasn't much time to accomplish what he needed, but God would be faithful if this was truly of Him. He worked the second shift on Thursday so he planned to catch John at the lumber store that morning.

Entering Windwood Lumber and Hardware Store was like stepping back in time to the days of penny candy and pickle barrels. Walking on the gray cement floor, he passed a short aisle of sticky fly traps, cattle dusting bags, and fireplace matches before arriving at the long counter which held a cash register and the elbows of two older men in denim overalls. Under the glass top were yellowed newspaper cartoons about farmers and politics, unchanged for years.

The two men, though customers, regularly occupied themselves here until it was time for coffee downtown. No employees were in sight, so Tony interrupted the farmers' crop gossip to ask where John was.

Following their directions, Tony made his way back to the old two-story lumber shed. John was on the other side of a large yellow forklift, stacking two-by-fours.

"Well, hello, stranger." John took off his glove and shook Tony's hand.

"Hi, John. Finding a lot of bent ones?"

"No more than usual. A few of these would make a dandy boat frame."

John smiled and Tony stumbled for more idle words. In the gaping moment, he plunged in head first.

"John, I'm real sorry for the way I acted when you told me about Sarah."

"Say no more, Tony. No apology needed. I'm sorry to have been the one to tell you. I'm not very good at that kind of stuff."

"No, John, I'm glad you did tell me, and I'm sorry I acted like a jerk. Actually, I've been a jerk the last few days, and I'm sorry for not being there to support you. Sarah was a very special friend to you and Melinda."

"Thanks, Tony. You're certainly forgiven. Have you got time for a cup of coffee?"

Tony shifted his feet a little nervously. "I'd like to talk with you for a minute if you can, but could we just stay out here?"

"Sure, what's up?"

"I was wondering what you were going to do now with the Russia mission trip—is it still on?"

"The team talked it over, and we still feel like we need to go, for Sarah's sake now, more than anything," John said. "Why, did you have a thought on it?"

"Yes—uh, I mean—no. I think that sounds great, but will you try to fill Sarah's spot?"

"Oh no, Tony. I don't think we could with only a month to go." John paused as he realized what Tony might be getting at.

"You see, I was wondering," Tony's words did not come smoothly. "I've been really praying about this the last couple days, and I think God might be wanting me to consider going. If that could be possible."

"Tony, are you serious?"

"The day of Sarah's funeral, Grandma Davis and I talked a long time about how God works in ways we cannot understand. She told me that as we seek to follow Him, things begin to clear and make some sense. I realized God might have been pricking my heart about this Russia trip after Sarah's death, but I was so mad, I couldn't see anything but my own self.

"Grandma Davis helped me see that I might be able to help the Russia team. Not that God had Sarah die so I could join the team, but I do wonder if God would have me go in Sarah's place." He paused. "What do you think?"

"It's an incredible idea. We had no inkling of anyone joining the team this late. It would have to be approved by the church, but I know there would be no one against you going. It's just the logistics of it all. It's quite late to be making travel plans."

"I know. I've thought through some of it. That's where God will have to show His plan. If it's meant for me to go, He can work out the details, true?"

"True, Tony, true." John paused to think it over. "It won't be easy. For instance, do you have the air fare, about twelve hundred dollars?"

Tony smiled. "That's the first miracle we'll have to ask for."

* * * * *

"Renat was so nervous and fidgety, nothing like the way I remembered him, Oksana."

Slava had been speaking to his wife about his visit with Mr. Chulstarisk, his rainy walk back to town, and his shadowy visit with Renat. Oksana sat listening without interrupting, glued to every word. Widow Gina was seeing a friend, and the boys were just in bed as Slava and his wife sat in the small kitchen sharing cups of strong tea.

"So what do you think?"

"It's scary, Slava, especially with what Renat said. Did he really mean we should move out of town?"

Slava held back his response. *She's frightened, but how could she feel any different? She's thinking of her children and home—God bless her for that. Can I really expect my wife to stand up to whatever this is we're facing?*

As he was quiet, Oksana did her thinking out loud. "But we can't leave here, I know that. I just wish I knew what God was doing. It doesn't make sense to me that He would have us in this much trouble. Could it all be directed at our church?"

"It has to be, Oksana. Someone really wants to see our church fail. We shouldn't be surprised, I suppose. We're bringing Jesus Christ to Bolshoigorsk for the first time, and our success is riling up some enemies. Why would we think there wouldn't be opposition?"

"My only concern is to be sure this isn't God closing the door on our ministry for some reason. Can we be sure that He isn't trying to direct us another way?"

Slava was thankful for his wife's honesty. Without doubting their call to Bolshoigorsk, she wanted to be completely confident that the ministry was in God's will. Oksana would fight this opposition if she had to. She was just exploring every angle, a valuable quality Slava knew God had given his wife.

"I have really sought the Lord over this, Oksana. I am convinced that Mr. Chulstarisk's and Renat's comments came out of lies and fear. God couldn't be closing the door. We need to stay in the battle here, but—" he hoped to soften the impact of his next words. "I can only imagine that it will be more difficult for us before it gets any easier. I don't know what we are up against, but if it can take my job, control the city government, and cause Renat to tremble, it must be very big."

Oksana was quiet. He knew she was worried about him and the children, wondering about her home. Where will the money come from for food? He silently prayed that she would share his conviction that God would help them rise above these challenges.

"We must stay here, Slava, and bring Jesus Christ to our people in Bolshoigorsk." Oksana spoke the words softly but firmly.

He reached out to take her hand. "I love you more than you could ever know." No man could put this marriage asunder.

"Oksana, let's pray just now. It is His strength holding us together."

Holding hands at the table with heads bowed, a loud knock at the door broke the silence before a word was uttered.

"Gina wouldn't knock, would she?" Oksana asked.

Slava released his wife's hands to go and see who it was.

Opening the door, khaki green uniforms of three men caught his attention before he even noticed their faces. With a billy club drawn, the front man gruffly said, "You're coming with us, Gdansk!" Grabbing Slava's arm, the policeman jerked him out of the doorway.

Oksana raced to the door. "What are you doing?"

The men roughly carried Slava down the stairway. She bolted after them, yanking the sleeve of the first policeman she reached.

"Get back, woman, or we'll take you, too!"

Slava yelled, "It's all right, Oksana. Stay with the boys. They can't keep me long. Pray."

The policemen laughed.

She continued to follow them to the ground floor. Slava was no longer resisting and briskly walked beside the policemen as they nudged him along.

"Where are you taking him? Where are you taking my husband? Please, just tell me where!" Her pleas were ignored.

It was barely past dusk. The night air was cool, though Oksana burned with worry and anger. Slava wasn't struggling, but the police still shoved him into the back seat of the dated military sedan with enough force to cause him to grimace. He flopped across the seat like a rag doll.

She screamed, "Where are you taking my husband?"

The driver matter-of-factly responded. "Your husband is under arrest, woman. You can visit him down at the station in the morning."

The car sped off with a single revolving red light flashing from the car top.

Oksana watched the blinking beacon fade in the midnight street, dazed and unsure. She stood frozen, her mind replaying the past sixty seconds.

It was Gina who interrupted her ten minutes later, finding her staring down the street.

That was when Oksana broke down.

*****

Oksana let Gina coax her back up to the flat, concerned that the boys might have awakened. They were both sound asleep, however.

She told Gina all she knew. "But all they would say was that he was arrested. They said I could see him tomorrow. How could they do this? What has he done?"

Gina was without an answer. Recent events had bewildered the elderly woman. Oksana could see this arrest sent her reeling all the more. The stress the Gdansk family was placing on her quiet way of life was taking its toll. Oksana had to impose a bit more.

"Gina, I have to go to the police station. I have to see Slava. Would you watch the boys while I'm gone? I promise I won't be more than a couple hours."

It would be dangerous to go to the station. It could land Oksana in the same mess her husband was in. Gina certainly realized all this.

"You be careful, dear. I'll stay with your boys. Please, get a message to me if there is any worse trouble."

"Thank you, Gina." They grasped hands tightly. "May God bless you for your help."

"And may God give you strength, dear. Please be very careful."

Oksana grabbed her blue shoulder wrap, tied a gray scarf around her head, and kissed each of her sleeping boys quickly before racing down the stairs to the dark streets of Bolshoigorsk to find her husband.

She could make it in twenty minutes or so. She never had cause to go the police station before, but it must be only a five minute walk east of the market she daily attended. If she hurried, she could mark off another minute or two.

The crisp night air nipped at her face and fingers. The farther she walked, the more alone she felt. Soon she was away from the rows of apartments with outside lighting, approaching more commercial paths with a street light only every few blocks. The lights were little comfort, creating eery shadows around trees and buildings. One beacon lit a drunken man lying on a bus stop bench. Oksana passed him as he slept his troubles away.

No cars were out this late; the roads were empty. Oksana decided to walk in the street to avoid any more sidewalk bums. The shadows were less fearful out here. She complimented herself on such a clever idea as she raced down the path in her quickest walk. Up ahead was where she needed to turn to reach the market.

Rounding the corner, she slowed her gait. Five shadowy figures were in the street twenty yards ahead of her. Even from this distance she could tell they were all men—and all drunk. Three of them staggered forward toward her while another man to the side had just given the fifth man a shove, causing them both to fall into the gutter. They burst out with an alcoholic laugh.

Oksana stopped, hoping to not draw their attention. It was too late.

"Well, well, well. Look what we have here, boys!"

The one in the center gave a long cat call, causing each man to look up. Though she couldn't see faces, she knew their drunken eyes would not let her escape.

She made a weak attempt to ignore their bellerings, but alone in the shadowy streets, their comments rang sharply, shattering any security.

Lord help me! Oh Lord, help me!

The two men who had fallen in the gutter were up now. All five of them walked toward her, coarsely shouting. They passed congratulatory back-slaps to each other as if at the climax of a hunting trip. Oksana hated most the dark laughter that echoed expectantly between the empty downtown street buildings.

Easing over to the sidewalk, she hugged the wall of a closed café and questioned whether to run ahead and hope to pass them, or break into a sprint the opposite direction. Their speed would be compromised, but each of them was a foot taller and wider than her. If one of them caught her, it would all be over.

Suddenly one of the five was shoved ahead by the others. He began a tipsy jog to her. He had been elected to take the first shot. It seemed he had a clear one.

Oksana stopped in her tracks and turned to run.

Suddenly the man, now an arm's reach behind her, said in a drawl, "Oh, 'cuse me fellas. I hadn't seen you with the girl."

She turned to see her attacker, his blood shot eyes showing fear as he gazed to the left and right of Oksana, just inches above her head.

He sees something around me. She looked at either side of her; only endlessly empty sidewalks in both directions.

The other four joined their friend, but he was pushing them away. "Let's go guys, let's go, quick!"

The four looked toward Oksana, though not really looking at her. They saw something next to her. Briefly halting with puzzled looks, their faces then showed the same fear as the first man. They all turned and bumped into each other clambering down the street away from Oksana.

They saw someone with me.

She was not alone. Turning toward the police station, she began walking along the sidewalk again. A joyous prayer came under her breath, praising God for His protection.

The streets were still dark, the shadows still foreboding, but Oksana walked with assurance. Her pace was steady as she grasped the mystery of her angelic protection.

The lighted globe on the police building was three blocks ahead. She wondered what she would say when she got there. It didn't really matter now. She was walking with the angels; she felt a large degree of invincibility.

A figure stepped out of the police station and began to walk toward her.

Two blocks away, he walked quickly. Her mind started to race. *If it was one of the arresting policemen, would he recognize me? Or could it be a prisoner, just released?*

Come now, Oksana, she told herself, *you know you're safe.* She slowed her pace. *But God, please be there to help me again.*

The darkness of the street surrounded her. She felt safer staying hidden in the darkness. Stopping, she peered at the stranger. He walked steadily with no evidence of drunkenness. Now a block away, the figure slowed to a stop, looking toward her.

He can see me!

The man began to walk again with a quick step. Oksana broke into a sweat, making another plea to God. Crouching against the building, she hid her face in her wrap waiting for the angels to take over again.

"Oksana!"

The call pierced the darkness. The figure was running toward her. She knew that run—and that voice.

"Slava!" She stood up just as he reached her with an embrace that lifted her off the ground. Grabbing his shoulders, her fingers dug into his back. She shed huge tears of joy.

"Oh, Slava! I'm so thankful it's you!"

He was crying too. "Just hold me, Oksana. Just hold me."

They stayed wrapped in each others arms, enjoying the security of the embrace. Finally Slava loosened his grasp to look at Oksana's tearful eyes. They had never looked so incredibly beautiful.

"I was so afraid I might not see you again, Oksana."

She nodded. "I wasn't about to let that happen."

"You walked down here by yourself? That was a crazy thing to do," Slava spoke gently.

"No, Slava, I had angels with me."

"Ah, yes. Praise the Lord, for it looks like so did I!"

They hugged each other again, lingering in the shadows of the street. In their embrace it really didn't seem so dark after all.

Arm in arm, they walked home. Slava described what had happened at the police station. In the car ride downtown, the police were abrasive, not telling Slava anything about his arrest. They made crude jokes about jail-life. At the station he was sat down before an older grizzled officer who seemed less gruff, and Slava was surprised at his own calm demeanor.

"I was told I was arrested on a suspicion of subversion to the government. He asked if I understood the charge and I said 'no'. He told me I would have to spend the night in jail, but that I could respond to the charges in the morning. The old man muttered something about wishing he didn't have to do the day shift's job. He honestly didn't seem to understand any more than I why I was there."

"So why were you released?"

"That's the strange part. I was taken into the basement, a dark, damp ugly place. It reminded me of an old Bolshevik dungeon. At the bottom of the stairs they handed me to this scary man, the jailer, I suppose. He was huge and had only one eye working. The other one gazed off to the side leaving a white socket. He grabbed my arm—I can still feel it—like I was in a vise, and shoved me into a jail cell. He grunted words I couldn't understand, but it was something like 'better not hear a sound out of you.'

"There was one bare light bulb in the whole room, and I could see three or four other cells. I think there was someone in the cell beside me, but he was sleeping on a cot and didn't move an inch. I wondered if he was dead."

Oksana shuddered and grabbed Slava's arm as they walked along. "It sounds horrible."

"It was. Anyway, this jailer sat back and flicked the switch beside him to turn off the overhead light. It was pitch black. I thought that was how I was going to spend the night, so I sat down on the cement floor of my cell and decided to try to pray the night away. The first place I sat was wet, who knows from what. So I knelt instead. I couldn't have prayed more than five or ten minutes before there was a commotion at the stairs. An officer flicked on the light, and walked past the jailer to open my cell.

"He was a younger man, and he told me abruptly to follow him. I walked out of the cell and past the jailer up the stairs. At the top of the stairs he said, 'I hope you've learned your lesson about testing the government. You will not want to have to visit your cell anymore, right?'

"I quickly agreed, and he gestured for me to leave. Before anyone could change their mind—I could feel that monstrous jailer wanting to grab me from behind and toss me back in his cell—I got out of there."

Oksana was without words, wondering how Slava avoided spending a night in such a pit. It had to have been the work of God.

She shared her story about her intense desire to see him, the five drunks, and the heavenly protection she received.

"I don't know if anyone would ever believe you," Slava said.

"Me? Your story's outrageous itself. Whatever we're up against, it's clear we're on the right side." Oksana stopped and turned to Slava. "There's no way we can quit our ministry now."

Slava hugged his wife to seal the assurance they both felt.

Chapter 10

Tony's visit with John at the lumberyard was encouraging. Hope surged with the possibilities. Yet, there was one other matter.

He sat in the Camelson's living room. John was still at work, but Tony was there to see Melinda. He needed a woman's point of view.

"After I blew up at her, she ran away in tears. I was so consumed with myself, I hardly cared, Melinda." He related his encounter with the young lady on Sarah's steps the day she died. Now five days later, Tony was hoping Melinda would have some idea how he could ever find this girl and apologize. Her shocked face would not leave his mind; he had been plainly cruel to her. He was burdened to seek her forgiveness—if he could find her.

"After she ran off, I noticed she had dropped this letter to Sarah. I picked it up and took it with me." He handed the sealed envelope to Melinda.

"Maybe we should give this to Sarah's family." She handled the envelope delicately, as if it held a priceless treasure. "Should we open it ourselves?"

"I don't know, Melinda. I thought maybe you might know her. If you don't, my only clue is in that envelope. If we send it to Sarah's folks, it might be days before we find out who it's from. What if something in there might upset her family?" Tony waited a moment and then suggested his idea. "I really need to find this girl, Melinda. I treated her horribly, and though God forgives me, I will not forget her face until I can resolve it with her. With you as my witness, can't we open it? Then we'll mail it right off to the Townsends."

"Okay, Tony," Melinda agreed. "Open it. I'll help you find her any way I can." She handed the letter back to him.

He carefully tapped the contents of the envelope to one side. Tearing the corner, he opened the letter which would never be seen by its intended recipient.

His darting eyes glanced at Melinda. She nodded and he pulled out two sheets of pink stationary filled with writing. As if they had just opened an ancient tomb, they silently read the neatly written script:

> Dear Sarah,
>
> Although we're getting together later today, I wanted to tell you some things before then. I hope you don't mind reading this.
>
> I have never had anyone be so kind to me as you. You found me at my lowest, and somehow, you knew just what to say and do. Instead of being the one to take my life, you became the one to save it.
>
> Sarah, I have a hard time talking about myself, yet you seemed really interested in knowing about me—even the parts of me that aren't so great. Well, there's a few things about me that would be hard for me to say to you face-to-face, so I'm going to tell you them here.
>
> When you found me wanting to kill myself, you need to know that it wasn't the first time I have had those feelings. I have been a problem in other people's lives for a long time. Especially with my mom and dad. They never seem happy, and I feel like I'm always making them argue. Sometimes I think it would be better if I wasn't around.
>
> But when I talked with you, Sarah, I felt different inside. I felt like there was really something worth living for. I can't explain what it is, but I don't want to end my life now. I want to find out how to make it better.

There's something about your life that I would like to understand. I think if I spend some time with you, I will figure out what it is I need.

Well, I guess I'll close now. Thank you for saving my life, Sarah. And thank you for spending time with me. I hope I can become a woman much like you.

Sincerely,

Hillary Wells

"Whoa," Tony sighed.

"Hillary Wells," Melinda whispered under her breath.

"You know her?"

"That's who Sarah was talking about."

"Sarah told you about her?"

"Yes, I guess she did."

"Come on, Melinda—spill it!"

"Sarah called me the very day she died. She said she had just met a girl who was in a lot of trouble, and she wanted to talk with me about her before they met again. That girl was Hillary Wells."

"So this Hillary was just getting her life together because Sarah made friends with her. Then I go and explode in her face with the news that Sarah died." Tony dropped his head, wishing to fall off the earth. "I really made a mess out of this one."

"But there's more, Tony. John told me a couple of days ago that Dr. Wells' daughter tried to commit suicide and almost died in the hospital. I think that happened the day before Sarah's funeral. That has got to be this girl."

"Oh, great," Tony muttered. "So I drove this girl to commit suicide with my stupid words."

"Stop it, Tony! You had very little to do with this girl's suicidal tendencies, that's very clear. It sounds like she's had a long series of problems, the least of which included you. But, you could have a lot to do with helping her out."

"How do you mean?"

"Because of this letter. We know a good deal about this girl's problems now, and maybe what she needs."

"So you're suggesting—"

"I'm suggesting we go to the hospital and visit her. Just be honest with her. Sarah's gone, and I think God made sure you would receive this letter so you could fill in for her to help Hillary."

Tony tried to imagine himself speaking with Hillary. He spoke hesitantly. "But you've got to be a major player. I can't become the kind of friend this girl needs."

"You're right. Let's go together and see if we can talk with her. Maybe later I can get her involved with some of the girls at church."

"God's behind this thing. That's for sure. When do you want to go?"

"How about tonight, about seven o'clock?"

"I'll pick you up. Thanks for helping me out."

"Like you said, if God's behind this, we can't get in His way, can we?"

Tony nodded, recalling the similar sage words from Grandma Davis.

* * * * *

"So how's my daughter doing today?" Dr. Joseph Wells stood beside the double doors of the intensive care unit with his friend and partner, Hank Bingham.

"She's had a good day, Joe," Hank replied. "We've been able to wean the Lidocaine completely, and she's not so sluggish. We're certainly out of the woods as far as the overdose is concerned." His voice trailed off.

"Yes, I know what you're saying." Dr. Wells asked the next question more to himself than anyone else: "Where do we go from here?"

"She needs serious counseling, Joe," Hank said firmly. "I think you and your wife need to be involved in it, too."

"But you know how we've tried that, Hank. It just doesn't seem to do any good."

Joe, you've got to do something or we'll be right back here again, or maybe worse." Hank was a good friend. No one else could talk to Dr. Wells like this and get away with it. "You know we almost lost her this time."

"I know it!" Joe snapped. "Don't you think I want her better?" He looked around to be sure the nurses hadn't heard him. Lowering his voice he said, "I just want to be sure we do the right thing, Hank. Maybe we need to send her to a psychiatric unit, like in Chicago, or I hear there's a good one in Texas. God knows our local people can't help her."

"Joe, all I can say is, she needs a lot of help. I think it will have to involve the whole family." He hesitated for the right words. "You never know. It might be just what you and your wife need, too."

"Dr. Bingham," Joe reared back stiffly. "I am thankful for your care of my daughter, but I ask you to keep your business confined to her health, and hers alone!" He turned abruptly and walked toward his daughter's room.

Hank stood, sadly watching his friend's life disintegrate before his eyes. "Only a miracle can save that family," he sighed. Slapping his hands against the double doors, he left the I.C.U..

As the doors swung wide, a college-age man pushing an attractive, thirty-ish brunette in a wheelchair had to jump back to avoid being hit.

"Excuse me!" Hank barked.

"I wonder if there's an emergency?" Melinda asked as they watched the doctor's white coat flutter down the hall in the breeze of his steps.

Tony shrugged and opened the door for Melinda. At the nurse's desk, they were asked if they were family. They replied, "friends." Though not completely true, it was their hope.

The nurse considered it for a moment. "Well, Hillary's parents are in the room, so I suppose you can visit as long as they wouldn't mind. Please limit yourselves to ten minutes, though. Hillary still needs a lot of rest."

"Thank you, we'll keep it short," Melinda replied.

Tony took a big breath. This was going to be more difficult with her parents present.

"She's down three doors in room six." The nurse pointed left.

Melinda and Tony moved down the hall, speaking to each other in soft tones.

"Melinda, are you sure we should do this tonight, with her parents here?"

"Tony, we've prayed. We've asked God to give us the words. We've asked Him to guide each step. I think now we have to see what He has in store for us and respond as wisely as we can. Besides, I know Dr. Wells. He's my doctor. He's quite easy to talk to."

Tony was impressed and thankful for the faith and confidence of this woman. "Okay. If God's behind this, I'm ready for it."

"Just keep listening for God's voice, Tony," Melinda counseled. "Speak words you're sure are from Him."

She gently knocked on the door labeled six and poked her chair and her head in. "Is Hillary up for visitors?"

Tony followed Melinda through the door. The room was lit by one long fluorescent light extending the width of Hillary's bed on the back wall. Her parents sat in two chairs across the room.

"Why, hello, Mrs. Camelson." Dr. Wells jumped to his feet. "This is a surprise—I didn't know you knew my daughter." He stood and gestured for her to come in.

"Actually Dr. Wells, I haven't met her, but my friend here has." She wheeled herself in and Tony, shoulders drooping, walked in behind her.

Hillary's lips tightened when she saw Tony.

Dr. Wells, not sensing the tension, played the host, introducing his wife.

Melinda nodded at Mrs. Wells. Approaching the bed, she held out her hand. "It's nice to meet you, Hillary. I hope you don't mind our visit."

Hillary's eyes were still on Tony. Realizing she had been spoken to, she lifted up her hand to acknowledge Melinda.

"It's nice to meet you, too." Hillary's words were hesitant. Her eyes kept darting back to Tony.

"And this is Tony Barton," Melinda quickly added. Dr. and Mrs. Wells politely shook his hand.

"Hillary and Tony met a few days ago," Melinda continued. "We had to do some searching to catch up with your daughter."

"Hillary," Tony interrupted. "I feel terrible about the way I treated you the other day. I didn't know who you were, and I had just learned about Sarah myself. I was pretty upset, and I guess I just kind of blew up about it all. I'm so sorry you had to be on the receiving end."

Hillary looked over this young, handsome man; he had to be at least five years older than herself. She couldn't believe her ears—was this guy apologizing to her?

She was unsure what to say. Her parents looked quizzically at Tony, but kept their questions to themselves.

"I know we never really met, Hillary," Tony filled the uncomfortable silence. "But I just wanted you to know that I am sorry I spoke so harshly to you that day. Would you please forgive me?"

Hillary wondered if she was dreaming. *This guy wants my forgiveness? There's got to be a catch somewhere.* She ignored the presence of her parents, and spoke quietly but directly to Tony. "Why are you doing this?"

"What?"

"Why did you really come to see me? Why are you apologizing to me?"

Hillary was questioning all of life right now, but to the forefront came this new question: *Why would a young man I have never met want to apologize to me? Even Dad wouldn't do this. There's got to be a reason. What's he after?*

* * * * *

Tony felt a stirring in himself. He recognized it immediately, although he had not sensed it for several weeks. He was being prompted to share about Jesus to this girl. But right here, right now—after all she's been through? *I hardly know her, Lord. Are You sure?*

"Yes."

It was only audible to Tony, but he distinctly knew the Holy Spirit answered his question affirmatively.

The room seemed crowded enough with its five occupants, but if one could see the angelic motion, it was overflowing. Fortas was hovering high overhead, assisting the Trinity in giving Tony confidence. Spiritual gifts utilized by humble and God-fearing souls were dynamic times in the Glory.

Hillary's guardian, Kison, nestled close to his charge, counseling her to keep an open mind. She was a tough one, but she had been considering spiritual ideas since Sarah's death, especially struggling with the futility of life. Over the last two days, Kison had encouraged her to keep questioning, keep searching for reasons why.

Her parents' guardians were present also, with related directives. Her parents were hardened to spiritual truths, except that Dr. Wells' angry response to Hank Bingham had opened a sore wound. A deep awareness of *I do need help* had been forced to the surface for the moment.

With the soil of souls before him sown, watered, and fertilized to this point, Fortas cheered Tony onward to sensitively speak the words of the Holy Spirit.

* * * * *

"Hillary, I am here for one reason only," Tony began. "Sarah was a dear friend of mine, as I understand she was to you also. She had mentioned your name to Melinda, and she was looking forward to seeing you again."

Hillary's eyes shifted to Melinda, who gave a nod of concurrence.

Tony continued. "As special as Sarah was to us, the Lord chose to take her. I still can't figure out why He would, but over these last few days I have learned a lot. Maybe you saw that Sarah knew God—extremely well. She didn't brag about it, but her life showed it more than any words could say. She knew Jesus Christ, and served Him every step of the way.

"Sarah showed me a lot about Jesus, Hillary. She showed me how He loves and cares for me. I understood from her that Jesus came to bring us hope and life. She believed in His power and wisdom, and it gave her a tremendous desire to live. You saw how much Sarah enjoyed life, didn't you?"

Hillary nodded her head gently. She remembered fondly the joy she felt after spending the evening with Sarah. Her love of life was contagious.

"I know that Sarah's joy in life came from her trust in Jesus. We learned together how Jesus can make our lives fulfilling, but when Sarah died, my faith in Christ took a nose dive. I could not come to grips with how her young, bubbly life could end. I could no longer trust God."

Hillary's eyes left Tony's. She began to stare at her bed sheets. Her hands grasped the linens nervously.

Not more "just trust God" talk, she thought. *I don't need any more preaching, thank you!*

Kison moved beside Hillary, gently encouraging her to consider what Tony was saying. "He's not a preacher, Hillary. He's just a guy, not much older than you. Aren't you surprised he's even here to see you? C'mon, give him a chance."

I don't need this! I don't want to hear this! Her knuckles tightened around her blanket as she argued with the voice inside her. She tuned Tony out, wrestling within herself. Her thoughts were interrupted by Tony's next words.

"But when I realized Sarah was dead, I thought God had really blown it." The words were spoken slowly, Tony's voice cracking.

Hillary looked at him. He was reliving his mourning. His grief was sincere.

"Christ had done a lot to change my life," Tony said more solidly. "But I was ready to turn and throw it all back to Him, saying, 'I don't want it!' I told God, 'If this is what You're about, I'm looking elsewhere.'

That's when you saw me, Hillary. I was throwing my life back in the face of God, backing out of my relationship with Him."

Hillary's mind started whirling. She was in a time tunnel, remembering a day six years ago when she lay on her own bed and said similar spiteful words. Years of Sunday School had told her of a loving God and His Son, Jesus, who came to save the world. She had prayed a ten year-old's prayer, that Jesus would save her folks' marriage and keep them from fighting. That prayer didn't work, and she told God then the same thing she heard now: "If this is what You're about, I don't want it!" It had been her spiritual motto throughout adolescence.

Tony's words echoed into her thoughts as he continued. "But Hillary, Jesus proved His love to me again, as He waited right there for me." His speech began to break again. "Jesus waited for me to let my anger die. He gave me friends and encouragement to understand that He knew what He was doing." Tony took a deep breath. "He surprised me, bringing people into my life who could explain to me what He was doing."

A tear rolled out of Hillary's closed eyes. Her countenance was softened and Kison stroked her hair with comfort only an angel can provide. She saw herself in Tony's words, almost able to speak the desire from her own heart as Tony shared his.

"Hillary, I wanted to have my relationship with Christ again. I had thought I could go on my own without Him, but I knew it was a lie. Then, I felt His love surround me."

Another tear coursed down her cheek.

"Because I had doubted Him, I asked Him to forgive me. He did. Immediately. But Hillary, He reminded me that you had seen my anger." Tony's words came softly, his voice comforting. "You see, He loves you every bit as much as He loves me. He knew it was wrong for me to speak to you that way. Because you are so special to Him, I knew I couldn't treat you that way. So I had to find you. Talk to you. The one reason I have come tonight is to ask you to forgive me. It is the love that Jesus has for you that prompted me."

Emotions around the room hung in the air like a foggy night, framing this portrait of God reaching down to one He loves.

Tony stood quietly at the bed. His eyes did not move from her as he waited, an eternity if need be, for her to take hold of her emotions. And take hold of her Lord.

Hillary's head was bowed, her cheeks glistening with tears.

Her mother reached out to her, though she could not understand her daughter's cry.

Melinda moved in front of Tony so she was eye to eye with Hillary, reaching for her still closed hand. Hillary released her grasp of the sheets and took her hand. She released her emotions at the same time, weeping out loud.

Taking a step back, Tony realized the women had a better handle on what was needed right now. He turned, almost running into Dr. Wells standing behind him.

"Excuse me," Tony whispered. Looking into the doctor's eyes, he saw tears.

"Young man, that's the first time in a long while that I've seen my daughter cry. Your words meant so much." Unable to speak, he turned and quickly walked out of the room.

Tony looked back at Hillary. She was quietly talking with her mother and Melinda. There was no room for him here. He stepped out.

In the hall, the only trace of Dr. Wells was the swinging entrance doors to I.C.U. Tony left to wait for Melinda in the car. The best thing he could do now was pray.

* * * * *

The next evening was Tony's first meeting with the Russia team as a member. The church board had unanimously approved his appointment on the team, and the mission agency immediately began work on obtaining his visa. Electronic communications with the Russian consulate confirmed that his travel arrangements could be secured within the three-week deadline.

Tony was obligated to complete the series of studies on cross-cultural mission work that the rest of the team had been assigned over the past nine weeks, but he was eager to do it. He met with different members of the team to understand the Russian culture, communication with translators, and specific mission goals of the team.

The only remaining concern was money.

"How can we help Tony raise the support he needs to fund this trip?" John asked the group. "We have all sensed the Lord's call on his heart to join the team, and we can expect the Lord to work this out. However, the fact remains that we have to buy a plane ticket tomorrow, or it will be too late to confirm Tony's seat on the flight with us." John nodded across the table for Paul Jonas to continue.

"John asked me to outline our expenses and support-raising thus far," Paul began. "Everyone on the team has met their support goal, with two hundred and forty-four dollars to spare. The money from Sarah's support has been held separate—most of her support came from individuals outside our church family, primarily people from her hometown. Tony asked that her money not be given to him, as he feels that those dollars were given by people who specifically knew Sarah. He doesn't feel right about taking that money. At present, we are planning to offer those funds to her parents to give to a ministry of their choice." Paul looked around the table to identify any disagreement. "Whether or not we agree with Tony about Sarah's support, I have to respect his faith in trusting God to provide. On the other hand," he eyed Tony, "We need some wisdom on what to do about the twelve hundred dollars we need for his ticket by tomorrow."

Embarrassed to have the whole group discussing his finances, Tony maintained his resolve that he would not use Sarah's money. If God truly wanted him on the team, God would make a way.

"Does anyone have suggestions about other contacts Tony could make, or other sources we have not considered?" John asked.

Everyone was silent, a wisp of shallow faith floating in the air. The money had not been easy for anyone on the team to raise. Tony felt the silence holding obvious questions: Was this really such a good idea? Do we have to ask for more donations? Was God being unfairly tested?

Mrs. Alice Hensley, a portly lady with feisty vigor, broke the silence. "Well, Tony, I wish I could turn around and just hand you the amount you need, but you all know I can't. However," she scooped the last syllable deeply. "This is where we need to trust God, like Tony is. I'm sure we'll meet obstacles while we are in Russia. Perhaps God is trying us out right now; seeing if we are ready."

"If that's true, we'd better turn our attention to Him," John responded. "Claiming the faith of Tony and Alice, let's pray over these funds. Then we'll continue on with our meeting."

Everyone in the group kneeled at their chair to pray, as they had done many times for special requests of their Lord. Though Mr. and Mrs. Hensley took a little extra time to get settled on their arthritic joints, Tony noticed that it seemed very natural. He realized he was involved in a group that sincerely sought the Lord's will, and were willing to respond to His direction without hesitation.

The spiritual comradery of the group was obvious, forcing him to consider the loss they must have felt in Sarah's death. While he tried to focus on praying, he felt awkward assuming a position on the team that she had filled so well. As prayers broke out on his behalf, his heart was filled with a sense of inadequacy. *Lord, help my faith to believe You really want me to be here.*

Mr. Hensley was first to pray. "Our Father, we bring to You our need for this young man. Father, You know our desire, and You have directed our hearts. We trust You, Almighty God, to provide the money we need for Tony to go to Russia. Father, we thank You for leading Tony to join our team, and we are so encouraged by his faith in You. Almighty, may we see Your hand work in his life powerfully to provide. In Your holy name, Amen."

Paul Jonas and John each followed with similar prayers that sought God to act. "Thank you for Tony. Please provide for him. Encourage our faith like Tony's. Use him mightily on our team."

Tony's legs quivered the whole time.

After the prayer, everyone rose, and John suggested a five minute break before they began their study for the night. Tony stepped over to him as the others broke away.

"John, this is really humbling. I hope I can fit in with the team."

"You've already made a big splash with all of us, Tony. The whole group is excited about your faith in God. I think your zeal is contagious to the rest of us."

"Man, that's not how I feel right now. I wish I knew how God was going to pull this off. We need to hear something real soon."

"I know, Tony. We can't sweat it, though. Just keep yourself in God's grace. Like last night—Melinda told me about your testimony to the Wells girl. She said she really saw your gift of evangelism in action."

"Yeah, that was really something. I can't take any credit, but the Holy Spirit was sure working overtime. It was great that Hillary could open up to your wife. I'm sure God's got a hold of her life now."

"I haven't seen Melinda so excited for quite a while. It makes me all the more thrilled that you will be on the team. God will use you in a special way." John squeezed Tony's shoulder tightly. "We better get on with the meeting."

John brought everyone back to the table. They opened their loose-leaf binders to section ten. The night's topic: Government Church and Religion in Russia.

"This might be a sleeper for me," Howard Matson, the youth pastor, whispered to Tony as they sat beside each other. Tony smiled back, himself curious to learn how religion was practiced in Russia.

John was just beginning the discussion when a knock sounded at the door of their room. Melinda wheeled in, wearing a big smile. "May I interrupt this meeting for an important announcement?"

She wasn't just smiling. She was about to burst.

John stopped, puzzled. "Sure, honey, come on in. What's going on?"

"Well," she tried to drag out her news. "I just visited Hillary Wells and her parents again." She fingered a white envelope in her hands. "They were very touched by a special visit one Tony Barton paid them last evening." Her smiling singsong voice made Tony feel especially restless. She was almost giggling.

"Yes, go on, Melinda."

"Dr. Wells was especially impressed with our Mr. Barton here, and he asked me if there was anything he could do to thank Tony for what he had done to help his daughter. Sooo," she made the one syllable sound like three. "I mentioned to him your need for the Russia trip. He in return wanted me to give you this."

Tony opened the flap and peaked inside.

Slapping the envelope down on the table, he looked like he would explode.

After two, maybe three seconds of silence, he let out the loudest whoop the Windwood Community Church walls had ever heard.

"I gotta get outside, folks," he gasped. "This is too much!"

He ran past Melinda, and the group heard the slam of the front door, followed by a longer, louder wwwhoooop.

Paul Jonas reached over to the envelope and pulled out a light green business check, written to Tony Barton.

"Twelve hundred dollars!" he announced.

Chapter 11

Slava was getting used to the bumpy bus trek to Nizhnekamsk. The three-hour trip gave him a chance to pray over his next strategy.

His meeting with Pastor Hatir had been planned during their phone call two days ago. Slava could not give him much news, except to schedule this time to get together. Phone lines were too often listened to by hidden ears; a confidential call was impossible. The only option was to meet in person, so Slava boarded the bus again a short two weeks after the last pastors' meeting.

The bus was crowded as usual, the bench seats lined with two, sometimes three people. Several men standing in the aisle had to grab the seat backs as the bus lurched sideways, dodging potholes. Conversations with strangers were unheard of, but a few visiting friends provided a distraction from the grinding gears and exhaust explosions coming underneath the overworked vehicle.

Slava glanced around the bus when he first got on, but hadn't notice the familiar face of one of the passengers until they were standing to exit the bus at Nizhnekamsk.

A common ability among pastor-types is never forgetting a face. Slava had surprised himself many times by being able to later recall a person whom he might have met only briefly. It opened the door to trust and confidence among many people he spoke with.

This time, as he glanced at the man getting off the bus ahead of him, he knew he'd seen that face before, but it was not in church. The hair on his neck suddenly bristled.

The man was the uniformed guard from the city building who was called to assist him out the door when he had tried to meet with Dontestansk. Rather than khaki military greens, he was now dressed in a blue plaid shirt and brown pants, but that was him.

A hot flush crossed his body as Slava lingered on the bus an extra minute, watching the guard disembark and walk across the street. The blue plaid shirt headed down the road out of sight.

Still perspiring, Slava stepped off the bus, the cool spring air dousing him with a chill that joined the fear he'd suddenly felt. He could have been followed, but he'd never imagined it. The man was gone, but couldn't any of the other thirty-some passengers also be there to spy?

He stood to the side of the road watching every person get off the bus. Several on the bus were loners like him, but everyone went to other places as soon as they stepped off. Still standing ten minutes after the bus pulled away, he was convinced he was alone.

During the eight block walk to Pastor Hatir's flat, he chided himself. *No more cloak and dagger ideas. I cannot create more imaginary problems. Lord, take my fear away. Help me be confident in You.*

The streets were not crowded, even the roadside stands received little business. Slava stopped at one to admire the liter bottles of Russian carbonated orange drinks sitting alongside the Coca-Cola. Though tempted to quench his dry mouth, he knew he shouldn't afford it. Beside the beverages were a dozen varieties of American and European candy bars, then rows of trinkets. Scarfs in shades of reds, browns, and greens, lacquered black and gold wooden spoons decorated with hand-painted flowers, and lines of wooden dolls with round faces and rounder bodies covered the tables.

Slava turned off the main avenue, walking uphill through simple residential apartment buildings. He reached Vahitova Street, Building Five. Climbing to the third floor, he rapped on the door of Flat Twenty-Three.

"Come in, come in, Brother Slava!" Pastor Gregori Hatir gave him a brisk embrace and Slava immediately felt safe.

The odor of fish broth joined the sounds of frying potatoes, both coming from the small kitchen just behind Mrs. Hatir. She briefly waved before returning to her meal in-the-works. He sat down on a small plastic chair beside a table dressed with fresh cherry juice in two glasses and a small platter of sliced dark bread. Gregori joined him, gesturing to enjoy a snack before they shared an afternoon meal together.

"It is a special treat to have you in our home, Slava. Please, eat, and tell me how your family is doing. Have there been further problems since the fire?"

"My family is very fine, Brother Gregori, thank you. But yes, we have more problems."

Slava told the stories of his job termination and Chulstarisk's peculiar threat. He continued with the alley meeting with Dontestansk and his sudden arrest. Hatir asked only a rare question, listening intently.

On his third piece of bread and a refill of cherry juice, he finished with his surprise release from jail, including the divine protection his wife had received.

"By our great God in heaven, Slava! I cannot believe all you have gone through!"

"Ah, God has been so faithful. I feel great encouragement to continue in this battle. Oksana and I have a strong conviction from the Lord. We must keep our ministry going in Bolshoigorsk. God will protect us."

"Brother Slava, your faith moves me," Hatir paused. "I am so distant from your circumstances that I must respect your sense of what you should do. You're certainly aware of the dangers. It must be our Lord's strength that keeps you directed." He spoke with the humility of a servant. "So what can I do to help you?"

Slava was thankful Hatir let him take the lead. "I need to have you find out some information for me if you can, even this afternoon."

"Certainly!" Hatir, ten years Slava's senior, exhibited a childlike enthusiasm. Slava wanted to remind him of the seriousness of the opposition, but was afraid of insulting his mentor. Food again relaxed his concerns.

"Let's eat now," Gregori invited. "Tell me what you need me to do."

Mrs. Hatir was placing soup bowls in front of them before Slava could answer. The graciousness of the Hatirs was soothing after the past days.

During the meal Slava related his acquaintance with Ilya Lyamova, who had lost his job at the refinery a couple of years ago. He was imprisoned, the last Slava knew, here in Nizhnekamsk. By all appearances, Ilya had been similarly framed by a supposed drunken brawl, and Slava shared how he had been unable to visit him in prison.

"I think Ilya might be able to shed some light on who is running these conspiracies in Bolshoigorsk, but I'm afraid if I show my face at the prison, it might get back to the city officials. I would land in jail again."

"So you want me to visit Ilya and find out what he knows?"

"Are you able?"

"I must leave right away," he responded without hesitation.

"I'll stay here, waiting and praying for you, my brother."

After Gregori left, Slava went to the small apartment window to see him stride down the street. He would have to catch a short bus ride out of town to reach the prison. Slava prayed his travel would be uneventful.

The newly green trees across the street were just beginning to fill their form with fresh leaves after the harsh winter. *Lord, may Gregori have an easy time meeting Ilya. May their meeting bring news that will be as fresh as the Spring You are making.*

As Slava silently prayed, his eyes rested on the shape of a man standing beside one of the trees across the street. Not conscious of the figure, his stare was without focus during his prayer.

Then the figure moved out of the tree's shadow. Slava recognized his blue plaid shirt and brown pants.

"The guard," he whispered, jolted out of his prayer.

* * * * *

A loud, mechanical buzz made Tony rise out of his sleep like a shot. He hit the clock with the red digital numbers reading three forty-five in the morning. "Ten more minutes—please," he groaned, deftly pressing the sleep button in his usual morning ritual.

But this morning was different.

"Wait a minute! Three forty-five? I gotta get going."

He dragged his body out of the bed that had held him for only three hours, stepping groggily through an obstacle course of jeans and shirts that had been worn over the past week. Finding his way to the bathroom, he flipped on the light and hit the shower controls. Warm streams woke his tired body. This would be his last hot shower for two weeks. A couple extra minutes of the nozzle's sharp spray beating his head and back made him ask himself if he was sure he was ready to go to Russia.

Too late to change your mind now, he told himself.

He dressed in a blue striped t-shirt and jeans. 'No jeans in Russia, everyone, but you can wear them on the international flight and change before we hit foreign land,' were John's packing instructions. The high price of jeans in Russia made people notice American clothing, distracting them from the message of the gospel.

Throwing together his toiletries, he left the mouthwashes and colognes behind. 'Even toothpaste is a luxury over there, so be discrete,' were the directions.

He went to a pile of four separate gallon-size freezer bags stuffed with sets of clothes, arranged in order of their wear. "This is really driving me crazy," he mumbled. The rest of the bedroom resembled the aftermath of a tornado. Organization was not his forte, but he tried to follow the rules as best he could.

Shoving the end of a vacuum hose into each bag of clothes, he turned on the machine to suck out the air. Pinching the zip-locks tightly, his clothing was shrunk to freeze-dried size. He packed the stiff bags snugly into the nylon duffle.

With a couple minutes to spare, he looked around his bedroom. Clothes strewn across the floor were hurriedly thrown into a closet, making his best effort to tidy up. The honk of the horn outside released him from his misery. Grabbing his bag and a smaller carry-on, he headed for the door.

As he turned back one more time to hit the light, he glanced at the photograph tacked to the wall, showing a beautiful smiling blonde sitting in front of a fireplace. He sat beside her in the picture, his arm at her waist.

"This is for you, Sarah."

Howard Matson laid on the horn a second time just as Tony emerged from the apartment.

"Are you crazy, Howard? You're waking the whole neighborhood!"

"Hey, man—it's a gorgeous night! What's everybody asleep for, anyway?"

They both laughed as they loaded Tony's bags.

"Are you ready for this?" Tony asked sincerely.

"Not in the least." Howard answered frankly.

"I thought this would be easy for you," Tony said. "Being a pastor, you're used to evangelizing. This is your livelihood."

"Not missions, Tony. Can't say God ever called me to this. To be honest, the biggest reason I'm here is because none of the other pastors would go."

"What?"

"'Fraid so. We had to have a pastor on the trip, and I drew the short straw. We'll make the most of it, don't worry. I just have some problems with this stuff. We're spending an awful lot of money to send six folks to Russia for two weeks. Do you really think that's the best use of God's money? I can think of other ways to spread the gospel."

A splash of ice water couldn't have shocked Tony more. He didn't know Howard very well, but from a distance he always felt they shared common interests. Their ride to the church became hushed and tense.

"So you really think this will be fruitless, Howard?"

"I guess we'll have to wait and see."

* * * * *

The rest of the team was standing beside the circle drive of Windwood Community Church when Howard and Tony drove up. Although only five minutes late, the young men took all kinds of kidding, relieving some of the tension as they prepared to hop continents.

Pastor McMahon was up at the early hour to see his delegation off, and loaded the van with the luggage. The rest of the team stood in a circle that grew quiet from a combination of jitters and sleepiness.

"How was it saying good-bye to your wife, John?" Paul Jonas asked softly, standing beside his team leader.

"A little rough. How about you?"

"She was in good spirits, but I know these two weeks seem like a long time to her."

"I think you're right. Katie Ann will keep the time passing quickly for Melinda, I expect. But you know, I'm really going to miss them."

"Yep, same here. Same here."

Enveloped by loneliness, the whole team pondered their adventure with a certain degree of self-pity for what each person was leaving behind. Pastor McMahon broke the silence by calling out for any last luggage, and the group shuffled toward him for prayer. Even here, the prayers were subdued. Words were difficult in expressing the myriad of emotions and inward desires. Thankfully, Pastor McMahon gave a corporate prayer of travel mercies and blessings for the families and the team, anchoring the most important sentiments of the group.

It was time to go.

A two-hour drive and an hour-long commuter flight brought them to Chicago's International Terminal by ten-thirty that morning, right on schedule.

* * * * *

Brael kept an eye on the guard outside the third story window even more closely than Slava. The blue plaid shirt never left the spot beside the tree. An hour and half had passed, and Mrs. Hatir had only once interrupted Slava to be sure he wasn't hungry. He did not want to worry her, and left her alone to her business.

The guardian angel sat near the window, keeping Blue Plaid in constant view. He spoke frequently to Slava's thoughts, trying to help him reason.

"Just be thankful you didn't try to visit the prison yourself, Slava. You'd be spending your days in Siberia."

I know that, Slava answered to himself. *But what if someone also followed Gregori? What if he's in danger?*

"It's you they're watching," Brael argued.

Lord God, I hope that's true, Slava prayed. *Please bring Gregori back safely. May he have helpful news for me, please, Lord.*

He moved again to the window, surveying the street. A figure hurriedly walked toward the flat. Hatir!

"Ah, praise God you made it, Gregori!" Slava greeted him anxiously at the door.

"A scary place, that prison is, Slava. It feels good to be home."

"Yes, well, I hope I have not endangered your home by coming here. I am afraid I was followed. There's been a man watching your apartment the whole time. See him leaning against the tree?"

Gregori saw the man's back turn to walk in front of the tree, looking directly at the front door of the apartment building.

"That's a guard from the Bolshoigorsk city offices, the one who escorted me from my foiled meeting with the city officials. I saw him get off the bus when I arrived here."

"So they're watching your every move?"

"Apparently. So tell me—did you find Ilya? Do we know any more about who 'they' are?"

"Slava, I'm sorry. I have bad news." Gregori dropped his head. "After waiting an hour at the prison visitor's desk, they informed me Ilya Lyamova was dead. Apparently died in his cell. 'Unknown causes,' they said."

"He was an innocent man, Gregori."

"I know."

"We shouldn't be surprised, with everything else that has happened."

"Slava, there's something else I must tell you. I should have mentioned it when I first saw you, but you unloaded enough problems that I couldn't bring it up."

"What is it?"

"The American team that is coming to visit you, they have had a tragedy. One of their team, the nurse, died in a car accident, two weeks ago. I just received word of it yesterday."

"Oh, no." Slava's eyes were glued to Gregori for more of an explanation.

"It shocked the team immensely, but they're still coming. A young man has signed up to take the girl's place."

"That they would still come is amazing."

"Yes, Slava. They have great faith that God desires to use them over here, but we will have to be very sensitive to their feelings about the loss of their friend. I hope it will not distract their thoughts too much from the ministry at hand—especially with what they may be walking into in Bolshoigorsk. Are you concerned that it might not be a good idea for the Americans to come to your church right now?"

"We have thought about that. The Americans could make a large contribution to the church, especially now. We need to gain credibility before the community and the city officials. The Americans' visit will provide that."

"Yes, but Slava, don't expect too much from the Americans. We need to consider their safety in Bolshoigorsk."

"I know, I know. But this could be exactly what God has planned, to use the Americans to help lead our church out of this mess. God has protected Oksana and I mightily these past weeks. I want to trust the Americans to Him as well."

"But don't put God to the test."

"Of course not, but I can think of no other way to salvage my ministry outside of the influence of the Americans. If it was not for their visit, I would have to consider resigning from Bolshoigorsk. As our friend outside demonstrates, these people are serious. It is a dangerous business."

"Precisely, Slava. That is my concern for the Americans. If something should happen to any of them, we'd have an international incident on our hands."

Both men paused at the stalemate. Respecting each other's arguments, a decision still had to be made. The Americans were to arrive in three days.

"Here's what I'll do, Slava. We'll leave things as planned for now, and we'll commit ourselves to praying constantly for the Americans' protection. But, you must promise me that at the slightest threat to the Americans' safety, you will get them out of Bolshoigorsk."

"Agreed. I expect to see God work, but I will not risk the Americans foolishly."

"We need to let the Americans know exactly what is going on as soon as they get here. They'll need to be on their guard twenty-four hours a day."

"As will we all, Gregori, as will we all."

* * * * *

The angels nodded in agreement. They realized even more so that their guardianship required the highest caliber. Remaining close to their charges, they sought every benefit from the two pastors' prayer.

At the 'amen,' a guardian spoke to Gregori's conscience. "Don't forget about the vase."

* * * * *

Gregori jumped up from his knees. "I almost forgot, Slava. I want you to have something." He reached into a large-bellied tarnished brass vase kept high on a shelf in the room, pulling out a bundle of rolled up Russian bills.

"Our church keeps an emergency fund for families in need, and God has prompted me to give this to you. I will not accept a refusal, so please put the roll in your pocket. With God's blessings, have a safe ride home."

"I don't know what to say, Gregori. You can't appreciate the timing of your gift. We really didn't know where money for our family would come from."

"Praise the Lord, Slava. He's taking care of you in remarkable ways."

Slava gave Gregori a strong embrace and moved toward the door, calling a thank-you to Mrs. Hatir before departing.

Outside, he saw the guard in his peripheral vision. Nonchalantly strolling down the street, the blue plaid shadow moved behind him.

It was an uneasy feeling. Slava first felt fear. The further he walked, the more his tag kept his distance. Fear dissolved into anger, every sense of privacy was disappearing from his life. His anger seeded an uncharacteristic bravery.

Picking up his pace slightly, he distanced himself a couple blocks from Blue Plaid. He approached the street near the bus stop, pausing again at the roadside stand. Pulling out his roll of bills, he handed a five-hundred ruble to the sales lady. Blue Plaid hesitated a block away and turned to look in a shop window.

Slava spoke to the sales lady and discretely pointed out the man with the blue plaid shirt and brown pants. Would she please offer a soda to his friend as he passed by her table?

Walking down the road more slowly now, he kept the scene behind him in focus. Perfectly, Blue Plaid approached the table. The lady caught his attention. His eyes were taken off Slava for an instant when he was handed the free liter bottle. That was all that was necessary.

Breaking into a sprint, Slava raced down alleys and paths, bolting opposite directions at each fork he came to.

Ten minutes later, he knew he was successful. Across the street from the bus stop, hidden inside a small bakery, he watched out the front window with a cup of hot strong tea in his hand.

The bus arrived on time, and Blue Plaid appeared with it. He stood near the hood with squinted eyes, watching the early passengers board. Unsatisfied, he darted back and forth across the open market area. He walked toward the bakery, but Slava was able to stay well out of view behind curtains. Watching him pace left, then right down the sidewalk, Slava had to smile at the liter bottle still in his hand.

Another five minutes and the bus would be leaving. It was time to go. Blue Plaid had made his way down several buildings a block away, entering a large bar. It would be naturally crowded this time of evening.

Slava left the bakery, his eyes glued to the front door of the bar. Walking slowly, he made a broad circle within the market and came around the back of the bus out of view from the bar.

No sign of Blue Plaid.

Boarding the bus, he took a rear seat, keeping the bar in view. The bus's engine fired as the driver began to pull away just after Slava was seated.

As the bus drove past the bar, Slava saw the door open. Blue Plaid jostled the tight crowd to make it through the doorway. He took four jogging steps toward the bus, but it was useless. The man clutched his soda and with slumped shoulders turned away.

Slava sat back in his lumpy seat and smiled with delight.

Brael watched with Slava, joyous over his work. He gave a big congratulatory wave to the six angels standing outside the bar.

Chapter 12

"The Americans are here! They're coming down the hall!"

The young teen raced in with the news for Gregori Hatir, Slava, and three translators from Moscow. They were waiting in a small room off the lobby of the Nizhnekamsk hotel where the American team had spent the past night. Word was they had gotten in about two a.m. Now six hours later, Slava could hardly wait to board the bus and bring the Americans to Bolshoigorsk.

The three translators, Tonya, Nadia, and Luda, all girls in their early twenties, had arrived two days ago in Nizhnekamsk. As students at a Moscow language school, the opportunity to work with Americans was just as exciting for them as for Slava. After three years of college level English studies, they would actually get to try out their skills with real Americans. Most of their teaching had come through British-trained Russians or other Eastern Europeans, so this chance to spend two weeks with Americans was an opportunity of a lifetime. It did not matter to them the nature of the Americans' business, they were just thrilled to have been selected.

Pastor Hatir had spent yesterday briefing the girls about their positions as translators and the importance of accurate interpretations. From past experience, he was able to counsel the girls to ask frequent questions of the Americans if there were any misunderstood words. It was of utmost importance to translate as exactly as possible, without adding any loose interpretations.

In his time with them, Hatir discovered that none of the girls understood Christianity, which was disappointing, but not surprising. These girls were from upper class, Russian-educated homes and had learned from childhood that God was a myth. Without hesitation, he politely addressed the girls' ignorance of God, and instructed them on some basic terms common in Christian thought. He showed them his Bible, teaching them how chapters and verses were organized.

They ogled over Hatir's copy of God's Word, having never seen the book before. Their eyes lit up as he had them each take turns finding different passages. Helping them read portions of Scripture, he could tell many questions were formulating in their minds. There would be plenty of time for that over the next two weeks. Right now, his job was to familiarize these girls with enough common phraseologies of Christianity so that they could be effective communicators of the gospel as expressed by the Americans. Though he sensed their excitement, he knew they had no idea what kind of experience they were about to embark on.

Slava had just met the translators himself an hour ago when he arrived in Nizhnekamsk. They seemed like pleasant girls, although very nervous at the moment. So was he. The Americans were just around the corner!

The door to their room opened and a line of six filed into the room, led by their Russian host from Hatir's church. Slava held back, watching Hatir rise immediately to greet them.

They don't look too odd, he thought to himself.

Hatir motioned for him to step forward as introductions were jumbled together through the translators. Names were tossed back and forth, and the Americans were initially confused with which name belonged to whom. Laughter was frequent and broke the formality of the moment. Just like he had been told, the Americans loved to laugh.

Using short phrases to speak through the translators, Slava asked Nadia to address a question to John and Tony.

"So you are having a good trip?" It felt like childish talk, but it seemed understood.

"Yes, everything has gone fairly smoothly," John responded as Nadia interpreted again. "We were held up in Moscow several hours waiting for Aeroflot," he added. "That was a very bumpy one."

Nadia paused over what word to use for "bumpy." She began to speak the words in Russian to Slava, and he looked quizzically when she translated the flight as 'filled with mounds.'

Looking at John, Nadia asked, "Bumpy?"

Tony saw the obvious confusion. "You know, like 'rocky'?"

Nadia faithfully translated in Russian to Slava. "Yes, it seems their flight was filled with stones."

John and Tony looked at Slava to see if he understood. He had no idea what they meant. Shrugging his shoulders, he smiled and tried another question.

"Nadia, ask them if they liked the hotel here."

Nadia asked, and John and Tony both nodded and spoke well of their accommodations. Nadia translated their responses, and Slava nodded with a sigh of relief over his first success at communication across the languages.

He gestured for them to wait, and he would find out how soon they would leave for Bolshoigorsk. Stepping away, he spoke quietly to Gregori about visiting with the Americans about recent events. They had earlier decided to tell the American team leader only. He could decide how much the whole team would need to know. The plan was for Slava to visit with John, and Gregori would take the rest of the team on a short walking tour of Nizhnekamsk.

* * * * *

"What's going to happen next, John?" Tony asked.

"It sounds like Slava wants to meet with me before we get on the bus. The rest of you can go with Gregori. He wants to show you the town."

"Do you want some company? This translating stuff isn't exactly easy."

"If you don't mind, it might be a good idea. Let me ask Slava if that's okay." Speaking with Nadia, John had her ask Slava, who readily agreed.

As Gregori escorted the group outside, Slava walked over and gestured for John, Tony, and Nadia to sit down.

"It is a tremendous privilege for me to welcome you to Russia," Slava began, with Nadia translating. "God has richly blessed us with the opportunity to have you come to Bolshoigorsk. We are looking forward to wonderful and mighty things in the next two weeks."

John and Tony modestly nodded their heads in agreement. Tony felt a twinge of concern that expectations here might be too high.

"There are some things we need to discuss before we arrive in our city," Slava continued. "With your permission, I would like to pray before I share these."

Slava spoke a few quick words to Nadia, and she translated that he would pray in Russian, and she would not translate this. They would please join him in an attitude of prayer. Gregori had earlier said small group prayers were best this way, so that the translation would not detract from the communication with God.

Tony bowed his head as Slava began a rush of unintelligible words, but there was no doubt this was prayer. Raising his eyes slightly, Tony looked at Slava as he was praying. The fervency on this young pastor's face added dimension to the intensity of his speech. His language was soft, almost melodious, as he addressed their heavenly Father. Without understanding a word, Tony felt he could agree with every thought.

Still in prayer, Tony happened to glance at Nadia as well, and saw her eyes peeking out. They traded embarrassed smiles, and bowed again. He tried to focus on the prayer, despite her captivating smile.

John was praying now, beginning spontaneously at the end of Slava's prayer. He was also touched by Slava's prayer, and offered praise to God for what was about to come in their two weeks in Russia. As the "amen" sounded from John, Slava and Nadia both repeated in their tongue, "A-meen."

Tony raised his head and again caught Nadia's eyes. Her lips curled more naturally this time, and he offered a confident smile of his own. *That's an amazing face,* he thought as Slava began to speak to them again.

Beginning with a brief history of the Bolshoigorsk church, Slava gave an overview of his ministry thus far. The information was not new to John and Tony, but it was good to hear it directly, in confirmation of the materials they had received in their training about Bolshoigorsk. Then Slava shared the more recent news of the mysterious fire in his flat, his job termination, the threats from his boss, Chulstarisk, and the peculiar warning from Renat Dontestansk. With only a few questions of interpretation, Nadia did an excellent job of communicating.

Tony did not feel too uncomfortable with the news thus far. These were the kind of stories he had heard happened to Russian Christians. Even though communism had fallen, the oppression of Christianity was common. Slava's report was feeding his adrenaline, and he was anxious to begin their ministry.

Then Slava told about his arrest and being followed to Nizhnekamsk. Tony's excitement of the adventure changed as he saw in Slava the fear of the jail cell. This tale was more extreme. *Shouldn't our mission council have warned us before sending us into something this hot?*

As Slava's story unfolded, Tony could see the surprise on John's face. It was especially clear in Nadia's translation that these were unusual circumstances. She was even shaken by what she had to speak. Slava concluded with words of caution on how they could not trust anyone in Bolshoigorsk. All that he had shared must be kept in strict confidence for the safety of himself and his family.

Suddenly the door to their room sprang open and the foursome all jumped.

"The bus is here and we're ready to go!" Gregori announced excitedly with Luda translating behind him. He toned down his remarks as he saw the subdued faces before him.

"I see Slava's news has been unsettling. But we must go now. Let us continue to talk on the bus. Please—we know that God is behind your visit with us. Let us all have faith in His direction here."

Tony looked at John and received an only half-reassuring smile. Shuffling out the door, each one thought the same thing. *God, I hope You know what You are doing.*

* * * * *

The American team, with translators, Slava, Gregori and luggage, filled the small bus chartered for the trip to Bolshoigorsk. The ride was filled with jolts, swerves and stops that kept the Americans laughing. It was a typical journey for Slava, but for the Americans, it was an exhilarating addition to their list of experiences.

Tony yelled to Nadia, gesturing into the air as the bus jiggled over a deep washboard stretch of road. "This is bumpy!"

"Ohhh, bumpy! I understand!" She spoke in Russian to the other translators, and they all laughed together at the earlier inadequate interpretation describing the Aeroflot flight. Slava caught wind of the girls laughing, and realized what the Americans had been trying to say.

"Boompy!" Slava said with his Russian accent, and the busload all laughed again.

The group carried on with light chatter and further introductions as the young girls enjoyed honing their skills with translating. The three-hour trip seemed to pass quickly for everyone.

In Bolshoigorsk, the Americans were dropped off in pairs at their host homes, with one translator joining each household. Tony and John were last, with Nadia as their translator. They were staying with Slava's family at Aunt Gina's home. Gregori would spend the night there as well, before leaving in the morning to return to Nizhnekamsk.

It was going to be a houseful.

* * * * *

The next morning, Aunt Gina's guests were all up early. The house was readied to serve as the meeting place for the rest of the team and translators.

John was sorry it had been a short night for him and Gina's other guests. They were up well past midnight discussing the situation Slava was in with his church. It was a valuable time, however, and they were able to speak honestly about how the Americans could best serve. John immediately received the trust of Gregori and Slava, and mutual respect was evident as they considered their options.

"Our greatest goal right now is to become registered with the local government," Slava had said as they sat around the small table sipping strong tea. Nadia translated effectively as he continued. "If the government will formally recognize us, people will be much more likely to visit our church."

"So how do you register as a church?" John asked.

"The city council must vote to approve the registration," Slava responded. "Right now the only registered church is the government church. If the people of the community would appeal to the council, they would register us. Right now, it's difficult to let the people know we even exist."

"Perhaps that is where we can be of most use," John suggested. "I understand we Americans are somewhat of a novelty here. Could we draw attention to the church and its benefits to the community?"

"That's exactly what we hoped for," Gregori said. "You are in a valuable position to bring our church into public focus, without requiring Slava to be visible himself. If the people will support the church as you present it, Slava will gain much credibility as its pastor."

"Perhaps we could visit the city officials ourselves," John suggested. "Would they be open to a meeting with us?"

"Very good idea," Slava agreed. "Tomorrow I will show you the city offices and you can make an appointment to see the mayor. I would think he would be honored to host American visitors."

"And could we visit the government church?" Tony offered. "Maybe they could help us with the registration."

Slava was quiet for a moment. He peered at Tony with a frown, and then looked away, mumbling to Nadia. She said, "They have not offered any help, but Slava says you could try. He's not very hopeful."

Obviously, Tony thought.

Despite the late hour and exhausting travels, the Americans carried an excitement around the table as more ideas circulated about how they could work effectively for the cause of the church in this community.

After much discussion, it was decided that in the morning the Americans would go to a local city park in Bolshoigorsk and try to meet as many people as possible. As long as Slava was not visibly associated with the team, the Americans could take the liberty to share freely with the community. They also planned an outdoor meeting for the following night, to be held at the local soccer field. It was the off season, and Slava thought he would have no difficulty reserving it. As the Americans met people, they could invite them to the field for a revival-type meeting. It seemed like a good place to start, and the focus would be on the Americans. A meeting with the mayor and a visit to the government church would be arranged. This would be the strategy for the team's first two days in Bolshoigorsk.

Now, the next morning, as the team came together in Gina's small living room, there was an obvious sense of anticipation. The Americans were ready to put their weeks of training to use. John loosely filled everyone in on Slava's job loss, and the animosity the church faced from an unknown circle. He did not mention Slava's arrest, as he felt such scare tactics against Slava would serve no purpose for his team.

Laying out the plan of gaining public credibility for the church, John expressed the goal of achieving the government's registration for the church. He could tell the team was ready to go to work in the city park today, and the outdoor meeting tomorrow would be a huge thrill. Looking into the eyes of his team members, he could see every one of them ably equipped to begin this ministry. The only thing left to do was pray.

* * * * *

The spring morning sunshine glistened in the dew on trees and bushes as the Americans approached the park. After walking through streets lined with pale buildings, facades chipped and peeling from decades of neglect, the park looked like an oasis in the desert. Its rich, innate beauty created a stark contrast from the manmade poverty of the city.

The appeal of the park was enhanced, however, by what could not be seen. This day, the block was a haven set apart by God. The perimeter was lined on all sides with protecting angels facing outward, securing the sacred ground against any enemy. Among the invisible, only angels of the Kingdom were allowed entrance, and they flowed in freely.

The Americans entered the grounds, quickly splitting into groups of two with their translators. In addition to guardian angels, other winged seraphs accompanied each group.

The angels knew the humans would not be prepared for what was to come. Beginning immediately, they ushered in Bolshoigorsk souls lost and searching in spiritual voids. One of the first under divine guidance was a young woman who approached Mrs. Hensley.

"American?" she asked in broken speech.

"Yes, I am," Alice replied with a nod and a smile.

An immediate barrage of words burst forth with Luda ready to translate. "She asks why you have come to Bolshoigorsk."

"Please tell her we have come to talk with her about our God."

As Luda translated, Alice saw the young woman's eyes brighten. A short phrase uttered under her breath was translated. "This is what I'd hoped for."

"Tell me about yourself," Alice gently asked. "What is your name?"

The Russian woman gladly answered, followed by Luda's caring translation. Alice listened intently. She then offered her own short story, in five minutes reflecting how Jesus Christ had become Lord of her life. The words flowed smoothly and lovingly; the young woman was enamored by Alice's warmth.

With unexpected ease, such conversations broke out across the city park. The Americans hardly had to move from their places as one conversation led to another. With leaflets and brief testimonies shared over and over, Russians openly encountered Christianity for the first time.

The Americans were cautious about pushing for salvation commitments, yet, several souls were ripe for this moment. Angelic celebrations of praise echoed from the park as a handful surrendered their lives to Christ for the first time.

Overwhelmed and overjoyed at the end of the day, the Americans left the park with nearly two hundred contact cards from individuals they had spoken with. Visiting with each other, they were incredulous at how each one had experienced the same tremendous response. Amazingly, almost every person they shared with agreed to come to the outdoor meeting planned for the next night.

The group walked down the street three blocks to the soccer field where the rally would be held. Mrs. Hensley suggested they spend some time in prayer there, and everyone excitedly agreed. Bolshoigorsk's first exposure to the gospel in nearly a century had gone without one sour note. A time of worship seemed a fitting postlude to the day.

A few Russians tagged along with the team, mostly young people hungry to spend some precious extra time with these Americans who held out so much hope and joy.

Reaching the soccer field, the team, translators, and straggling Russians sat down in the lower section of the twenty rows of stands. The wood seating was well worn, with the choicest seats found between splinters and droppings.

John stood in front of the stands, ready to address the team with a few announcements before they would pray and be dismissed to their host homes for the evening. As he was gathering everyone's attention, Paul Jonas pointed. "It looks like we have company."

John turned to see two men in khaki soldier uniforms walking on the field toward him. They were obviously not there for a prayer meeting. Motioning Nadia to come to his side, he asked, "Who is this?"

"The police," she replied with a hush.

The high emotions of the group were quickly subdued as word was whispered around of the visitors.

"Nadia, please greet them politely for us, and ask how we may help them."

A flurry of Russian words flew out of the lead policeman's mouth and Nadia translated. "They say we must leave this place at once, and they ask to speak with the one in charge."

"Tell them that's me," John said.

Tony moved down from the stands. "I'm with you if there's any trouble," he whispered.

Another barrage of the policeman's foreign tongue was thrown to Nadia, who, yet unshaken, shared the interpretation. "The Americans' activity in the park today is a breech of the security of the local government. Bolshoigorsk is a peaceful community, and the Americans' propaganda has upset the people."

"What?" Tony exclaimed.

The policeman spouted another sentence and Nadia repeated it. "Under authority of the mayor, we must insist you contain your visit in our community away from any public areas, or you will be asked to leave."

"Stay calm, and translate carefully for me," John quietly said to Nadia, moving with her closer to the policemen. He gestured for Tony to stay back and spoke directly to the police. "We did not mean to offend your peaceful city by any of our activities today, and we wish to apologize for any harm we have caused." He nodded for Nadia to translate and then continued. "With all respect to you and the mayor we will certainly abide by your wishes."

The policemen both nodded with understanding. Their posture softened slightly. John knew they were surprised at this acquiescence.

"But may we make one request of you?" he asked.

Nadia translated, and the lead policeman gestured with his hand to continue.

"We ask to meet with your mayor, and give him greetings from America. We would like to tell him how much we have enjoyed our visit to Bolshoigorsk thus far."

The policeman muttered an abrupt phrase, and Nadia relayed. "He will ask the mayor and contact you later if he agrees."

"Thank you very much." As Nadia translated, John held out his hand to shake with the man. The officer uncomfortably let his hand be grasped, and then motioned for the other officer to shake hands.

"Tell him where we live, Nadia, so he can get a message to us."

Nadia spoke to the officer, and he gave a curt response followed by a surprising smile on his face. The two officers turned quickly and walked away.

"What did he say?" John asked.

"He said he already knew where you lived."

John raised his eyebrows at Nadia and they walked the few steps back to the group. "Nice work under pressure," he said.

"I would say the same to you, John."

Back at the stands, John addressed the group. "Okay, everyone, we will have to postpone our prayer time for later."

"What do you mean?" Paul shouted back. "We've been praying here the whole time!"

"Thank you," John sighed with relief. "And praise God. Right now, however, we must leave. Let's meet at Gina's so I can fill you in, and then you may go to your host homes. Translators, please encourage our

Russian friends here to go to their homes. Let them know we hope to see them tomorrow."

John tried to cover his doubt as much as possible.

Chapter 13

"So how did the Americans respond to you?"

The deep, husky voice spoke with a quiet severity that unnerved the young policeman reporting to his superior.

"They seemed respectful and immediately left the field. The whole group went directly to Gdansk's flat, stayed together there for about an hour, and then broke up to their host homes. There was no further trouble."

"That is good. Yet, we must watch them very closely. Those Americans have many tricks." The voice's intensity lessened, and the officer hoped this meant his boss would relax. He looked cautiously at the massive, tall man across the table, trying to read eyes darkly hidden in the shadows of deep orbits and overgrown eyebrows. In the silence, he knew he must ask.

"Father, there is something else."

"I must know everything—tell me now."

"The Americans requested a meeting with the mayor."

The large man was quiet for a moment. The officer debated if he should run for his life or wait for new orders. Choosing the latter, he sighed with relief as his boss spoke calmly.

"I think that can be arranged. Yes, in fact, I think that might even be helpful. See to it that the mayor extends an invitation to the Americans—tomorrow, if possible. Tell him to call me as soon as he knows the time of this little welcoming reception."

* * * * *

The following morning the team met again at Aunt Gina's home for devotions before beginning their day. Each one had wrestled through the night over the prohibition from meeting with the people of Bolshoigorsk. Their mission seemed fruitless if the police prevented them from witnessing.

Heads hung low. The excitement felt at yesterday morning's devotions was greatly tempered this morning. John held the burden of bringing the team together to renew their hope—except he wasn't sure he had a solid grasp of it himself. Was it fatigue, the stress of cultural adjustments, or true desperation that made him question his own purpose for even being here?

Gina courteously busied around finding a seat for the six team members and three translators. The cramped living room served as the temporary bedroom for Slava's boys in addition to Tony and John each night. Each morning bed mats were rolled up and suitcases shoved aside to make the room livable again.

John watched Gina closely, waiting to see her express some degree of frustration over her small apartment being turned into a combination hotel and meeting hall. He only expected that she, at sixty-two years of age, having lived her past 10 years as a widow, would reach the end of her rope and insist on some time for herself.

He wanted to be sensitive to her first sign of concern, but there was no need. Gina loved all the activity, thriving on the opportunities to help, from the early morning dressing of the Gdansk boys to serving tea for the men's late night planning sessions. This Russian woman was of high character, and John confirmed in his mind her giftedness—this was true hospitality.

John found her busily but contentedly attending to the breakfast dishes. In the next room, the team began singing a simple Russian praise chorus the Americans were learning. The song moped along without enthusiasm.

This woman just quietly goes about her work, never missing an opportunity to serve, John thought to himself as he watched Gina in her kitchen. *This is the heart I need to have, willing to accept whatever God brings my way.* He watched her intently, trying to learn from her actions how he too could work so dutifully in any circumstance. She caught his stare and shooed him out of the kitchen with a wholehearted laugh. Whatever he could glean from watching her would have to wait. It was time to lead the team.

"Praise God for your hearts that are able to sing and bring joy to the Lord this morning, everyone," he announced, sounding more encouraged than he was. What could he say to change the bleak outlook on their mission? "Paul, are you ready to share your devotional with us this morning?"

Each team member took turns leading a devotional during these morning meetings. Paul nodded with a modest smile and clutched his Bible.

I'm punting this to you, John thought.

Paul began his devotional as Tonya, the translator who stayed at his home, interpreted. John watched her as Paul shared. He could tell the whole truth of God was foreign to her.

What was she seeing of the reality of God? Nothing!

Paul discussed the undeserving nature of man to receive anything from God. He related how man commonly approaches God with expectations that he should receive something.

"Even today, we as a team want to come before God and say, 'Why have You allowed the police to halt our ministry here? We have worked hard and have come all this way to Russia, and now will You just allow the door to close?'"

As Paul spoke, John was pricked by these words that had formed unspoken prayers throughout the night. Besides the team, even Slava and the translators appeared to hold on to each phrase.

"But who are we to question God?" Paul continued. "Who are we to say we have a better plan? Remember John's message at Sarah's funeral back home? Remember how he posed before us the question of, 'Is God in control?' Is that not the question we face now?"

The words pierced John. The sermon he was receiving was the very one he had given a short month ago.

"'I know that God can do all things; no plan of His can be thwarted. Surely I earlier spoke of things I did not understand, things too wonderful for me to know.' Is this not the answer to our questions this morning? Can we not depend on God to carry out His plan for Bolshoigorsk? Is this not the grace and mercy of God, that He is faithful to complete what He has begun here in Russia, and even in each of our lives?"

John heard a loud 'amen' from Mr. Hensley, and looked around to see everyone in the room nodding in agreement. There was a lengthy silence as he realized Paul had finished.

"Thank you, Paul," John stammered. "You truly hit a chord with me." He paused to collect his thoughts. "I have to be honest with you all, I was pretty discouraged with what I woke up to face this morning. I don't know about you, but I've been wondering what on earth we're supposed to do here if we can't even witness. I felt like we had been abandoned—by God. I'm disgraced to have to admit this before you. I'm humbled, needing to hear the very words I had said such a short time ago."

The Americans gave John understanding smiles. Their faces showed the same contriteness.

"Maybe it would be good for us to pray. Let's direct our prayers toward confessing our lack of faith, our doubts of God's work. Let us appeal to God for forgiveness, and commit ourselves to place our trust in Him."

The team quietly shifted to a position of prayer, and Tony was first to begin a sincere prayer of confession. John noticed momentarily that each of the three translators awkwardly had their heads bowed, yet still watched the team carefully during Tony's prayer. It was of no matter to him what they were thinking, however, and he returned to silently pray in agreement with Tony.

* * * * *

The cornerstone of the Christian faith was being reinstated in this small room. God's forgiveness was being handed out freely to those who sincerely asked with repentant hearts.

His angels in this small corner of the globe were offering up holy praise to Him, supported by the sentiments of these prayers. The purity and righteousness of God was extolled in the worship of these angels, and the Comforter came to flood the room with peace. Conviction was the Holy Spirit's greatest tool. This response to His promptings brought about the cleansing of souls and forgiveness of sins. As if a haze was lifting off the room, countenances began to shine with hope and promise. The incomprehensible security of the Spirit cleared away doubt.

As Mrs. Hensley broke out in a chorus of 'Holy, Holy, Holy,' she had no idea she led her team in singing with the angelic choir surrounding them. The six human voices in the room did not impressively resonate, but the heavens heard a magnificent chorale of worship that transcended any orchestral performance. The small group in the modest room of a concrete building, on a dirt street, in an unknown town, of a Godless country, had just opened a window to heaven that allowed its rays of unseen brilliance to flood the waiting souls below with joy and mercy.

* * * * *

After nearly three-quarters of an hour of this praying, John's conversation with his Lord was interrupted as he heard the apartment's front door open.

He broke from the team to attend to the door, where he found a group of Russians entering with smiles, shaking his hand and giving Russian greetings.

Who on earth are these people?

Seven people had entered, moving into the living room with more at the door as John continued his confused combination of handshaking and smiles. He yelled for Nadia to come to him.

"Please—find out who all these people are!" he said after she had finally worked her way to him down the tight hall. At least twelve had now entered, with three more yet outside.

She quickly spoke to one of the younger women walking in and then returned to John. "They are people from the church. They've invited their friends to come meet you." Nadia gave a little laugh. "It looks like you'll have something to do this morning after all."

The final person, a teenage boy, entered and made his way into the living room after shaking John's overly squeezed hand. The Americans were clearly overwhelmed, with Tony and Mrs. Hensley still wiping their eyes from tears shed during their prayers. Slava was greeting several of the group with smiles and eager faces surrounding every guest.

John quickly spoke to his team members. "These are people from the church here or their invited friends. They've heard of our witnessing in the park, and have come to meet with us. Let's break into groups with a translator, and enjoy God's blessing of our new friends!"

The team all responded back to John with elated smiles and quickly went to work. John sought Slava, and with Nadia moved into the bedroom where Oksana was dressing the two boys.

"Please, Nadia," John said. "Ask Oksana to stay with us." With a humble smile, Oksana moved beside her husband.

"Are you as surprised as I am about this morning's visitors?" John asked Slava.

Through Nadia's translation, Slava replied, "Very much so. Natasha, one of the girls here, is a believer. She told me, 'if the Americans can't come to Bolshoigorsk, we will bring Bolshoigorsk to the Americans!'"

"This is just grand! But what will the police say?"

"As long as we are in our own homes, they should not care," Slava responded.

"Slava, do you have any concern over your family's safety because of our meeting like this?" Before Slava could answer, John asked Nadia to add, "I want you and your wife to know I am very concerned for you."

"I am thankful for your concern, but it is as Brother Paul has just said, 'No plan of God's can be thwarted.' I feel we are within the law, and we are ready to receive whatever God has in store for us." Slava looked at his wife, and she gave him a nod of agreement combined with her smile.

"With your permission, then, we will meet with these that have come and share as much as we can in this home today." John paused to allow Nadia to translate. The Gdansks smiled with approval.

"Would it be possible to still meet with the government church?" John asked.

"I think if perhaps two or three of you went, it would be received well," Slava replied. "Whenever you are ready I will have someone show you the way. The bishop is almost always at the church during the day."

"This afternoon should work," John said. "Can we plan for then?"

Nadia translated, and then responded back to John. "After lunch would be fine."

"Great. Well, Nadia, let's get back to our guests, shall we?"

In the next room, a groundswell of conversations had begun as John and Nadia stepped into the cramped living room. Mr. and Mrs. Hensley were showing photographs to a group of four Russian girls, all in their early twenties, with Luda translating. The pictures of their family back home served as great conversation starters. The glossy color prints were unique in Russia, as those who could afford cameras only had access to black and white film. The bright colors and American styles were fascinating to the Russians.

Paul Jonas was with Tonya, speaking with a group of younger boys, perhaps ages ten to fourteen. They were in rapt attention as he was building a small balsa wood airplane. After winding the rubber band tightly, Paul sent the plane airborne to the complete delight of his audience. The plane crashed into the wall across the room, the boys laughing and scurrying to get the plane ready for another flight.

Tony was at the back of the room with a group of six Russians and no translator. He eyed Nadia as she and John entered the room.

"Nadia, Nadia, over here! We need you badly!"

Nadia left John and came alongside Tony. He asked her, "How do I ask these people their names?"

"Say, '*kahk vahss zahvoot?*'"

Tony tried it, puckering his lips together on the last syllable. The Russians all laughed.

"How'd I do, Nadia, how'd I do?"

"Not too bad for a foreigner," she smiled broadly. "I think they can figure it out."

Each of the Russians excitedly offered their names to Tony, and he immediately pronounced them, massacring each one. It delighted the Russians to hear his American accent attempt their names, no matter how it sounded. Tony, while embarrassed at his inadequate dialect, sensed his rapport building quickly.

"Ask them why they are here, Nadia."

She did so, and translated the response of a young man. "We wish to study the Bible with you."

Tony was stunned. He had no idea these young people, perhaps in their late teens or early twenties, would be there solely for Bible study. No need for friendship evangelism techniques now—they were ready to dive right in.

"Well, great! Let me grab my Bible." Tony reached over for his burgundy leather-covered New International Version, and saw at the same time four of the six in his group pull small paper-covered books out of their pockets. The books were thinner than a half inch, no bigger than his pocket-size Russian phrase book.

"What kind of Bibles are those?" he asked.

Nadia asked, and interpreted their response. "They say these are the four gospels. They received them a few months ago from a traveling preacher. They ask if these Bibles are acceptable to you?"

"Oh definitely, definitely!" Tony was immediately humbled looking at the tattered booklets in each of their hands, worn with frequent use. A couple of the books were in two or more pieces; the bindings were poorly constructed. Though pages were loose, he could tell by the way each person delicately held their gospels that they made every effort to keep each book intact. As he opened his own Bible, he felt like he was turning the pages of a huge family heirloom in comparison.

"What would you like to study? Any specific questions?"

One of the girls spoke, and Nadia told Tony, "Sveta asks if you could explain what it says in the Gospel of Mark, chapter three. If I understand her question, apparently Jesus would not greet his own mother or brothers, but instead said each one in the crowd with him was his mother and brother. Why would he seem so rude?" Nadia asked the question as much for herself as she did for the girl.

"Uh, yes. That's a good question." *Wouldn't you know they would ask a question like this!* "Uh, well, let's look at it here. Yes, Mark three, verse thirty-one. Nadia, ask one of them to read it out loud, would you?"

Tony hoped she couldn't tell he was trying to stall. He didn't have the foggiest idea what to say. *Lord, give me an answer, please!*

Nadia had one of the young men read the verses, and she listened while sharing a gospel with one of the others. Tony stared at the verses in his Bible while the Russian version was read. When the story was finished, every eye looked at Tony, waiting for an answer. He could feel Nadia's gaze penetrate him, ready to be enlightened—but he had nothing to say. He glanced up for help, but the rest of the Americans were all involved. *Please Lord, I need to say something now!*

"Nadia, ask them what they think it means."

It was cheap, but it would gain him precious time to think.

Sveta, the girl who asked the question, spoke right up. "Isn't Jesus trying to say that he is related to all men and women as the Son of Man, and that all people are important to him?"

With a huge smile, Tony sighed. "Yes, yes, Svee-yeta! I believe you're right on!" Everyone giggled as Tony's pronunciation of Sveta's name fell far short.

Nadia translated Tony's remark, and Sveta appeared pleased that her answer was approved. These young people had a grasp of Scripture, Tony realized, but needed affirmation that what they were learning on their own was accurate. He decided to continue right where they were.

"Let's read from here in Mark a few more verses, and I will ask someone else to tell me what it means, okay?" Nadia translated.

"Sergei," he butchered the name again as he pointed to a young man beside him. "You start reading through verse eight of chapter four." Everyone smiled, and studied their gospels closely while Sergei began reading.

Tony took a moment to realize he was leading his first Russian Bible study, and it was going pretty well. He gave quick thanks to God and followed along in his Bible. Excited to see what his group would come up with in the next verses, he was perturbed when John called everyone in the room together for an announcement.

"We just had a couple more visitors at the door here," John began, this time with Tonya translating for him. "These guests had to leave, but I just thought you all would like to know they came to tell us we are invited to meet with the mayor today at three o'clock!"

Exclamations and backslaps filled the room with the great joy and anticipation this news brought to the young church. Tony saw again how much these people wanted the Americans to be successful in their ministry.

"Oh Tony, this is wonderful news!" Nadia spoke the words with more elation than expected from someone who barely understood the purpose of the church. She only knew that this was what the Americans had hoped for, and she was ready to share the joy.

He casually put his hand on her shoulder. "Thanks for being together with us in all of this."

Her shoulder tensed; her eyes shot quickly into his own. His friendly intent communicated more than he had meant, but before he dropped his hand he could feel the muscles of her arm relax. Still holding her gaze, he thought he could read her eyes saying, 'I don't mind.' Yet, she quickly turned away from him and began talking Russian with one of the group.

Lord, help my focus stay with Your design for this trip, Tony prayed as his mind was swimming. *I can't allow myself to rebound into some relationship over here. It's too soon, Lord. It's not right.*

He continued his silent prayer, trying to repress the shivers that crawled up his spine. Nadia walked away across the room. He couldn't stop staring. Then suddenly, she turned around and met his eyes, as if she knew he was watching her.

He hastily glanced another direction. *Lord, help my focus stay on You.*

Chapter 14

John suggested that he and Paul meet with the mayor. Tony still wanted to pursue a visit with the Bolshoigorsk City Church and Howard volunteered to go with him. While the mayor's visit came with an overture, the government church visit would be more delicate. Tony suggested he visit the church as an interested tourist rather than seeking an invitation. John agreed.

The Hensleys would stay at the flat with Slava and continue the Bible studies with the church people and their friends. Because of the importance of both meetings, John asked the team to spend an hour together praying and fasting during their usual lunch time.

Slava told the fifteen or so people still at his flat about the prayer time and suggested they leave for an hour, but everyone wanted to stay for prayer. The translators were encouraged to take a break as well, and Slava thoroughly explained to them that they would not be needed. Still, the three women did not wish to leave.

"I am sorry, John, but it appears everyone wishes to be with the Americans," Slava said as Tonya translated. Her smile at the end of the translation gave away her own eagerness in having every moment with the team.

"Well, okay, Slava," John responded. "But let me give everyone some ground rules, if you wouldn't mind."

"Not at all. Please, do as you wish."

John asked Tonya to have the group assemble together for a short announcement, and she continued to translate for him.

"I understand everyone here wishes to stay for our time of prayer and fasting. You are most welcome to be with us, but we want you to understand what this time means to us."

As Tonya translated, John could see everyone in the room give him their complete attention. The group was so willing to please the Americans, he felt he could ask them to jump into the lake and they would do so in the dead of winter. He hoped his words would change their blind obedience to a specific understanding of their purpose.

"This is a time we wish to set apart especially for God. Our meeting with the mayor and our visit to the Bolshoigorsk City Church this afternoon are vital to the Lord's ministry here. We wish to make a special effort to come before God with clean and devoted hearts, and seek His mercy and guidance in our activities. The Scriptures give us numerous examples of this pattern of praying, and we desire to follow these. It is a time when we surrender ourselves completely to God's will, and trust Him to provide us with His wisdom for everything we need. Skipping our lunch meal will be a small example to God of our desire to depend on Him for our most basic needs."

John looked around the entire room to be sure everyone was with him.

"Coming before God in this way is a very serious gesture that we do not wish to take lightly. Therefore, we ask any of you to feel free to leave for an hour or so if you do not feel ready to spend this type of time before God. There is no reason to feel embarrassed, and you will be welcome to return at any time. If you do stay, each of you will be asked to pray silently, making every effort not to bother anyone else. Feel free to quietly read Scripture, but mostly, we encourage you to get alone with yourself and God, and seek His face and His desires. Let's take a short break so you can get settled here or leave if you wish."

John could tell this was new for the Russians. He quickly prayed to himself, *Lord, I don't want this to be a show for the curious. Please be honored by our time set aside for You.*

No one left, and the group sat quietly in various places throughout the flat. Mr. Hensley passed out Russian Bibles to those who did not have one. John led the Americans in a worship chorus, and Slava followed with a beautiful chorus from the Russians. A sweet solemnness filled the room as heads were lowered to pray.

* * * * *

If eyes could see, the quiet, somber room would view two hundred angels sweeping across the heavens to attend this special time. Some of the pray-ers could almost sense the motion in the room, and the presence of God was soon felt in their prayers. The angels flew across the room in a kaleidoscope of patterns, shifting each moment with a dizzy blur of activity. Every movement was synchronized from above, as the worship of this group was magnified in glorious ways to honor God.

In a variety of unseen ways, the angels ministered to this small group of believers and seekers. Faith was increased, doubts were discarded, strength was found, and encouragement freely given to all who asked. Prayers were delivered from people of many unlike backgrounds, yet their requests were similar toward seeing God's will occur in Bolshoigorsk. The angels communicated to their charges with confidence that their prayers were answered.

The time moved as quickly as the angels, until a moment when many of them suddenly shifted their flight and came to an area of the flat inside the bedroom. Something unearthly was happening in the heart of one of these pray-ers, and the angelic activity was shooting off like a fountain into the heavens. Majestic somersaults, flips and twirls in huge patterns from the floor to the high heavens were exalting the glorious event. The angels' song was a joyous and mighty symphonic chorus of hallelujahs and amens.

All the attention focused on a young lady crouching in her chair. She hardly looked like the focus of a celebration as she began weeping openly, tears staining the pages of her Bible. Yet, fireworks were going off in the heavens.

* * * * *

"Mrs. Hensley, you'd better come see Luda," Tony said quietly, interrupting the lady on her knees in the kitchen.

"Why, Tony?" She was surprised to be called out of her prayers. "Is something wrong?"

"No, I think something very right is going on," he smiled as he helped her up and into the bedroom.

As Mrs. Hensley walked in, she saw Luda, her face wet with tears. Nadia sat beside her on the bed. As Luda's eyes raised, Mrs. Hensley could not mistake the look on her face. Luda exclaimed to confirm what Mrs. Hensley saw. "I believe—I've just met Jesus!"

* * * * *

Luda had made her commitment to believe in Jesus Christ. Mrs. Hensley visited and prayed with her. By the time they came out of the bedroom, everyone had caught wind of something happening and were waiting expectantly.

Luda said she wished to share with the group, that she would speak the words first in English and follow with her own translation in Russian. "My time of quiet prayer led me to consider the message that I translated so many times in the park yesterday. Ever since I first spoke the words about the love of Jesus and His death for sins, I knew that His death was for me. Last night, Mr. and Mrs. Hensley helped me to see what the Bible says about Jesus before they went to bed. Now, during this prayer time, I was overwhelmed with my unworthiness before God." Her speech broke as tears began to flow.

"I felt so awful trying to pray to God when I knew I was a sinner. That's when I saw Him—just in my mind, you see—but I saw Him. I saw the face of Jesus, with rich and longing eyes that said to me, 'I love you, Luda. I died for you.'"

Luda had to stop as her emotions overflowed. Standing beside her, Mrs. Hensley took her into her arms.

Amens were heard across the room in both languages, mixed with sniffles from many of the witnesses. What had happened to Luda was real, and everyone in the room could sense the awesome presence of God's hand of salvation fall on this woman.

"I wish to try to speak again," Luda continued with more composure. "When I heard those words from Jesus' mouth, I knew they were for me. Jesus died for me, and His love for me, well, His love for me is—how do you say in English—splendid, magnificent, wonderful, marvelous! All those words and more." She followed with the same words in Russian.

Slava approached her and hugged her shoulders. He addressed the group through Tonya. "This is wonderful! We are so excited with you, Luda. But, I must ask the Americans to please prepare yourselves; the time for your visit with the mayor soon approaches."

John, startled as he looked at his watch, forced himself to break up their celebration and call the Americans together, assigning translators to the group. The Hensleys were happy to stay with Luda and the other Russians, while John asked Tonya to ready herself for the mayor. Tony and Howard, as the delegation to the government church, would have Nadia as translator.

The latter threesome left for the church with a couple of their new Russian friends, Sergei and Natasha, as guides. It would take them almost twenty minutes to reach their destination, and Tony was glad to have the time to visit about the past hour.

He anxiously asked Nadia, "What did you think of Luda's decision?"

"I am very happy for her," Nadia replied with a distant tone in her voice. "She seems to have a great joy."

Howard joined in with a question. "Do you understand what has happened to her?"

"I believe she has had a—how do you say—a 'spiritual revelation,' yes?"

"Yes, I suppose those would be the right words," Howard responded.

"And that is why I am happy for her," Nadia continued, speaking offhandedly. "This was something she was wanting, I am sure."

"But do you ever wish for the same thing in your life, Nadia?" Tony asked hopefully.

"I cannot say that I do."

The trio was interrupted by Sergei who directed them down a different street. He gave Nadia a question to ask the Americans, and Tony and Howard took it as a sign that it was time to leave the present discussion. They began talking about favorite American foods with Sergei and Natasha for the rest of the walk. While Howard visited, Tony walked slowly behind the group, struggling over Nadia's lack of interest in her own salvation.

How can she be so blind, Lord? Doesn't she see her need for You? From the back of the group, his eyes stared at the gleam of her dark brown hair covering her shoulders. The sun made the natural bronze tones shine golden as she strolled down the street in a carefree walk. *Lord, I have such a burden for her to know You, but she doesn't give an inkling of desire. Please open her heart to You. Please show her who You are.*

As he continued to watch her, his prayer became introspective.

Why am I so drawn to her, Lord? I find myself wanting to know all about her, understand her. She seems so cool to any spiritual talk, but I want to visit with her, be around her, share more of myself with her. Lord, help me sort through how I can best touch her life for You.

His daydreaming prayer was interrupted by Sergei's shout and pointing finger ahead of him.

At the end of the street was a huge, looming building. They were still two blocks away, yet the structure rose out of the gray complexes around it as a shining castle. The building was at least six stories tall, with bright white plaster walls. The front facade framed a huge arch extending across ten-foot high double doors at the top of the entry's stairs. Above the magnificent entrance, Tony's eyes were drawn to the beacons at each of the top corners of the building. Large domes in the shape of gigantic upside-down onions, each painted a brilliant blue, crowned each corner structure. In the center of the roof, an even larger dome surpassed the height of the others and was covered with shimmering brass. The point of this onion shape held a towering golden cross easily marked as the highest point of the town.

The afternoon sun caused the center dome and cross to beam with a blinding glare. Each member of the group shaded their eyes as they gazed at the immense building. It boldly stood as a fortress of riches and superiority compared to the crumbling facades surrounding it, a miniature Taj Mahal in the midst of slums.

"It's beautiful!" Tony exclaimed. "Howard, get some pictures of this." But he was way ahead of him, already snapping.

Sergei had walked ahead while the rest of the team had stopped. He came running back, impatiently motioning for them to come.

"Nadia, tell Sergei to wait a minute, we want to get some good shots of this," Howard said.

Nadia spoke with Sergei, and he responded. "This is not so special—it is just the work of man. Please don't offend God by giving it so much attention."

His words caught Tony off guard. The boy was surely no more than eighteen years old, yet he had some strong impressions of this church.

Tony called him over. "Sergei, this is a beautiful building. Wasn't it made to glorify God?" Nadia translated.

"Yes, I am sure our forefathers built it to God's glory, but it only serves man now."

"What do you mean, Sergei? How do you know so much about this church?"

"My family goes here. I used to. I was even baptized here, but I am embarrassed to admit it. I did not know Jesus Christ as my Savior then." His head hanged shamefully.

"So why did you leave?"

"A friend introduced me to Slava, and he told me about Jesus. I met with Slava several times, and learned who Jesus really is. Soon after this I became a true believer." He spoke more boldly. "When I told my family I was a Christian, they kicked me out of my home. My old church friends turned away from me."

Howard approached the conversation with Natasha. "Where do you live now?"

"I live with my grandfather, when he is not drinking. Sometimes other families let me sleep at their homes, like Natasha's." He gave a gracious smile to Natasha and she blushed.

Tony continued, "So Sergei, you do not believe this church preaches about Jesus Christ?"

Nadia did not need to interpret his response. Sergei spoke a strong and definite "*Nyet!*" with a thrust of his hands.

"You just gave us a whole new meaning to our visit here. Let's go see if anybody's home."

They turned and walked more slowly down the street. Tony slipped over to Howard to speak with him quietly.

"What do you think of his story, Howard?"

"I don't know. The boy definitely has a gripe with his church. I know of the Russian Orthodox church. They have a solid theology that I can't quibble over. You know, you see the same thing in America. Someone gets upset at a church and goes to another one. It doesn't necessarily mean the church is all bad."

"Yeah, but in America you don't usually get kicked out of your house."

Nadia interrupted them. "I think I can explain Sergei's story to you"

Tony looked with surprise that Nadia would have a comment.

"You see, the government church in Russia is very wealthy. Many poor people give their money to the church. They think it pleases their God. But the church uses the money to look—how do you say—beautiful. It angers people like Sergei to see people act so foolishly." Nadia spoke the words with a strong resolve of her own.

"It sounds like it angers you too," Tony responded.

"Yes, of course."

Tony and Howard remained silent in rhetorical agreement as they approached the front steps of the gilded church. Now the wondrous architecture seemed more ominous. The group moved up the steps without a word, and Sergei opened the huge wooden door, gesturing for everyone to enter.

The darkness inside was blinding until their eyes adjusted. The small foyer was lit by two weak lights mounted on opposite dark paneled walls. Tony could not tell if he shivered from the chill in the humid air or from apprehension.

Sergei led the team a short distance to another entrance door, this one beautifully scored with a huge symmetrical cross in the maple door. He again ushered the group through.

Tony caught his breath as they entered the sanctuary. The circular room was not huge by diameter, but the arched ceiling rose at least another story high, giving the room an astounding depth. The walls held small lit candle sconces, creating the dim glow of a dark, mystical atmosphere. Walking along the lines of wooden pews, Tony caught a faint scent of an unknown incense wafting in the air.

The flickering candles reflected on bronze plaques hanging every few feet along each wall. Tony stepped to the side to view one more closely. It was a poster-sized brass plate, imprinted with a two-dimensional outline of a roundheaded haloed man in Slavic armor, wearing a skirt and cape, holding a spear. His costume was painted with reds and greens against the golden background. At the bottom was an engraved Russian word labeling the picture.

Howard whispered over Tony's shoulder, "Do you know what these are?"

"Some kind of decoration for the church?"

"Yes, but much more. They're called icons. They portray events or people from Scripture. Sometimes they're famous saints from the church's history. It's an important part of this religion."

"They're beautiful, and look—they're all around the church walls."

"I remember a professor I had in seminary. He said icons were used to remind the people of the tradition and history of the church, and were revered as holy objects. They served as a reverent testimony of how God had worked through certain people to uphold the faith. Some churches got carried away with icons, even assigning spiritual powers to them. Like, maybe you could be healed by looking at this plaque. Apparently some fringe religions even go so far as to say the actual spirit of the person in the icon exists within the art. A prayer to the icon can be heard by that spirit."

"Whoa—that's too weird. Do you think this church believes that?"

"I doubt it. But it does seem this church has had some problems taking things too far."

The others walked over and Tony asked Nadia to read the title on the icon.

"It says 'Saint Demetrios.'"

Sergei spoke and Nadia responded in English, "Sergei says this was a Byzantine saint who fought for Christianity in the tenth century. The icons on the side walls are all saints, and the front icons are from the Bible."

Tony had not looked at the front of the church as it was so dark, but now that his eyes had adjusted he could see this wall covered with elaborate drawings. As they walked up together, Sergei stopped them in the aisle a few pews in front of the icons.

"Sergei says we mustn't go too close to the icons or we could desecrate them," Nadia said. Tony moved with Howard a few steps back just to be careful.

As he gazed more closely at the images, Tony realized the front wall was actually a screen, with large double doors in the center. There were four rows of large separate icons painted above the doors, extending the entire width and height of the wall. Each figure faced toward the center doors, most kneeling in a position of prayer, except for the scenes in the third row which held various depictions of what appeared to be the same two people, a man and a woman. Mary and Jesus, Tony thought.

With what Howard had said about icons, Tony felt an eerie chill, imagining the figures in the icons each holding a spirit. If it were so, dozens of eyes were peering at them just now.

"Is this the iconostasis?" Howard asked Sergei.

"Yes. You can see the icons here illustrate the Bible." Nadia interpreted Sergei's response. "The top row is the Old Testament patriarchs and the next row, Old Testament prophets. The third row shows events from the life of Christ that are celebrated here as holy days. The fourth row depicts Christ in the center, Mary on one side, John the Baptist on the other, and other archangels and saints extending out behind them, all representing the Last Judgement."

"So what's behind the doors?" Tony questioned.

"The priest enters these doors to prepare the Eucharist, the bread and the wine of Holy Communion. It is felt the doors represent the division between the divine and human worlds, and only the priest may enter."

"So you don't want us knocking on that door," Tony said with a smile.

From the back of the church a surprising voice thundered in English. "That would indeed be a disgrace!"

Everyone turned quickly to see where the voice came from, but the figure remained hidden in the darkness of the rear foyer. The voice spoke again, this time in Russian. The inflections were foreboding. Tony felt a chill that was definitely not from the temperature.

Sergei responded to the voice in Russian, seeming respectful and unsurprised. Tony marveled at the maturity of this young man. He handled himself with much confidence.

The conversation between Sergei and the voice continued in normal tones, but the shadowed presence and pretentious speech did not reassure Tony. He moved closer to Nadia and asked her what was going on.

She whispered back, "This is the bishop of the church, a Father Federov. He knows Sergei and is questioning him about who we are. Sergei has asked to introduce us."

Sergei looked at Tony expectantly. He gestured for him to meet the priest.

Tony stepped up the center aisle and looked toward the figure, trying to speak with more confidence than he felt.

"My name is Tony Barton, and I'm from America. We were just visiting your beautiful church—I hope you don't mind."

Nadia began to translate, but the voice interrupted her, this time in English.

"Excuse me young lady, but I understand some English; save your breath. Mr. Barton, it is a pleasure to welcome you to our community." The pleasantries were contrasted by the deep snarl in their sound. "And who is your friend?"

Howard stepped up beside Tony. "I am Howard Matson, and it is certainly our privilege to meet you, sir."

Finally, the figure stepped forward into the dim light to show himself. His face was yet shadowed in the candlelight. A black miter topping his head revealed little of his face except for adding six more inches to his six-foot frame. His eyes were hidden under prominent ebony eyebrows shading the broad pits of his orbits. As he walked down the aisle, his pitch black full-length robe moved smoothly and quietly; it was a well-rehearsed pace. He did not speak, and no one else knew what to say in the uncomfortable silence.

Stopping right in front of Tony, the man towered over him. His voice echoed in the chamber again, ending the muted tension.

"And what brings you to visit our church, Mr. Barton?"

Tony began to speak, but his voice cracked, exposing the intimidation he felt. The priest's words were polite, but their tone caused Tony to lose his breath. Something in the air tightened like a noose around his neck. Clearing his throat a couple times, he turned his head to cough and heard Howard step in, thankfully.

"We are here to bring you greetings from Christians in America, Father—," Howard hesitated, hoping to prompt an introduction.

"Excuse me," the bishop said. "Of course I should introduce myself. I am Father Federov, Bishop of the Bolshoigorsk City Church." The introduction was more of a proclamation.

Howard continued, "Father Federov, we greet you in the grace and mercy of our Lord Jesus Christ."

A sudden interruption thundered from the bishop. "How dare you speak so flippantly of one you know so little about!"

Standing a pace behind Howard, Tony's speech was still lost in his own distress.

"I do not mean to offend you, Father Federov, but as a pastor myself," Howard continued, cautious but clear, "I wish to speak with you as one who serves the same Lord as you."

"Do not even pretend to suggest yourself worthy of serving the Lord God as I do," the bishop roared, his words ringing across the sanctuary. He turned and threw a furious barrage of Russian words at Sergei.

Seeing Sergei shrink back, suffering the same ridicule that forced him out of his own home, Tony knew he had to redirect the conversation. As soon as the priest stopped long enough for a breath, Tony looked directly into the dark caverns holding the priest's eyes and mustered a voice to bear words. "We come only with the purpose of sharing the love of Christ with your community."

"Again you take the holy name in vain!" The bishop approached a rage. "You must stop at once speaking of our sovereign God with such—such peasant language." A tirade of Russian flew again as he spoke this time to Nadia.

"He says to mention the name of the Lord is intolerable in his presence," Nadia shakingly translated. "Your speech insults his wisdom and position as bishop of Bolshoigorsk."

Howard tried again. "Please sir, can we not together agree that we search the same holy Scriptures to understand God? Can we offer you a peaceful greeting from our country?"

The priest angrily resorted to reply in Russian, forcing Nadia into the uncomfortable interpretation. His tone evidenced his disagreement.

"I do not believe you are going to find any grounds to visit with him," Nadia related his words quietly, her voice fearful. "He says you are illiterate of the true Scriptures, and that you mock him and God in suggesting you could possibly understand them."

The bishop saw Nadia finish and addressed Howard in English. "If you truly seek God, what do you know of Saint Cyprianos, Origen, or Chrysostomos?"

The question was offered accusingly, and Howard shrugged his shoulders with his response. "I know John Chrysostomos as a fourth century theologian."

"Ha! You see!" The priest, making sense only to himself, felt satisfied with his argument. "You cannot even speak correctly of the holy fathers of the church. Don't attempt to speak to me of God if you cannot even speak of the saints who have instructed us. You waste my time! I will give you a single verse to dwell on from the holy Scriptures. Read the holy words from the Gospel of Saint Matthew, chapter twenty-three, verse fifteen. You will find yourselves there. But for now, I must insist that you leave."

With finality he spoke gruff Russian to Nadia. The visit was over. "He asks us to quickly find our way out. We are not welcome to return."

"I can't say I feel any differently," Tony whispered to Howard as they quickly made their way outside.

The bright sunshine hit their eyes with refreshing light as they came down the outside steps away from the church. Tony felt released from bondage as he left the building.

"I've never been so thankful to get out of church!" Howard agreed.

Sergei and Natasha were quiet and shaken as they looked to the two Americans for their response.

"Was that a good example of what this church is like?" Tony asked Sergei.

"Yes, quite so," Nadia responded from Sergei's answer. "Father Federov does not approve of anyone speaking of the Lord by his given name, Jesus. He believes it is far too informal for man to address God's Son personally. That is why he was so offended."

"Why did he ask me about the early theologians?" Howard asked.

"The men he mentioned are saints of the church. Their teachings are considered infallible, according to Father Federov. He believes the validity of the Bible is found in its teachers, such as these men."

"You mean to say that he would use the teachings of an early theologian to defend the Bible?" Tony asked. "Shouldn't the Scripture serve as judge over a man's words?"

Nadia carefully translated the question to Sergei, and he responded affirmatively, *"Dah."*

Tony held his gaze with Sergei, seeing the long history of hurt and disappointment that the bishop had caused this young man.

"Why is that so important?" Nadia asked. "Why do you believe your Bible has the final truth in everything? You treat that book as if it was one of those icons."

"Nadia, as a Christian I must look to God as the source of all truth," Tony responded. "All right and wrong, all good and evil, must be determined by the wisdom of God, if He truly created and controls all things." He paused a moment to be sure of his words. "I understand this book to be written by God as a letter to me and all people everywhere. The Bible was given by God's direct guidance to show us His perfect plan. It may be hard for you to believe, but there is a long list of predictions in the Bible which have occurred exactly as they were recorded. As these prophecies have proved the truth of God's Word in ages past, I trust the Scripture to teach me and guide me now. Does that make sense to you?"

Nadia's eyes were fixed on Tony's and perhaps softened, if only for an instant. "Yes, I think I understand what you mean."

"When we depend on other men to tell us the Scripture, we must be sure that what they say agrees completely with this Word. The danger comes when we do not know the Bible well enough to compare it to what we might be taught. Many false teachers in the world pretend to offer words from Scripture, only to serve themselves."

Howard nodded his head in agreement as Nadia seemed to sincerely listen.

"Nadia, I am really sorry for what you had to see in there with Father Federov," Tony continued. "Something was very wrong in his manner. Please do not judge Christianity based on his example."

"Do not worry," Nadia responded. "I see a big difference in the Christ of your church and the one who was worshiped back there." She added a reassuring smile.

"Good," Tony felt his blood flow warmly through his veins. *She's doing some soul-searching!* He let his smile linger back to her for a moment before Sergei interrupted. He was holding out his New Testament gospels, asking Nadia to read something.

"Sergei found the verse Father Federov wanted us to read." She took his booklet and translated the verse he pointed to. "'Woe to you, teachers of the law and Pharisees, you hypocrites! You travel over land and sea to win a single convert, and when he becomes one, you make him twice as much a son of hell as you are.'"

"Ouch!" Howard said, feeling the sting of the words. "That's a good example of how a teacher of the Scripture can misuse it."

"Exactly," Tony agreed.

"Nadia, read the very first part of that chapter," Howard added. "These are Jesus' words, and I believe the first verses tell who He is addressing."

Nadia turned back a page and began reading in Russian for Sergei and Natasha, then she followed with the English translation.

"It says, 'The teachers of the law and the Pharisees sit in Moses' seat. So you must do everything they tell you. But do not do what they do, for they do not practice what they preach. They tie up heavy loads and put them on men's shoulders, but they themselves are not willing to lift a finger to move them.'"

"Judge for yourself, Nadia, who is more like the Pharisees—us, or Father Federov." Howard spoke the words not expecting an answer. "We'd better head back to the flat and see how the Hensleys are doing."

"Howard, wait just a minute," Tony said. "Before we go, let's pray. This church's problems are much bigger than we can handle, but I would guess that unless something changes, Father Federov will never be supportive of Slava's ministry."

"You're right. Nadia, tell Natasha and Sergei we're going to spend a moment to pray here."

The group held a brief vigil still in the shadows of the magnificent architecture that only an hour ago had left them awe-struck with its beauty. Now the temple's proud and greedy facade was clearly apparent. Their prayers sought the Lord to bring humility, love and mercy to its halls. It seemed a feeble effort to Tony, but he knew this was how God worked.

He just didn't realize God would work so fast.

As the group began to walk away from the church, they heard someone call to them from behind. "Americans, Americans, please wait—"

Tony turned to see a middle-aged nicely dressed woman waving at him across the street, with a younger man and girl walking with her. As they approached, their serious faces gave no clue as to who they were, but their clothing was finer than what he was used to seeing in

Bolshoigorsk. The front lady spoke Russian words to which Nadia quickly responded, and they had a brief exchange before Nadia interpreted for Tony and Howard.

"These people are from the Bolshoigorsk television station. They have been searching everywhere to find you. They would like to interview you for their news program, as soon as possible."

Sergei was waving his arms excitedly and speaking rapidly, all smiles, but Tony hesitated.

Nadia spoke quietly to Tony. "Sergei says this is God's answer to our prayers. He says you could tell all of Bolshoigorsk about Jesus on the television."

"Yes, I understand, Nadia. But I want to be sure this would do no harm to Slava and the church here." He thought a moment more. "Ask the news people if they understand we are missionaries, here to speak about Jesus Christ. Tell them that is what we would want to talk about in an interview."

While Nadia related his words to the TV crew, Tony spoke with Howard.

"What do you think?"

"I don't know, Tony. It sounds like a great opportunity on one hand, but I wish we could run it by John and Slava to be sure."

"I agree. Let's see if we can set a tentative time, and try to find John."

Nadia returned to Tony. "They say that your religion is exactly what they want you to talk about. They want to hear about the Christ Americans worship."

"Wow," Tony exclaimed. "Nadia, tell them we need to check with our team, but that we would like to set a time now."

Nadia communicated the message, visited with the lady briefly, and spoke to Tony. "They would like to meet with you at a restaurant near here at four-thirty today. They have given me directions."

"Four-thirty! Howard, that's only a couple hours from now. Do you think we can make it?"

"Let's do it, Tony. We might have to postpone or cancel, but if we turn it down now, we may never get the chance again."

"Okay. Nadia, tell them we'll be there." Tony followed her and gave a smile and handshake to each of the crew. He blustered out a sloppy thanks in Russian, and they all laughed.

"Tony," Nadia joked, "You should leave the Russian to me, yes?"

Chapter 15

Slava sat back on the thin cushion of the metal folding chair, lost in his own thoughts. The people around him studied a chapter from the Gospel of John, but his mind was not with them.

Mr. Hensley led the study, with Luda enamored to the Scriptures as she translated for him. Slava counted twelve others around the circle from his church besides three newcomers. Each one held rapt attention to their teacher, but Slava kept drifting away.

This man really understands God's Word, Slava thought. *His teaching comes with such wisdom, full of background information that clarifies his words. It would take me years to learn the Scriptures like that.*

The rustling of pages interrupted Slava. Everyone was turning to a new verse. He looked beside him to see where Oksana turned and followed suit, but his actions were mechanical.

These Americans all seem so in control, so sure of themselves. Their faith and boldness put me to shame. Having them want to visit the city church—I don't think I could ever have visited that place—if only because of all the stories I've heard about their bishop. I was too scared. I was afraid of being made a fool. So I just went ahead and let the Americans go and do what I should have done a long time ago. He fidgeted in his chair, throwing his fingers through his hair. *Well, Lord, I hope You can use them more than me.*

A small crash and the cry of a child came from the kitchen. Both Slava and Oksana flinched.

"I will go," Slava whispered to his wife, and she nodded her head. He stepped away, thankful for an excuse to get out of the group right now.

In the kitchen his two boys sat beside a small pile of sugar on the floor, a broken bowl to their side completing the story. With crystals sparkling their cheeks and fingers, both boys froze when their father entered. The two-year-old, Andrei, immediately began a guilty cry. Vladislav, at age five, knew where he should point his finger.

Quickly shushing them both, Slava scooped the costly sugar grains back into a new bowl.

"Vlad, you cannot eat sugar like this. It is much too expensive; it will make you sick."

"But Father, the Americans said that they put sugar on many things. One man said he sprinkles it on toast with something called seena-, seeno-, seenomun, or something like that. Why can't we do that?"

"We live very differently than the Americans. There are many things that they do that we just cannot. Sugar and other spices—like cinnamon—are just too expensive here." Slava inwardly groaned; his son was becoming just as jealous of the Americans as he.

"We have to be thankful for the blessings God has given us, without always looking at what others may have that we want." The words pained him to speak, as much to himself as his son.

"But Father, why did God give the Americans so much more than He gave us? Why are we so poor and they so rich?" Vladislav's big brown eyes stared innocently. The questions burned a hole in Slava's own heart. He stopped spooning the sugar and sat on the floor, pulling little Andrei on his lap.

"I don't know, son. I don't know." The words came with defeat. "We just have to remember to be faithful to God with what we do have. God surely provides just what we need." Slava looked at his two boys and realized aloud, "You and Andrei are God's blessings to me, in greater ways than any money could buy. I have no reason to complain to God about how we live when I think of you two and your mother. So don't worry about what we have compared to the Americans. I feel very rich just sitting here with you."

Slava reached over and gave Vladislav a big squeeze with Andrei still in his arms. He fell to the floor, dog-piling his boys on top of himself. The boys squealed with delight, having their father love them on their level. This was more grand than all the sugar in the world.

A commotion at the front door interrupted the wrestles and hugs. Slava stepped out of the kitchen with Andrei still grabbing his shoulders and Vlad wrapped around his waist. He felt empowered to rescue the world as he wore his boys' embraces as heroic medals.

Tony and Howard had just entered. Nadia called to Slava to come into the living room for the full report. The Hensleys broke up the Bible study to also hear what happened.

"We've got some good news and some bad news," Tony began. "Let's start with the bad. Slava, hold onto your hat when I tell you about your neighborhood church. It's not exactly the beginning of an ecumenical society here."

Nadia began to translate, then looked quizzically at Tony. "Hold onto your hat? He's not wearing a hat, Tony."

"Excuse me, Nadia—another American expression. Let's start over."

The front door abruptly opened again. This time a lady from the church entered, half out of breath. She excused herself for interrupting and handed a note to Slava.

"Pastor Hatir from Nizhnekamsk just called at my home and asked me to give you this message right away, Slava. He said he could not talk long, but that you would understand these words. I raced over as quickly as I could."

Slava read the slip of paper silently: 'Ilya's family found. Federov is source.' He crumpled the note into his palm. "Well, let's hear about your visit to the Bolshoigorsk City Church."

* * * * *

Five miles away, the mayor's secretary was respectful and polite. John, Paul and Tonya were asked to wait twenty minutes or so, but everyone was cordial. Ushered into a large dark walnut paneled meeting room, they found themselves alone beside a huge oval table of polished mahogany. At one end of the room, a lighter brown desk was butted against the large table. Two neatly organized stacks of papers rested on one side of the desk, and four separately colored telephones lined the other. After they found their seats in black vinyl upholstered chairs around the table, a young girl surprised the group, courteously serving strong coffee and shortbread cookies on delicate china dishes. She left just as quickly, efficient but nervous.

Around the room were framed black and white photographs of individuals presumed to be former officials of the city. As the threesome waited for the mayor, the frowning portraits stared directly out of their frames, communicating an eerie feeling that they were being watched.

After a long ten minutes, three men entered the room. Introductions passed through Tonya and greetings were extended both ways.

Mayor Dmitry Babekov was a short round-faced gentleman, fifty-ish, with more the appearance of the local baker than a politician. A lengthy tuft of hair was swept across his scalp. He nervously kept adjusting it as he shook hands with the Americans. It appeared he had already had a long day.

The other two men were taller and younger, flanking the mayor on either side. While the mayor was in a white shirt with rolled up sleeves and a loosened tie, these two, one blonde, one dark haired, were smartly dressed in suits. They were of few words, and John puzzled over their presence. Tonya described them as the mayor's attendants.

Gesturing for his guests to be seated, Mayor Babekov moved to his desk, his suited companions sitting on either side of him at the table. As the Americans took their seats at the opposite end, John felt the wide distance between them. He spoke first to try to gloss over any mistaken first impressions.

"We are thankful for the opportunity to meet with you, Mayor Babekov." John kept his eyes directly on the mayor as Tonya translated. "It is a great privilege to be in Bolshoigorsk and now meet you. We want to apologize again to you and your officials for any difficulties we may have caused on our arrival."

The mayor responded to Tonya as translator, but John did not take his eyes off the man. He wanted to communicate beyond words that his intentions were sincere, but also earnest.

"The mayor says he is very pleased to be able to meet the Americans. Had he known you were coming, he would have invited you to visit him earlier. He asks for the purpose of your visit here."

So much for pleasantries, John thought as he formed his answer. "Mayor Babekov, we have come to visit our friends here in Bolshoigorsk. Our friends have established a church in your city, and we wish to encourage them in their ministry to the people. While here, we have found the citizens to be most pleasant and hospitable, and we would like to have an opportunity to meet with as many as possible." John paused to let Tonya translate, then he jumped in with his punch line.

"We would like to learn what people here feel is important about life in Russia, as well as share about our lives in America. Would you permit us to hold a meeting at your soccer stadium for this purpose?"

The mayor's answer was quick and verbose. John thought he heard the word, 'nyet,' but had to wait for Tonya to give the full answer in translation.

"The mayor says he does not think this would be possible."

John did not allow himself to show his dismay as Tonya continued. "He said he is concerned that such a meeting could stir the people into a controversy, that the group we are visiting here has attempted to do this before. He says Bolshoigorsk is a peaceful community. It is his job to protect this peace."

The mayor added additional Russian words, gesturing with several sheets of paper in his hands. His hand mopped his scalp nervously, but his tone of voice remained smooth. The two suited gentlemen were leaning forward on the table, causing John to anticipate some sort of attack as he waited anxiously for the translation.

"The mayor says when he reviewed your visas, he read that you were tourists. Now it appears that you have specific business here. He asks if this is true."

John hoped his face did not appear as white as he felt inside. *Was that true? Did the visas say 'tourists'?* He couldn't remember. The team filled them out months ago, following a rote format the mission agency gave him.

Paul had been quiet until now, and offered to respond.

"Mayor Babekov, I recall marking on my visa that I was a teacher, not a tourist," Paul spoke politely. "I believe that is how all of them read. By profession, each of us are employed in various capacities, but we are trained to be teachers—teachers of the Scriptures. The opportunity to meet with your community will help us to learn more about your way of life in Russia. We believe as we visit here, we will learn more about the God who created us all."

The mayor seemed unsatisfied with Paul's response, but let the visa documents lie beside his hands. He then spoke directly to Tonya. She responded with a few statements in Russian, and he posed another question to her. Her response caused them both to laugh, which surprised everyone, and brought short smiles to the faces of the suits flanking the mayor.

John felt uncomfortable watching this interplay without a notion of what was being communicated. The lead he had hoped to maintain in the conversation was quickly evaporating. *What private stories are they telling—dumb American jokes? Surely Tonya would not jeopardize our position here.* He felt he had to try to take some control of this conversation.

"Excuse me, Tonya, but would you please ask the mayor something else for me? Tell him we would like to learn about his city. Ask him to describe what strengths he sees in Bolshoigorsk."

Redressing her position as translator, Tonya gave a quaint smile to the mayor with a brief statement that brought a smirk to his face. She then took a more serious tone, asking John's question.

After clearing his throat, the mayor took another sweep at his hair and responded without the edge that his other comments had. The two suits relaxed and appeared distracted as the mayor gave a lengthy answer.

"The mayor says the people of Bolshoigorsk are proud of their city for many reasons," Tonya responded. "But he would especially emphasize the strong work ethic of the people. He feels the citizens contribute greatly to the success of the city, whether it is in selling their own garden produce at the city market, or working at the oil refinery."

"We noticed the refinery when we came into town our first day here," John again spoke directly to the mayor as Tonya translated. "It is a very impressive factory."

The mayor beamed with pride that Americans would compliment his city, and the suits sat back with much less attention to the conversation.

"Conversely, would you identify any weak spots in your community that you are trying as a government to improve?" John hoped the mayor would bite for the worm he dangled.

The two suits watched the mayor more closely with his initial response, then relaxed back in their chairs, apparently satisfied with his words.

"The mayor says he feels quite comfortable in stating that Bolshoigorsk does not have any serious problems. His government spends most of its time developing new strategies for the city's growth."

The mayor didn't even nibble.

"In America we continue to work on growth, but we have to give adequate attention to some national concerns, such as alcohol abuse, drug problems, the changing economy, family breakdown, and such," John persisted. "Do these things not concern you in Bolshoigorsk?"

John threw his hook back out. This time, the mayor bit.

"Well, of course we have those problems, everybody does," Tonya replied with the mayor's answer. "But it is a very difficult thing—alcohol, drugs, divorce, poverty. There are no easy solutions, yes?"

The hook set in and John began reeling.

"Yes, I completely agree. But in America, we have found the church offers a variety of resourceful solutions. They are best met on a local level. In our country, the church is ministering to people with these types of needs, and doing more for them than the government is able to. That's one reason why we would like to see Bolshoigorsk give their attention to registering the church we are visiting, so that they may reach into the community with support for struggling families."

"Ah, I understand," the mayor responded thoughtfully. "It is an interesting idea, asking the church to offer their assistance to those in need." John could see the mayor swallowing the hook. Maybe, maybe he could net him yet.

"Would you permit us to meet with you and the church's pastor, to show you a plan of how the church could minister to the people of Bolshoigorsk with special needs?"

John saw the mayor pause with serious consideration as Tonya translated the new proposal. Any response was quickly terminated, however. The blonde-haired suit on the left leaned forward and answered directly to John. With great surprise, John heard the words from the suit in English.

"Bolshoigorsk does not need American ideas to help solve any of our problems, small as they are. I believe the mayor would not be open to any such meeting with the church pastor you are associating with. Do you not know this man has been found in disrepute in our community?"

The words were spit in thick English, hitting John like a bolt of lightning.

"You—you speak English? Please excuse me, but I am very surprised to only learn this now." John held back his anger at the man's fluency. He felt deceived and mocked. The mayor cowered back in his chair, giving the floor to the blonde.

"I think your appraisal of Pastor Gdansk is unfair and only supported by false accusations," John continued. "Perhaps a meeting with him and us, face to face, would allow you to present your concerns directly, so that he could fairly address them." John spoke now to the suit in charge, willing to spear this shark if it would land him the catch.

"There is no reason to meet with your so-called pastor," the suit replied angrily. The spear missed. "The charges against him are clear and documented. I think it is best for our meeting to end." Standing, the suit grabbed the elbow of the mayor, bringing him to his feet. "I'm sure the mayor has nothing more to say to you."

The mayor stood deflated. Though he had not understood a word of the last several shared in English, his face expressed fear of his near acquiescence to the Americans. John felt pity for a man so controlled.

"Tonya, please give the mayor our thanks for his time." John stood and spoke the words sternly, trying to pierce the shark-mouthed suit with his glare.

Before Tonya could speak, the green phone on the mayor's desk interrupted them with a shrill ring. The mayor, relieved to be distracted, answered the call.

Gesturing for Paul and Tonya to follow, John moved quickly toward the door without a further word. Outside the city building, the three huddled over their new perspective on Bolshoigorsk government.

"Could you believe the way that guy came at you, interrupting the mayor?" Paul said. "He was ready to lunge!"

"I've never seen anything like it. Tonya, who were those two guys? What do 'attendants' mean?"

"I am not exactly sure. I suppose they could have been lawyers, or deputies of the mayor. Something of that sort. I certainly agree that they were most unfriendly."

"But you gained a little ground with the mayor, Tonya. What was the little joke you shared in there?" Paul asked.

"That was very unusual. The mayor asked me if you could be trusted. He asked me if I was in danger as a translator." Tonya began to smile. "I laughed at his question and told him you both were quite harmless, and that he need not be concerned for me." Tonya spoke more quietly, almost embarrassed to speak the next words. "He then offered me protection, and said one of his attendants could accompany me if I needed it. That is when you interrupted with your question, John. I was thankful you did. The way those two men smiled at me, I am sure I am in safer hands with the Americans!"

"Thank you, Tonya," John responded. "You did a superb job of staying calm in there. Paul, you did some quick thinking on that visa issue."

"Yeah, I was wondering how far he might push. They've done a little homework on us. It gives the impression they have an agenda, doesn't it?"

"I agree," John returned. "But did you think the mayor was softening a bit toward us? I really thought I would have won him over if it hadn't been for the other guy."

Tonya offered her appraisal. "From what happened in that room, I think the mayor is your least concern. We need to know who is behind those other two gentlemen."

Chapter 16

Back in the Gdansk's borrowed flat, Slava heard Tony's report of the government church visit. He realized the truth in Pastor Hatir's brief message: 'Federov is source.' The animosity of this man during Tony's visit evidenced the priest's agenda. Federov could not accept another church in town. Slava was a direct threat to him and the welfare of his congregation. If such bitterness raged within the priest from his position of power, his anger could explode into unexplained fires, unjust terminations and overly zealous arrests.

Slava, however, was numb to at last identifying Federov. He did not even fear the prospect of tackling this giant in the community. With the Americans effectively steering the mission, Slava continued to ride the wave to see where he would wind up in the wake of it all.

He was unconcerned about the Americans' television opportunity. Tony and Howard found it important to have his permission to go before the cameras, but Slava was comfortable suggesting they do as they saw best. It felt good to release his authority—perhaps God would use the Americans in even greater ways.

On the other hand, he wondered if his indecision was of a reluctant leader allowing the chips to fall where they may.

*****

John had not returned yet from the mayor's office, and Tony and Howard needed to get to their meeting with the TV crew. As Slava didn't offer much advice, the Hensleys were the only other source of counsel.

"So what do you think? Should we go now, or try to schedule another interview later?" Tony asked.

"If Slava doesn't care, I think I'd do it if I were you," Mr. Hensley offered. "It seems like a miraculous opportunity. I'd hate to see you turn it away."

"God will give you the words, boys," Mrs. Hensley said. "I think you should go. We'll hold the fort here until John and Paul return."

"But, Tony, you must be careful not to criticize the government or the church you visited," Mr. Hensley added. "That could cause us some serious trouble. Keep the focus on our mission here, and on Jesus Christ."

Tony and Howard nodded. Mrs. Hensley encouraged them with grandmotherly words. "You both will do just fine. We'll be praying for you here."

"We'll count on that, Mrs. Hensley," Howard said. "By the way, will the prayer meeting here be at the same time tonight?"

"Yes, six o'clock," Mr. Hensley responded. "Slava said we could expect a goodly number. I believe John is planning to preach."

"We'll do our best to make it back before then," Howard said.

Tony went over to Nadia to see if she would do the TV interview. She would be most comfortable interpreting as she was used to working with them.

"What? I cannot interpret on television!"

"Nadia, relax. You'll do wonderfully. If you can handle Father Federov, you can handle a camera. Please—we need your help."

"I am still not sure I am best suited, but if you wish, I will translate for you, yes."

"Great! Howard and I will change into suits, so if you want to wear something else, feel free." Tony gestured at her clothes, noticing it was the same black dress she had worn yesterday.

Nadia looked down from Tony's eyes. "This is the only dress I have. Is it not acceptable?"

"Ah, no, not at all. I mean, it's just fine, Nadia, just fine. I'm sorry, I didn't realize—" Tony stumbled for more words.

"It is okay, Tony. I take no offense." She hung her head, not looking at him.

He knew he had to redeem himself. "Nadia, really—you look great. I bet the camera will have a hard time staying on Howard and me when it will have someone as beautiful as you to focus on."

Nadia looked up, her dark brown eyes larger than Tony had remembered. She didn't speak for a moment, which made Tony feel awkward in her gaze. Then the words came softly from her mouth.

"No one has ever said such a kind word to me, Tony."

"Every word is true, Nadia. You are a beautiful woman."

Nadia blushed, but she did not look away. "And you, Tony Barton, are the kindest man I have ever met."

Tony felt as if the world's rotation had slowed a couple notches. Somehow, he moved into a separate dimension of time with this Russian girl. The crowded room was vacant for a moment—this moment—a grand moment, spent looking deeply into the eyes of a woman like no other. She was mysterious in her ways, yet delightful to be with. She held a confidence about herself while avoiding conceit, sensitive to those around her. His staring into her eyes communicated feelings that words could not convey. The emotion of the moment could only be broken from outside.

"Hey, you two! We gotta go to Hollywood!" Howard shouted from across the room. He was dressed in black slacks and a tweed sport jacket with tie. The jacket was a little rumpled, but he still looked distinctly American, with a touch of class compared to the dress of others in the room.

Tony split from Nadia long enough to call back, "I have to make a quick change, too. Give me two minutes and I'll be out." Returning his eyes to Nadia for a moment of closure, he received the rosy smile from her lips. He forced himself to break away.

Grabbing his suitcase, he stepped into the bedroom wishing for a cold shower. Rather, he donned a Goodwill jacket he'd bought for a dollar in America.

* * * * *

As he shook out the wrinkles of his vacuum-packed jacket, Tony had no idea of the angelic garments prepared for him at the same time. Powered by the prayers of dozens of nameless witnesses back home in America, Fortas and several others were giving Tony the armor he needed, just as they had for Howard moments before.

The two men were entering a battle they could not recognize. Though their trip to the government church had provoked earthly fear, the television interview held much more at stake. The angels had been coached about the spiritual ramifications of this visit. While their charges were oblivious to their actions, they carefully dressed the two unknowing soldiers for war.

Changing into his white button-down shirt, Tony asked himself what he would say to the TV cameras. Cinching his belt in the well-worn hole, he comprehended a simple answer from Fortas: "Just tell the truth. Only tell the truth."

But will I know the right words to say? Will I freeze up on the camera, or worse yet, start rambling like a talk show freak?

The angels applied their counsel as they placed Tony's breastplate. "You are right, Tony, in seeing the pitfalls. Humility is key. Keep in mind who paid for your life on the cross. You can do nothing without Him, but you can do all things with Him."

Fortas was at his feet as Tony slipped into his shoes. "Tony, speak words only in grace. Be careful to avoid any pretentious debates, and do not allow any arguing in this interview. Your purpose here is to bring peace."

Tony stood before his small travel mirror, stretching his arm into his jacket sleeve while Fortas slipped the inside band of a large shield over his shoulder. Tony checked his appearance, brushing his hair with his hand, unaware of the golden helmet being placed over his head. At the same moment he realized he needed to check over some terms with Nadia.

I better be sure Nadia is ready to translate some of the phrases Howard and I might use. Let's see—she needs to be comfortable with words like 'salvation', 'evangelize', 'saved by grace', the 'crucifixion and resurrection', and all. On our walk there, we can go over some words we might say.

Tony walked out of the bedroom, the angels admiring their military of two, dressed alike in armor. The Hensleys led a prayer over the two men and Nadia, a cluster of heralds flapping their wings like huge unfurled flags waving in the breeze. As the men left the flat, they were as well-equipped as Sherman tanks rolling into battle—almost.

The three walked out the door when suddenly the angels began to fly furiously around them, unseen, but making enough of a commotion to stop a brigade. This was not synchronized movement. The heavenlies were under alarm. Something was drastically wrong!

"I feel like there's something I'm forgetting," Tony said as they started down the street. Howard and Nadia paused with him.

Fortas shouted at his charge. The remaining angels stood shoulder to shoulder directly in front of the three, making a brick-solid wall.

"What is it?" Howard asked.

"I don't know," Tony responded. "I can't think of anything, but it feels like something's missing." He looked in his small duffle bag, loosely filled with a few snacks, a notebook, tracts, a water bottle, and several inexpensive pen and pencil sets—gifts from the Americans to the TV crew. "Nope, it looks like I have everything here."

The angelic blockade remained, with appeals in prayer to their Lord to break the mental obstacle that prevented Tony from hearing them. The enemy was already on the attack.

"We should be going," Nadia prompted. "It will take twenty minutes. We must hurry."

"Okay, let's just go on," Tony said. "It must not be important."

They all turned with Tony and took one step before he stopped again.

"Man, I just can't get over this feeling. Something's not right. Hey, I remember! I'll be right back!"

Tony dashed up the steps of the flat and in less then a minute reappeared at the entry, holding his burgundy-colored Bible high in the air.

Applause came from the angels. Tony appeared in full raiment, a long gleaming silver sword thrust toward the sky. Fortas joined the heralds, praising God that Tony's armor was complete.

"My Bible! How could I have forgotten it?"

"I'm glad you remembered," Howard responded. "You may need your 'sword of the spirit' in this meeting."

"Please, we must hurry," Nadia prompted again, yet unaware of the significance of the book.

"Okay, let's go," Tony said as they marched down the walk at a brisk pace.

"I do not understand," Nadia fumed as they walked. "Why must that Bible be so important to you?"

"God has specific tools for us, Nadia," Howard began calmly. "We depend on them so we can be victorious in every cause."

"Yeah, they're even called the armor of God," Tony added. "The Bible is considered the 'sword of the spirit' for our armor. God's word can pierce hearts to gain understanding like nothing else can. His word also sets a standard for our lives. With it we can separate lies from the truth. The message of this Book is our best weapon to show anyone who God truly is."

"So what is the rest of your armor?" Nadia asked.

The battalion of angels hovered low, adding spiritual conviction about the importance of this armor. Howard and Tony took turns describing the belt, shoes, helmet and breastplate to Nadia. As the men acknowledged the spiritual tools they were wearing, the angels saw their charges' breastplates glowing brightly. A blazing white cross formed across each of their chests.

They were ready for battle.

* * * * *

A short time later, Nadia pointed down the block. "There it is. That's where we are to meet them."

"Great, Nadia. We're right on time," Tony said. "What's the name of this place? Did you say it was a restaurant or something?"

"Yes. It is what you call in America a 'bar', no?"

"A bar! You've got to be kidding." Howard exclaimed.

"You mean this is where they serve liquor, Nadia?" Tony asked.

"Yes, of course. Is there something wrong?"

"No, Nadia. It's alright," Tony tried to explain Howard's surprise. "In America, bars are sometimes considered inappropriate places to go if you are a missionary. People in bars may drink too much and carry on. It isn't unusual for a bar in America to hold activities that demean women or lead people into sin. So here, it just seems ironic that we, as missionaries, will be giving our testimonies inside a bar."

"Oh, I understand," Nadia nodded nonchalantly. "I would have to say you will find Russian bars very similar to American bars."

Tony and Howard caught each other's eyes with Nadia's remark. It sounded like a dare more than a warning. They followed her across the street to the bar's entrance.

"Keep your guard up, Tony," Howard said quietly as they peered inside the door.

"You better believe I will."

* * * * *

Neither of them could feel the thick brass shields sliding from their shoulders down to their arms as they entered. Angels on either side of them adjusted the armor. They were protected from head to toe.

*****

The acrid smell of cigarette smoke combined with alcoholic breathings greeted them as they walked in the front door. The odors intensified as they waited for their eyes to adjust to the darkness of the room.

As Tony's eyes began to focus, he saw he was in a small, L-shaped room with a counter and stools to the right, backed by square tiled mirrors reflecting only partial images as several tiles were cracked or missing. To the left was the longer wing with several square tables and chairs set for dining. Toward the back the TV lady was positioning four chairs in front of a single floodlight. The bright beam burned Tony's eyes in the dim lighting of the rest of the room.

The lady noticed their arrival, and without leaving her post motioned for them to come. A young man aimed a video camera toward her, and now Tony could see a younger girl adjusting the light. Tony and Howard walked forward, approaching the brightness while hesitant to interrupt the light check.

"Hello," the TV lady said in broken but plain English. "I am glad you are able to come for the interview."

"It is our privilege to be here," Tony replied. "I am surprised to hear you speak English."

"I know only a few phrases, but I am learning more." She smiled with a friendliness that Tony had not noted before. "My name is Galina Listyev. And you?"

"I am Tony Barton, and this is Howard Matson." Howard stepped forward and shook Galina's hand.

"And is your translator with you?"

"Why, yes," Tony responded, turning around to introduce Nadia. "She's right—"

Turning away from the floodlight made Tony lose his vision into the darkness again, but Nadia was nowhere close. As his eyes adjusted, Tony was swept with horror. Nadia was across the room at the bar, squirming in the arms of a man forcibly holding her on his lap, another man laughing at his side.

Tony froze. Nadia's muffled scream forced a reaction before he could consider more.

"Tony!"

The word was unmistakable, despite the large hand smothering Nadia's mouth. The two burly men laughed obliviously with drunken drawls.

He ran across the room with Howard at his side.

"Take your hands off the woman," Howard barked. The men could not understand English. They were so drunk, they probably couldn't understand their own tongue.

Howard's words did, however, turn the two men around, where Tony could first see Nadia's face with grimy fingers pressed across her lips.

Her eyes were wide and red, tears smeared across her cheeks. The combination of anger and fear in her expression stabbed Tony. This woman was tough, but she was at the end of her courage.

The two Russian men stood, the one imprisoning Nadia using his large hairy arm to hold her against his overgrown waist. They were both as tall as Tony, but twice as wide across.

Howard spoke again, more quietly, more threatening. "Release her, now!"

Tony could see only blank angry stares from the men. Howard's words weren't working. He reached forward and grabbed the wrist holding Nadia. *God, help me!* The sweat and grime he touched made him tighten his grasp so he wouldn't slip. Pulling the massive arm toward him, he met eyes with his enemy.

Just as their stare down began, a sharp fire burned his left cheek. He spun back a step, still holding the man's wrist like a vise. He opened his eyes just in time to see a second blow heading for the same cheek. Tony ducked to the right, jerking the arm he held even harder. This time, Nadia broke free just as the ogre's knee shot up into his gut.

Tony fell to the ground with a mixture of nausea and pain. He glanced up to see the other man holding Howard by the neck tie. The man growled at him with yellowed teeth like a banshee.

As Tony stood to help his partner, Howard put his arms against the chest of his attacker, giving him a shove that sent him flying—literally flying.

The Russian flew three feet, cracking his low back on the edge of the bar before his body splayed across the counter.

Tony was incredulous. He saw Howard look at his own hands in disbelief. For several seconds, the figure on the bar didn't move.

A bartender touched the shoulder of the fallen Russian. He stirred and slid off the bar onto his feet, his body crumpling over as he rubbed his back.

Howard moved forward, immediately apologizing. "I'm really sorry. I didn't mean to push you so hard. Are you okay?"

The man looked at Howard, and Tony saw fear in the big man's eyes. He limped over to Tony's attacker. Without a word, they both headed out the door.

Looking over his shoulder, Tony saw Nadia cowering against the back wall and went to her.

"Are you okay?" they both asked each other at the same time.

"I will be fine," Nadia's voice was shaking. "But what about you?"

"Just a little stomach ache."

Howard approached them, holding his hands as if they were smoking.

"Did you see that?" he asked, oblivious to the injured before him.

"Man, I don't know what you're eating, but there's gotta be some Wheaties in there somewhere," Tony said.

"Incredible, simply incredible!" Howard said, ignoring Tony. "I know I didn't do that. I just know I couldn't have done that."

Nadia touched Tony on the cheek. "You're bleeding a little."

"Now that you mention it, it does feel like I've got a hole there."

The TV lady approached. "How is everyone?"

"I think we're all okay, Galina," Tony said, still watching Nadia to be sure she agreed.

Galina spoke to Howard. "How did you do that—" she motioned with her hands in the same shove Howard had given to make the Russian fly.

"I really have no idea. That was not my own power—it couldn't have been."

"How do you say 'angels' in Russian, Nadia?" Tony asked.

Galina's eyes perked and she gasped when Nadia translated.

"Galina asks if you really think it was an angel who protected you," Nadia translated, yet with a shaking voice.

There was no doubt in Tony's mind. "Tell Galina that whatever she saw, it was only by God's protection and might that we were able to save you and ourselves."

Nadia paused momentarily before interpreting, and Tony could see her emotions coming forth. Nadia translated his words, but immediately broke out in tears at the end of her sentence.

Her head looked for a shoulder to bury in, and Tony's was closest. As she leaned into him, he awkwardly put his arm around her. "It's alright now, it's okay," he murmured softly.

Howard came closer to the two. "Do you think she's okay?"

Tony squeezed her a little and spoke. "I think so. She's just doing what we all feel like doing."

"That's for sure. Tony, how could I have pushed that guy like that? Do you really think it was an angel?"

"I only know that I didn't have the strength to move my guy's arm like I did, Howard. Not to say I don't feel the cut on my face or my ruptured gut, but I had strength like I've never felt before. Did you feel the same way?"

"Exactly. I'm shaking like a leaf inside. That wasn't me."

Nadia lifted her head. "All I know is, you both saved me from something horrible, and I am so thankful." Another course of tears followed. "I must find a bathroom. Excuse me."

Galina followed Nadia to help her.

The young man with the video camera came over and gestured for Tony and Howard to come speak with the bartender. Through sign language, the bartender wished to offer them a drink on the house.

"A Coke sounds good to me right now," Tony remarked, pointing to the bottles behind the bar. Though served without ice, soda had not tasted so good for a long time.

Chapter 17

Back at the widow Gina's flat, the room held an overflow crowd of forty-plus people, come to see the Americans. Word of mouth was traveling, with many attending out of curiosity to hear the foreigners talk about their country and their God.

Slava was pleased with the attendance, but was shy about meeting so many new people. He greeted everyone as they arrived, then quickly introduced them to one of the Americans. Having never been to his church before, he assumed they must be more interested in speaking to one of the travelers.

The meeting began with John leading some lively American choruses. The Russians clapped their hands with the melodies, oblivious to the words, but enjoying the festivity. The young Russian ladies took their turn, leading a song that joyously rang out in Slavic tongue while the Americans listened in delight.

The singing ended too quickly, and someone caught Slava still waiting at the door for any latecomers. He was asked to come forward to give announcements and pray.

Embarrassed, he made his way through the standing bodies in the back, around the rows of wood plank pews squeezed full of people, to the front of the group.

"It is an honor to have so many of you here tonight," he stammered. Except for a few pockets of people from his congregation, he spoke to a room full of strangers.

"We hope you will find our time together encouraging and honoring to our Lord. I am grateful for the wonderful talents of our American friends, and know you will be blessed as you get to know them."

As the crowd politely gave Slava their attention, his confidence grew. He hesitated, then decided to air his convictions.

"Many of you know that the Americans have been asked by the police to not go out in the streets. We have been praying that these restrictions will be lifted. Earlier today, the Americans met with Father Federov of the City Church to enlist his support of their ministry. Unfortunately, Father Federov was reluctant ? no, I must be honest with you. Father Federov was completely against the Americans sharing their testimonies."

Slava's inhibitions dropped away as he continued to openly relate the events of the day. "Later, the Americans met with Mayor Babekov to seek the opportunity for our church to be recognized by the city. They were refused any opportunity to minister to the people of our city." Slava sensed afresh his leadership in this church. He began to address the crowd with more confidence.

"As we speak, two Americans, at the request of our local television station, are being interviewed for a broadcast tomorrow morning. Let us pray for these two brothers of ours, Tony and Howard. May God use them for His mighty purposes while they are here in Bolshoigorsk. Let us pray now."

Immediately ten people stood with heads bowed as those from the faithful congregation responded to their pastor's call. The remaining visitors slowly rose to their feet as well, some joining in prayer while others looked on in respect.

After the prayer, Slava motioned for John to bring the message of the night. He made his way through the crowd to the rear again, parking himself in the first available spot in the line of people standing in the hall. It was a lousy view, but at least he could hear John from here.

No sooner did he get settled when right beside him, the front door opened with one more visitor arriving. This face was no stranger.

"Renat!"

"Hello, Slava. I must be at the right place." The old friend entered, this time dressed in more casual clothes than the business suit Slava last saw him in.

"I'm sorry I can't offer you a decent seat for the meeting. We're very full." Slava gestured to the line of people standing in the hall. "I could offer you a cup of tea."

"I'd welcome that." The deputy mayor followed Slava quietly to the small table in the kitchen.

Slava sat across from his friend with two cups of hot strong tea. "So why did you come to our meeting? As much as you warned me to leave town the last time I saw you, I'm surprised to see you at our door."

"And I'm surprised you're even in town, Slava." Renat spoke in whispered tones, just as he had during the mysterious alley visit a few days before. "Yet, when I heard that your church was meeting every night this week, despite what you and your family have gone through, I just had to see for myself what it was that was keeping you here. Do you still have no idea what it is you are up against?"

Slava spoke quietly and calmly. "I have learned who is behind our troubles. Father Federov, correct?"

"How did you find out?"

"That does not matter. But what do you know? Why is Federov so strongly opposed to our church?"

"Slava, if I speak to you, you must tell no one."

"You have my promise."

With a darting glance over his shoulder, Renat began. "Father Federov has acquired a great deal of power in Bolshoigorsk. Since the downfall of communism, the local cities have lost support from the national offices. You've seen how the people here are disenchanted with the government. The church filled the vacated leadership over their lives.

"About three years ago, Mayor Babekov contacted Father Federov for assistance in rebuilding some of Bolshoigorsk's failing industries. To his favor, the mayor thought enlisting the help of the church would be popular with the people and bolster the government's fallen clout. However, Federov was able to seize the opportunity to bring the city to its knees, depending on the church for finances and support for every government action. The city eventually became more and more in debt to Federov."

"Including the mayor selling his position to Father Federov in the last election, yes?"

"Right. Federov was responsible for directing the people to vote for Mayor Babekov, which cemented his control over the top office in town. Now, Federov uses the government as a puppet for his whim and fancy. The people have been none the wiser until your church began to make a stir."

"Because the people who came to our church here would no longer be held under the influence of Father Federov, and he would risk losing his control."

"Exactly." Renat appeared relieved to have finally shared his secret with somebody. "I have heard rumors that Federov and his church have similar connections in other communities as well. You see, you are not only going against the city government of Bolshoigorsk. You may be up against powers from around the whole province."

"Renat, tell me honestly," Slava spoke in soft tones, but his words were intensely sincere. "How much do you want Bolshoigorsk freed from the reign of this man?"

"He is a crazy man, this Federov," Renat answered quickly, then looked away. "But there is little that can be done against the forces he has built."

"Perhaps, Renat, perhaps. My faith is not placed in the hands of Father Federov, and I believe there is a way to have freedom for our city."

"How, Slava? Surely you are not as crazy as the man we discuss."

"No, I am not crazy. Please just consider rising up at an opportune time in the future, to share your secret again."

"Don't ask me to be an idiot! That would be Russian roulette with the chambers filled."

"Please don't say no just yet, Renat," Slava continued in his same calm demeanor. "I do not know when, and I can't say how, but I just ask you to be ready to speak what you know is truth. That is all."

"I don't know. I still think it would be best for you to leave for a while. Take your family and settle away from here, where you can find safety. It is not my life in jeopardy; it is yours. For me and my family, I can handle Federov's government—it is much like the rule of communism for me. But you—this could destroy your future. Don't you see, this could destroy your very life. What is worth that, Slava? What drives you to fight this?"

Slava stood from his chair and gestured into the hallway. "Come with me, Renat. Perhaps you will find what it is you are seeking. Come."

They moved out of the kitchen into the hall, now lined with people sitting along the floor. John was speaking with Tonya translating. Slava led Renat, stepping over several legs, finding their way into the living room. In the back row, he asked a couple of people to squeeze together even more tightly, clearing a small space for Renat.

Renat blushed and shook his hands against the generosity, but before he could turn, Slava had grabbed his arm and brought him down to the seat with a slight commotion. He stood behind Renat with his hands on his friend's shoulders, leaning over with a whispered smile. "Don't move from this spot, or I'll have the whole place praying over you."

John had stopped speaking momentarily to be sure Slava was not needing to have his attention. With a nod from the pastor, John continued, and everyone who had turned to stare returned to listen to the American at the front of the room.

* * * * *

Slava's guardian angel, Brael, immediately went to work as Slava silently prayed for Renat. Combined with four angels, they worked

Renat's soul, breaking up the hardened soil of his dry and thirsty life. The angels prepared the ground of his spiritual heart well. He was readily plowed and fertilized by the words John shared. Slava's prayers at this very moment provided the flow of water refreshing the parched and dusty soul.

The angels worked quickly. From the ease of their labors they knew Renat was willing to receive the Seed of life. After no more than ten minutes, as John was concluding his remarks and preparing to close in prayer, the angels stepped back from their field work and watched for planting. The freshly overturned soil was evidence that Renat's eternal life could be sown tonight.

Brael watched Renat's shoulders soften and drop from their rigid position. Further into his soul, he could see a small spark of light begin to form. Yes! The conviction of the Holy Spirit! The Seed was being tenderly placed even now!

Rejoicing over the heavenly work, angels flew in rings around Renat, constantly changing oval diameters. In heaven's eyes, giant spirographic art was drawn, with wide arcs interlocked over small loops presenting the glorious picture of salvation being born.

A sudden interruption caused the angels' labor to abruptly halt. Salvation would have to wait.

* * * * *

The door burst open.

All eyes turned to the back of the room. Tony stepped into the room as nonchalantly as possible, Howard and Nadia behind him. Their quiet actions were needless.

"Tony!" John welcomed the interruption. "How have you fared with the TV station?"

Before Tony could respond, Mrs. Hensley interrupted. "Tony, you're hurt! What happened to your face?"

John then saw the cut on Tony's left cheek, a purplish swollen bruise rising below his eye. He quickly looked over Howard and Nadia, with no further injuries seen. Better yet, they were all smiling.

"Tony, come up here! Are you alright? Can you tell us what happened?"

Tony moved to the front as the room buzzed with questions.

"I'm okay, I'm okay, everyone. We all are." Tony paused to eye Nadia across the room. "Are you up for translating for me?"

Nadia smiled and translated the words of relief.

"We've come from an amazing time with the television people. God was present and powerful in that place tonight, let me assure you."

Mr. Hensley said, "Amen," and several Russians followed suit after hearing Nadia's translation.

"Unfortunately, the evening began with an altercation we had with a couple of drunks. You won't believe—we still can't believe it ourselves—how God protected us."

The room listened with rapt attention as Tony explained Nadia's attack, and how Howard was able to use angelic force to prevent further harm. Then he described how they had decided to go ahead with the interview, and how favorable it went.

"Galina Listyev was very positive in her questions about Christianity. She allowed us every chance to openly share about our purpose here. Howard was even able to clearly explain the Gospel. He did a marvelous job of defining how Jesus Christ is God's best and only plan to save the world."

Several people nodded with their excited approval as a tremendous sense of hope and expectancy filled the room.

"But there is even more good news! The TV crew was so interested in our story, they asked if they could come film us meeting as a church. When I told them we were meeting tonight, they said they would follow us here—I expect them to be here any minute." Tony excitedly watched for the joy he would see on the faces as Nadia translated his words.

Instead of joy, he saw faces turn to alarm.

Suddenly there was a hubbub of activity, with several people working their way quickly to the hall. The room became a mass of confusion.

"Wait, wait!" Tony shouted. "Nadia, tell them to wait—what did I say?"

Nadia was lost in a small cluster of bodies by the hall entrance. The room emptied as if there had been a bomb scare.

Slava stood in the back corner, trying to convince Renat to stay. He'd felt a softening spirit in his friend, and he pleaded for him not to leave.

"Please Renat, stay just a little longer. We can visit again in the kitchen."

"I cannot, Slava. If I'm caught here on camera, it would be the end of me. I'd be a fool to stay—immediate execution. It could endanger my family. I cannot."

In seconds he was lost in the mob of people heading out the door.

Less than two minutes later, the room was almost empty with only eight or so faithfuls remaining. Slava saw the Americans clustered together around Howard and Tony and stepped over to them.

"I'm afraid the people have been scared away by the TV," Slava said after asking Luda to translate for him.

"I understand that now," Tony responded, dejected. "I am so sorry. I thought this was a God-given opportunity for the church to really show itself to the community."

"Do not worry," Slava replied calmly. "I will trust with you that God is providing this chance to have the television exposure. If He was this faithful to you during the interview, we should be sure He will continue to be faithful, yes?"

Tony nodded his head slowly with the others. *How can this guy be so patiently optimistic all the time? I've created a disaster for the church tonight, and he still thinks it's God's design.*

"Slava," John spoke, nodding at Luda to continue to translate. "Perhaps we should meet the TV people at the door and tell them we would rather not have them film us here. Our services are very personal, and the filming would interrupt our worship too much."

"My dear American friends," Slava responded, "Why is it you suddenly have so many doubts? You have always been so sure of yourselves, so confident of God being ahead of every obstacle. I have leaned on you these past days, and you have been my support in trusting that God remains in control. But now? Now you seem to think we have failed, that God has lost the battle.

"Look here," Slava pointed to the few scattered people of his congregation milling about the open room. "These people have stayed, fully aware of the risks they are taking. These are the people of our congregation. These are the stones that make up the walls of our church. They are ready to show themselves, as am I, to the world. The people who left are scared, but they are not the building blocks of our church. We are glad to let them go. Let us show Bolshoigorsk who we are as a church, and let God use this opportunity to come into the lives of our community. I am ready to stand up and be counted simply as a Christian in our city. I invite you to join my brothers and sisters here in doing likewise."

As if on cue, a rap sounded at the door. The widow Gina opened it and welcomed Galina Listyev and the cameraman into her flat. Slava greeted the guests also, and introduced them to those in the room.

Tony, still standing with the Americans at the front of the room, leaned over to John. "What do you make of that guy? Is that faith or what?"

"I stand amazed, Tony. I stand amazed. If only I could be so bold and willing."

Slava approached the team with Galina, and Tony put on a smile and shook her hand. Speaking plainly and slowly he said, "Galina, let me introduce the Americans to you. This is John, and Paul, and Joe and Alice Hensley."

They shook hands with each other, then Galina looked around the room. "So this is the church, yes?"

"Yes, this is the church," Tony responded. "Please set up where you wish." Then he whispered to John. "What should we do now?"

Slava had already resumed his leadership over the body before John needed to answer. Gathering everyone together, he spoke with a young Russian songstress who immediately began a beautiful Russian hymn to the tune of 'Amazing Grace.' The Americans sat down and began to sing in English with the refrain. The video camera rolled, but its activity was soon ignored as the worship of this small mighty church took hold of its unified congregation. The praise went beyond the barriers of language to uplift and adore the Host of hosts. The people rejoiced in God's presence with them, His faithfulness to them, and His providence for them.

Chapter 18

Getting to sleep that night was difficult for John and Tony. It was after midnight before the flat was empty of its guests. Everyone finally found their beds—John under sheets thrown over the lone living room couch, and Tony in blankets on the floor beside him. With the two Gdansk boys asleep at the other end of the living room, Tony hoped the sounds of their slumber would lull him into a peaceful rest.

It didn't work.

His thoughts raced through the events of the tremendously long day. Was it just this morning that he had awakened with discouragement in not being able to share Christ in the streets of Bolshoigorsk? In the aftermath of his first Bible study, a threatening visit with the Bolshoigorsk City Church, and his first ever fistfight, in a Russian bar, no less, now he would be seen all across the city over the morning airwaves giving his testimony. Who could possibly sleep?

When he was finally able to process the day's events and put them to rest, his mind was flooded with new thoughts. These were honed to a point of conflicting emotions over one issue: Nadia.

How could he continue to be attracted to her? What common interest drew his feelings toward her? She seemed to deny the very existence of God! So why did he still have a desire to be with her, to be her friend, to be her close friend.

Earlier this evening when she was crying in his arms after the attackers had left, there was more than brotherly comfort being shared. When he faced himself honestly, he cared for her deeply. But she still seemed resistant to believing the Gospel. What would it take to break through her soul to the point of her salvation? Should he be more bold? Was he being too bold? Had he already offended her? Was she turned off to Christianity because of him?

His thoughts were interrupted by a tearful sob in the room.

At first he thought it was coming from the direction of the two boys. Then, in the pitch darkness, he knew it came from the couch beside him. It was John.

"John," Tony whispered. "Are you okay?"

After a muffled sniffle John responded. "I'm sorry, Tony. I hoped you were asleep." The sound of his voice was weak and shaky.

"What's wrong?"

"I'm not really sure. The same thing happened last night when I went to bed." A quiet weeping began again, and he could not speak for a moment.

"I just can't seem to control my tears." More whispered cries.

"John, like you feel homesick or something?"

"I don't think so, Tony. Oh sure, I miss Melinda and Katie Ann something awful, but I know they're okay. I think I'm crying more because of the people here."

Tony didn't understand. His silence prompted John to continue, when he was ready.

"These people are so incredible, Tony. They love so deeply, and treat us so wonderfully. They are so unashamed of their faith in God. I feel so undeserving of their kindness. I'm supposed to be the servant here, but they go far beyond any ideas I would ever have of serving. You know what I mean?"

"I think I do, John. It just shows in their life, doesn't it? They would do anything for us; so simply and humbly, like it was the ordinary expectation. Yeah, I know what you mean."

"And last night, it was the same thing. I just had to cry awhile. Don't ask me why. I'm really not like this." He lost it again.

"Let me pray for you, John. But don't let your tears get in your way." Tony reached up and patted John's arm. "I think you're just sensing the touch of God in these lives. It should bring each of us to tears if we're human at all."

"Thanks, Tony. It means a lot."

The two men remained in their beds, turning their hearts toward God.

Tony prayed in whispered tones of their thanksgiving. "Lord, we are so humbled that You would lead us here to be touched by these precious people in Bolshoigorsk."

John was succumbing again to tears.

"I thank you for John's tender spirit, and his sensitivity to these people's hearts. Help us to be servants like them, Lord."

Sobs continued from the couch.

"In your majesty and grace, we ask Your blessing on these dear people, Lord, that they may be able to continue in Your strength during these days—that You would allow the church here to flourish."

John's uninhibited, quiet crying began to move Tony.

"Lord, be with Aunt Gina especially."

This lady's heart really hit home with both men.

"Bring her such joy, such hope (sniff), that she would be sustained by Your presence."

Tony could not hold it. He began to weep also. Neither man could speak, but their hearts, fully exposed to God, conveyed their sentiments more than any words could.

God was glorified and praised through their tears. Peace was brought to both of them. They soon found rest.

* * * * *

Early the next morning, Oksana laid in her bed, wide awake. An hour ago she had awakened when Slava had gotten up and left the flat. Hard as she tried, sleep would not return.

His early morning departures were typical of late. She knew this was his time to pray and study. When she once asked him where he went, he had said he usually just walked around the outskirts of town, praying and thinking about his ministry to Bolshoigorsk. With the present company of the Americans, it was hard to garner time alone. Although she worried every time he left, he needed these sunrise ventures. What was good for him, she knew, was also good for her, their boys, and their church.

This morning, however, she was more restless about his absence.

It was useless for her to toss in the bed any longer. She quietly got up, stepping over the sleeping forms of Nadia and Aunt Gina stretched out on mats across the floor. In the hall, she peered into the living room where John and Tony were soundly out. Tiptoeing past them, she reached her two sleeping sons.

The boys laid in similar positions, their breathings paced almost equally. Both had rich black hair like their father's, except as Oksana stroked them, their curls were much softer. And those noses, little pug offshoots. Their dad's was short, almost too narrow for his face. She'd never noticed until now, but the boys' were just the same way.

These are my two young Slavas, she thought to herself. *Little replicas of their daddy. God, help them to be as devoted to You as their father is.* She adjusted their blankets and crept out of the room, into the kitchen.

Beams from the sun shone brightly through the window panes, yet not enough to warm the room. She lit the pilot light on the rusty water heater that sat above the stove. The wooden floors were chilly to her bare feet, but soon the heater would make the room cozy.

After setting a pot of water on the stove for tea, she sat at the small table and saw a note.

Oksana,
Gone for my walk. I hope to watch American interview on television at Yakovlevs. Will be home after that.
                 Slava.

Oh yes, the TV interview.

Although most homes in Bolshoigorsk had televisions, this congregation was not in the economic strata to enjoy such luxuries, except for the Yakovlevs. Oksana remembered months ago enthralled in watching the black-and-white screen when their family had been invited over for a special showing of 'The Sound of Music'. She dreamed for nights afterwards of the sights and sounds of large families, the Swiss Alps, and singing. Such splendid joy and frivolity. Americans were so lucky to have such wonderful diversions at their disposal. Could it be, as she had heard, that families there would have two or even three televisions in the same house? How extravagant!

Yet, for now, she would need to find contentment with her cup of tea and her imagination. Waiting for the pot to boil, her thoughts sped to dreamy lands of grassy fields amidst snow-capped peaks, children in matching shorts frolicking as she strummed a guitar. A fantasy land, so different from the dreary stucco buildings surrounding her view out the kitchen window. She would never know her musings first-hand, and could only pretend to experience it from the black-and-white pictures her mind recalled. Perhaps this was the closest image of heaven she would have. Holding on to the memory, the scenes passed through her thoughts often. Could heaven be more beautiful than this?

Yes, Lord, I look forward to such a day. Your heavenly home must be so glorious. I can't wait to see it! Surely my dreams are only half as wonderful as what it truly is. Lord, thank you for making my eternal home so grand!

"Good morning," a Russian voice interrupted Oksana's praying.

"Good morning, Nadia," Oksana greeted her with a smile.

"All the boys are still sound asleep, yes?"

"I believe so. Except Slava, he's out for a walk. Even Aunt Gina is still asleep, unless you saw her wake."

"Asleep like a baby, the Americans would say. May I sit with you?"

"Certainly. I have some tea brewing; let me get you a cup."

Oksana went to the counter and found the small container of crushed leaves she had dried from her garden. Placing spoonfuls of the herbs into the boiling pot, a delightful aroma wafted into the air.

"You have a wonderful family, Oksana. Your boys have been so darling."

"Thank you. God has blessed us with those boys. They are a great source of joy for us."

"I envy your home life, Oksana. You have found a grand husband, and I can tell he cares so much for you and the children."

"Another tremendous blessing, Nadia. I don't deserve it, but I feel very blessed to have married Slava." Oksana paused, seeing a wistful look in Nadia. "How about you? Any special man in your life?"

"I fear the life of a spinster for me," Nadia cracked a humble smile. "There is a man back in Moscow. If we continue, he would marry me, but—"

Oksana sensed Nadia's reluctance. She set the two cups of tea on the table and sat down.

"But you're just not sure it's right."

"Yes, I am not sure. When you married, how did you know, Oksana? How did you know Slava was the man for you?"

"I'm not sure I really did, at the time. It is more so now that I see how fortunate I am." Oksana could say more, but she sensed Nadia needed to talk. There was such social pressure on young Russian girls to marry. When a woman entered her twenties a sense of desperation took over.

"Nadia, tell me about your boyfriend in Moscow."

"Oh, his name is George," she began quickly, pleased to be asked. "He is really very nice. He has dark black hair and eyes to match. His father is a carpenter, and they work together. He—" Nadia faltered in what else she should say.

"He treats you well?"

"Yes. Well, I had thought he treated me fine, until I met these Americans. Oksana, do you notice how different they are to women? I mean, always asking to help, opening doors, offering chairs for us. Have you noticed?"

"Yes, the American men have been very generous to us. I am not so sure, though, that it is only because they are Americans."

"What do you mean? I had always heard that American men treat their women like babies. Is not this their culture?"

"Culture in part, but I think these men treat women with kindness because they are Christians. I know the Russian Christians here are very much the same way, don't you think?"

"I, uh, I have never met any Russian Christians." Nadia was suddenly shy.

"That's understandable," Oksana reassured her. "It doesn't surprise me. In our country, there just aren't many to be found, are there?" She smiled, giving a reasonable excuse to be ignorant of Christianity.

"That's true," Nadia's finger ran in a circle around the rim of her cup. Something was at the brink of her thoughts.

"So since you met the Americans, has it changed your feelings about George?"

"That's what I wonder, Oksana. This is all so new to me. Yet, the way I feel here in Bolshoigorsk—it seems my life is more full, more vital. Is it my position as translator, or the way the Americans treat me, or is it something more?"

"Let me ask you a question, Nadia. Is there one particular American that has made you feel this way?"

Nadia immediately blushed and looked into her teacup. Oksana knew her own assumptions were true. She waited for Nadia to honestly respond.

"He does seem especially kind." Her voice was quiet, but her eyes twinkled.

"I've noticed the same thing, Nadia. He seems very kind—especially kind to you."

"Oh, Oksana, so it is not just my imagination?"

"There is not much doubt in my mind. Tony has some special feelings for you. But with all you two have been through—"

Nadia interrupted, "You could not imagine what it was like to have him save me from those bums at the bar yesterday. It was like a fairy tale."

There was danger in these feelings. Oksana had heard about Tony's relationship with the American girl who died just before they came to Russia. She understood how fragile his feelings must be. Introducing a young attractive Russian to him just now, one who had never before been treated with such favor, could just be the fuel for a roller coaster ride of emotions for both of them.

But there was more at stake. Nadia's initial hearing of Christ's unconditional love, intermingled with the flirtations of a love lost man, could send a confusing message at a critical juncture in this young woman's life. Nadia needed a clear distinction between her search for acceptance, and her search for life.

"So Nadia, you find yourself perhaps attracted to Tony because he is nice to you, and because he rescued you yesterday."

"But it's more than that, Oksana. It is more than how he treats me. I feel different just being around him. I feel more like the person I should be. There is something about him, about his character, that makes me want to live—and enjoy living. That is a new feeling for me, something I've never felt with George."

"Nadia, I think that is where you are seeing Tony as a Christian, compared to George who is not. Tony has found the source of peace and strength for his life, and that is Jesus Christ. Could that be what draws you to him?"

"I am fascinated by his commitment to his religion, that is true. And I find it peculiar that he would direct so much of his life toward speaking to others about Christ. But I am not sure that I would want to lead my own life in that way. I must understand more."

Oksana set her cup down and clasped her hands in front of her. "I respect your cautious desire to learn about Christianity, Nadia. Yet, I encourage you to search your feelings. Are you attracted to Tony because of Tony, or are you attracted to Tony because of Who he serves? It is a very thin line that separates the two in your emotions." She paused to sip her tea. "Nadia, you are an extremely bright young lady. I admire the effort of all your studies; something I was never able to do. But I believe these days you are spending in Bolshoigorsk are not just rewards for your accomplishments. I believe you were brought here specifically by God, so that you would know of His love for you. Tony is a part of His plan to communicate His message to you.

"You mean God brought Tony into my life? That's a little hard for me to understand." Nadia fidgeted, grasping her cup tightly.

"I believe it with all my heart, Nadia. In Tony you see a grand young man who seems to have his life together. What you don't see, but what we both know is there, is his motivation to live a life worthy of His Lord. He has confessed to God that he believes Jesus Christ died on the cross as a punishment for his sins. He acknowledges that Christ rose from the dead, and lives eternally. And he has given Christ the rule over his heart. Much of what you see in Tony is a result of what Christ has done in his life. As much as you may wish to deny it, you hunger to know Jesus Christ in the same way. Yet, you feel you must understand everything about Christ before you believe."

Nadia remained quiet, sitting forward with her elbows on the table, ready to hear the toughest words.

"All your intelligence will never allow you to completely comprehend the truth of Jesus Christ. You must come to a point in your life where you are willing to accept Jesus Christ for Who He says He is."

A loud, pounding on the front door interrupted Oksana's words.

"Open the door! This is the police!"

Oh no, not again! Oksana stood frozen, unwilling to move. She motioned for Nadia to stay quiet.

John was out of bed and in the hall. Seeing the women in the kitchen, he gestured that he would answer the knock. Oksana shook her hands at him furiously.

Aunt Gina came out of her room just as the police thumped again at the door.

"Open the door or we'll break it down!"

With pleading eyes, Oksana tried to prevent the inevitable, but Aunt Gina moved to the door. "I am sorry, Oksana, but I must answer. Dear God, protect us all."

John could not have understood a word, but he moved with Gina to the door. Oksana hoped he would be a reckoning force for whatever would come.

As Gina cracked the door, Oksana ran to her boys, still asleep in the living room. She laid down, covering their heads and her's with sheets. Her ears strained for every sound.

First, muffled voices of men: the police. She heard them say Slava's name. *Oh God, please no!* Then Nadia's name. John's voice was next, shouting! A short startled scream had to be Nadia. Heavy footsteps in the hall. A new voice—Tony. He's upset. More footsteps, something banging along the wall. *What is it?* Now mixed voices. "Stay inside or we'll arrest you all!" A curt shout from the police. Tony yells. The door slams cutting him off. Silence.

Silence. Too long of silence.

"Oksana—Oksana?" It was Aunt Gina.

"Are they gone?" Oksana peeled the blanket away from her head.

Gina was kneeling beside her. Was that Tony being held by John behind her? Was he crying?

"Yes, Oksana," Gina said. "The police are gone. But they took Nadia."

"Nadia!"

* * * * *

"Is that man whistling?"

Slava heard the small voice ask her mother as he passed them on the sidewalk. No matter. In fact, it made him whistle his tune a little louder.

The lilt in his step was unmistakable. A passerby would have thought he was drunk if it was not for his quick-footed pace. He strutted like Scrooge on Christmas morning. It was a fine day. A very fine day.

The television interview was an incredible success. Slava left the Yakovlevs after raptly watching the program. He could not have gained better support had Mayor Babekov spoken himself.

Galina Listyev had devoted almost fifteen minutes to the Americans' visit. She introduced it with the heroic rescue of Nadia from the drunkards' grasps. Emphasizing the compassion and bravery of the Americans established all the credibility necessary. Then, Howard and Tony both shared their testimonies of Jesus Christ, right across the public airwaves. Bolshoigorsk's televisions had to be crackling with all the good news. Beaming the gospel right into Russian homes—homes that had yet to even hear of the existence of God! What a tremendous impact!

Slava was almost in a trot as he hurried home, recalling the interview carefully so he could relate it exactly for his wife and the team.

Galina's questions about the church were probing. 'What is your purpose here in Bolshoigorsk?' she asked Howard. With poise he told of the new church in Bolshoigorsk that shared the Americans' understanding of God, how they had come to encourage this small church in their ministry to the Russians.

'Why is the church you are visiting here unable to meet publicly?' was another great question. Tony carefully explained how the Bolshoigorsk government had not registered the church. Stopping short of saying the government refused to do so, Tony encouraged the TV audience to appeal to the government officials and request the church registration.

'Would such restrictions occur to such a church in America?' Galina asked.

'*Nyet, nyet, nyet,*' Howard had responded himself. He then addressed with candor the people's right to worship without government restrictions.

A very short clip followed of the church meeting in Gina's home, with quick pans of the congregation that were thankfully discrete. Galina ended the interview with her own commentary. It was complimentary, but the hitch she concluded with was especially remarkable. "Why would the Bolshoigorsk Council want to prohibit our involvement in such a compassionate ministry, one that has even caught the eyes of the U.S.A. half a world away? I join my voice with the Americans to ask the city council to approve the registration of this church immediately!"

Thank You, God! Thank You! This is why You brought the Americans here! You are the crown King of all. Forgive me for ever doubting Your providence in my life.

Slava broke out in a whistle again as he paced quickly down the street. Two more blocks and he would be home—what a celebration he would hold with the Americans!

Wham! From behind, the blow to his head sent him sprawling.

"Get up, infidel!"

Two uniformed police grabbed each arm and dragged him to his feet. A third held a pistol to Slava's stomach. "Try anything and you'll have a hole to plug in your slimy belly!"

Slava was struck dumb. His body went limp, more from surprise than pain. In under a minute, he was stuffed into a car.

Whether from the throbbing concussion, the ugly taste of blood from the side of his head, or utter shock, Slava remembered no more, lapsing into unconsciousness.

Chapter 19

Brael towered over the police assault on Slava, but withheld his power. Seconds later his angelic eyes saw two Americans running toward them. They were too late to catch the police car as it sped away with its prisoner.

Brael felt no disappointment, however. God's eternal plan was not to be altered. This was nothing short of the Master's work. Brael had no reason to doubt.

It was news that flashed across the heavenlies: Slava had been arrested. The angels involved all knew simultaneously and prepared themselves to give God the glory.

It was not so easy for their charges to embrace the message.

Back in Gina's apartment, Fortas was with Tony, who knew nothing about Slava's arrest. The angel's hands were full dealing with the accusations and guilt Tony tossed around about Nadia's forced departure. In his own world of self-pity, only Fortas could hear Tony's heart.

"Why, God? Why would You let them take Nadia? What did she do wrong? She was close, Lord. I just know she was close to believing. And now she's whisked away. What are You doing?"

Getting a word in edgewise was impossible for Fortas. It wasn't going to get any easier.

Paul and Howard burst into Gina's apartment without knocking. "We just saw the police arrest Slava!"

"No! It can't be!" John yelled. "This is crazy! Absolutely crazy!"

"They took Tonya earlier, right from our flat!" Howard said. "She wasn't even given a chance to speak. We have no idea where they went!"

Tony, exhausted from spent tears, said, "They took Nadia the same way. She's—gone."

"We've got to get to the Hensley's," John said. "Maybe we can reach them before Luda—" His voice dropped off. Joe and Alice appeared at the still open doorway. Their drooping countenances said it all.

"Luda was arrested this morning?" Paul asked to confirm the obvious.

"Yes," Joe said. "You mean they have arrested all our translators?"

"And Slava, too," Howard added. "Paul and I saw them pistol whip him before they took him away. We tried to get there in time to stop—" A sense of defeat took away his words.

"What about Oksana? How is she?" Mrs. Hensley asked.

"I don't think she knows," John replied. "She was pretty upset after Nadia was arrested here. Gina has her in the kitchen, but how can we tell her that her husband's been arrested? There's no one left to translate."

"How can we speak to anyone here?" Tony ranted. "We're useless without the translators!"

And so went the circus of bewilderment and worry before the angels. The six Americans left little space for the spiritual counselors to offer their gifts. What could be said, even by the heavenly vanguard, to offer hope?

* * * * *

Plenty.

There was no moping around the heavenlies. Battle stations were readied for the spiritual warfare taking place right at this moment.

Maliel was flying in circles around John, reminding him of his position in Christ, that nothing could separate him from His love, that no temptation had seized him beyond what he could bear. Maliel forged a one-way channel of scriptural truths from John's memory that firmed his foundation as the leader. "Cast all your cares on Him. And now to Him who is able to do immeasurably more than we could ever ask or think. If any of you lack wisdom he should ask God and it will be given. And my God will meet all your needs according to His glorious riches." Like rifle shots, the verses repeatedly hit John squarely, killing every enemy of doubt and dismay. John was finding his strength. He was the most receptive target of the angels' efforts.

A cluster of twenty or so angels hovered over Paul, Howard and the Hensleys. The foursome sat together, discussing how to let Oksana know about her husband. No one had any ideas of how to communicate without the Russian language. The angels imparted reassurance for when the humans would receive it.

"I will never leave you or forsake you," one of them spoke of their Lord to Howard.

No response.

Three angels pressed down on Paul. "Consider it pure joy, my brothers, whenever you face trials."

A blank stare returned.

Joe was next. The angels shouted one of his favorite verses. "Do not be anxious about anything."

They could not penetrate the barrier.

"My peace I leave with you," one of them offered Alice. Her ears perked as if she heard the words aloud.

"Yes, My peace I leave with you," the angel reminded her. Other angels moved toward her, speaking inaudibly. Alice's conscience was pricked.

"And the peace of God, which transcends all understanding, will guard your hearts and your minds in Christ Jesus."

The angels echoed a soft chorus of verses with a melodic chant. Alice's face showed her receptivity. She garnered every word and expression.

"Men, I can't tell you what I feel," Alice began. "But I must tell you the Scripture that keeps popping into my head. It's your favorite, Joe. Philippians four, verses six and seven, remember? 'Do not be anxious about anything, but in everything, by prayer and petition—'" she rattled off the rest of the verse.

"You must understand, I am almost hearing that verse spoken to me, it is so clear in my mind," Alice's eyes began to tear. "I really think God is trying to comfort us."

Howard immediately blurted out, "I will never leave you or forsake you." He looked surprised. "I'm not sure where that came from either, but Alice—everyone—that verse just hit me like a rock."

Multiple angels stayed tightly clustered around the four as they received the comfort of the Comforter to renew their fallen spirits. It was an indefinable moment as they simply sat and received the peace God offered them.

Across the room, Fortas sat beside Tony alone, distanced from the whirring angelic motions around the others. Tony wallowed in his private commiseration. Fortas had remained silent long enough.

"Tony, why do you think God has failed you?" The angelic question was asked with gentleness. It easily broke through the mental beating Tony was giving himself.

Oh God! It makes no sense that all this would be Your design. These people are so undeserving of punishment. They are so faithful to You. Why are they allowed to continue to suffer? Tony's questions were sincere, but Fortas knew they were superficial to his heart's true pain.

"But Tony," Fortas patiently whispered back, "I asked why do you think God has failed **you**?"

Tony's thoughts were driven by grief as he contemplated the question planted in his mind. With eyes tightly closed, his mind exploded with a silent response that only the heavens could hear.

This has nothing to do with me! I just can't believe, God, that You would force these people into so much pain, so much difficulty. Closing our opportunity to witness in town was the start, but now plucking Nadia right out of our hands just as she was opening up to your gospel, and causing Slava and his family so much grief. God, I just can't understand.

"Tony?" Fortas waited, his charge's soul vulnerable. This time, the cherubic language took aim as a searing hot arrow, spearing Tony's innermost being. "Tony! Why do you persecute the Lord?"

Suddenly a brilliance flashed before Tony's eyes. His eyelids remained tightly clenched, the burning radiancy blinding him. A broad beam penetrated his spirit, painfully but necessarily scorching the bleeding surfaces of long festering emotional wounds. Tony's hands instinctively flew up to hide his face. The fleshly protection offered no relief from the blazing streak of light that flared over his conscience.

"Why do you persecute the Lord?"

The questioned boomed in majesty and awesome power, dwarfing Tony as pure and achingly honest humility prevented any human defense.

My Lord, my Lord! Why do you think I persecute You? Tony's thoughts screamed to the heavens. His head was bowed, avoiding the beacon searing his eyes.

"You doubt the Lord's actions, you doubt the Lord's control, you doubt the Lord's sovereignty. When will you trust God to guide your every step?"

The angelic message beat like a strobe across Tony's soul. The intensity of the light rays grew stronger yet, causing an unusual pain. While unlike any physical hurt, Tony collapsed to the floor with a short, agonizing scream. The pain scorched his emotions.

The angels closed the window of heaven, shielding again the holy light of the Glory.

* * * * *

"Tony! Tony! Are you okay?" John was at his side immediately after he had fallen out of his chair.

"Is he breathing?" Howard exclaimed.

"Yes, I see him breathing, and he's got a pulse." John felt at Tony's limp wrist. "It's fast, but it's strong. But he's wringing wet with sweat!"

"He looks white as a sheet!" Mrs. Hensley pointed to his face, her other hand over her mouth.

John shook Tony's loose shoulders. "C'mon, Tony, wake up. Tony! Can you hear me?"

"Here," Paul came into the circle hovering over Tony. "Here's a wet cloth. Wipe his face—see if it will cool him off."

John took the rag and ran it over Tony's forehead. "God, please! Bring Tony around!"

Tony groaned in response.

"He's waking up!" John yelled.

Tony's head rolled back and forth with another slow moan. "Wha—what happened?"

"You blacked out on us, buddy," John said. "Open your eyes."

Tony's eyes cracked slightly, staring straight up to the ceiling. "Oh no!" he suddenly yelled. "Oh no. Oh my God!"

He tried to raise up quickly, but John grabbed his shoulders to slow him down.

"What's wrong, Tony? What's wrong?"

Tony's head bobbed right and left, a frightful contortion on his face. "I—I can't—I can't see! John! I can't see you. I can't see anything!"

* * * * *

The small chamber inside the Bolshoigorsk City Church was chillingly dark, like an underground chasm. A group of four met for a midnight briefing.

"Did Gdansk give you any problems?" The crisp voice boomed out of the shadowed face of Bishop Federov.

"That sniveling weasel? Not at all. He's been a limp rag. Does whatever we ask him—after I remind him of the pain of a gun smashed into his cheek." The sharp words came from a tall, muscular blonde man in a classy business suit. Next to him, the chubby mayor sat with nervous fingers clasped in his lap.

"Father Federov," the mayor volunteered. "Could I publicly insist that Gdansk leave his ministry? Perhaps he would respect my direction. I could speak to him in the strongest of terms."

Guttural laughter issued from the bishop, his head thrown back allowing the candlelight to illuminate his face. Federov's countenance appeared even more evil when lit.

"Gdansk is not blind, Babekov," Federov said, his face returning to the shadows. "He must be suspicious of both you and me by now. He is not the fool you take him for."

"But what kind of guy would stick it out after such a battering?" Babekov questioned. "His home is burned, his reputation ruined, and he's ripped away from his family. Who wouldn't think even his God is prompting him to leave?"

"Yeah, he still believes that his God somehow wants him here," the blonde muscle added. "How does he figure it? There's nothing in his favor whatsoever!"

The mayor's eyes darted across the room. His deputy was standing across from where he sat, shuffling back and forth. Babekov knew he needed something, some kind of information, to regain respect from Federov after the clumsy meeting with the Americans. Deputy Mayor Renat Dontestansk knew Pastor Gdansk better than any of them.

"Renat," Babekov spoke, "What do you think? Why can't we convince Slava to leave?"

Renat responded with a quiet, thoughtful voice. "He believes God is faithful."

"Don't be ridiculous!" Federov interrupted with a shout. "Babekov, is your whole office filled with fools like you? You all know how people are. Everyone trusts in God until they see God fail them. Gdansk is just a little stronger than we've seen."

He was speaking more quietly now. Babekov, shaking from fear, didn't like the dark minister's voice any better than when he was shouting.

"Indeed," Federov continued, "I was misled when I suggested some of these past deeds. Gdansk's faith is deeper than I had expected, but that is where we can get him. He believes so strongly in God that nothing outside himself could dissuade him. That leaves us an even better angle." Federov's voice became a sinister hush.

"What are you thinking, Father?" the blonde muscle asked.

"Instead of trying to destroy his faith in God," Federov hissed, "We can destroy his faith in himself. If God is so high and mighty to Gdansk, let's make him too low and miserable to be worthy of his God. We must make this insipid excuse for a pastor see his own failings, his own sin. If Gdansk is found guilty of sin, I'm sure we can convince him and his congregation that he must get out."

"But, getting Gdansk to sin?" Babekov said. "Can a brick float?"

"Ah, Mister Mayor," Federov snarled in an ominous whisper, his evil countenance in the full glow of the flickering candles. "He will sin—or he will die."

Chapter 20

"And so, we repeat that we do not know the charges that have been brought against Pastor Slava Gdansk, nor do we know why the Americans' translators were returned to Moscow," the attractive middle-aged newscaster reported over the television.

"Mayor Babekov has not returned our calls, and the police have released no information. In follow-up of our full coverage of this story, Station K2L will re-air the complete interview with the Americans, including video footage of Pastor Gdansk's church service. At Station K2L, we feel it is important for the people of Bolshoigorsk to form their own opinions about matters of religion. To this end, we encourage our viewers to stay tuned at three o'clock today for this fascinating exchange with our American visitors. This is Galina Listyev reporting."

Hoots and hollers were heard around the Yakovlev's home, the excited sounds and smiles convincing the Hensleys that the broadcast must have been favorable. Without the slightest notion of what had been said, they stood dazed by the elated gibberings from a dozen Russians surrounding them.

"Apparently some good words were shared," Joe Hensley shouted to his wife over the din. Alice nodded, sharing smiles and handshakes.

It was a lonely feeling. The Hensleys were the center of attention in a room of people who could not speak a word of English. They hoped their enthusiasm and gestures of love would tell enough.

The Americans had divided, with John and Paul making their way, apparently successfully, to the television station to find Galina. She understood enough English to communicate, and their prayer to find in her an ally for the church was answered. The Hensleys' job was to go with Oksana to Yakovlevs, trusting that Galina would broadcast a message of the morning's events so all of Bolshoigorsk, and particularly, Gdansk's congregation, would learn of the arrest.

From the coming and going of people, the Hensleys assumed messages were being sent to spread the word further.

Alice saw Oksana walk into the kitchen, supported by a couple of ladies. She was obviously in some distress and Alice followed them.

Entering the cramped room, Alice met Oksana's softened, wet eyes. The two were in each other's arms immediately, tears breaking over each shoulder.

"It's going to be alright; it's going to be alright," Alice consoled.

Oksana spoke softly into Alice's shoulder as they embraced. Alice saw the other two ladies in the room had bowed their heads.

Oksana was praying.

Hugging the anguished wife all the more tightly, Alice joined silently in the prayer circle, hearing the Russian women trade turns in their appeals to God. She immersed herself in the congealing souls of these contrite women as they powerfully worked to move the hand of God. This was holy ground, with heavy hearts pounding on the doors of heaven to gain direction and safety.

Countless prayer meetings had touched Alice in the past, but never had she experienced a fervor like this. The intimacy of this prayer language evidenced a passion for God that would make rich the most impoverished spirit. Not understanding a word that was said, she purposefully engaged herself in the selfless, yoked vigil that held no boundaries of time.

* * * * *

At Aunt Gina's flat, Howard had tried his best to get Tony to talk. His friend was adamantly mute as well as unwillingly blind. Peering into Tony's eyes, the glazed pupils gave no evidence of injury, but also no sign of vision.

Howard began as a nurse, soothing and comforting Tony after the others left, but his efforts met resistance at every offer of help. Tony tried to stand once, wanting to escape Howard's attention, but could not, and had to be lowered back to the floor with unrequited help.

"C'mon, Tony! I'm your friend. Tell me what happened!"

Tony was silent.

"You've got to say something—anything! Don't treat me like an idiot!" Howard was angry now. He moved right in front of Tony's sightless eyes. "Tell me, Tony! Tell me why you're blind!"

Tony remained dumb, even ignoring the heated air that ushered the biting words from his friend.

Howard resigned himself to kneeling across the room. Tired and exasperated, he turned to prayer.

* * * * *

The dank musty smell of the underground jail would have been tolerable had it not been for the pungent odor of excrement wafting past Slava every time the guard passed his cell.

At least he was somewhat acquainted with the surroundings and routine this time around. The guard was just as gruff, his one-eyed stare just as frightful, but familiarity removed a good deal of the shock.

Or maybe the blow he took on the side of his head jostled the cells of his brain enough to numb their function.

Or, as he hoped the most, he could claim his confidence in Christ, who had rescued him miraculously from the prison just a few days ago.

In any case, his capture yesterday morning had not created the panic and fear he would have expected from himself.

It had been more than twenty-four hours since he'd had any food or drink. The rubber hose at the corner of his cell offered a continuous trickle of water, but its spout rested on a drain that conspicuously served as the latrine. The gurgling sounds from the thin line of irrigation served as a constant reminder of thirst. Yet, Slava found himself able to tolerate the filthy conditions and do without, so far.

Even the jailer's rough habitus did not alarm Slava. With a body structure like a beer bellied gorilla, he was dressed in the same yellowed tee-shirt as the last time Slava occupied this cell; the same large holes showing the same dense hair on his bulging abdomen.

A man of few words, the watchman more often grunted and bellered at his prisoner. When those utterances wouldn't communicate his wishes, he used an eight-foot long rod of steel, thick as a broom stick, to whack the cell bars. The weapon, perhaps ripped from a line of bars in a lockup further away, made a huge gong-like reverberation across the wall of vertical irons. The deafening sound rang through the hollow chambers like a train whistle blasting through an underground tunnel.

It must be daybreak; the guard just turned on a bare bulb suspended from the ceiling outside his cell. It served as the sole source of light for the entire cellar. Slava might have gotten a few winks of sleep during the night while he sat huddled on the cold cell floor in pitch darkness, although his body could not attest to any rest.

He stood, stretching his wooden legs and arms. As he rubbed his hands together, he felt a few more stains of clotted blood come off his fingers, reminding him of his head wound. Lightly touching his temple, he could feel the tense bubble of swollen tissue extending from his ear to below his eye. Running his hand over the crusty scab at the edge of his cheek, he was at least thankful the bleeding had stopped. A quick rinse of the wound would surely help, but any thought of water only increased his thirst.

The cellar door clanked open, offering a hope of a drink this morning. The sound of two sets of footsteps clumping down the stairs encouraged him that life still existed beyond this hole.

It was two uniformed men, one a large muscular blonde, the other dark-haired. Slava could see them stare into his cell, but as soon as his eyes met theirs, they both quickly turned away.

With their backs to him, they spoke in terse whispers to the jailer, he answering with short grunts. The guard resisted the new orders, but the policemen argued insistently. At one point the jailer moaned a long sound and shook his head, plainly refusing the men. "He's not gonna hurt anybody," Slava overheard the jailer grumble. "Just let him be!"

The two policemen moved quickly, the dark-haired man grabbing the jailer from behind. The blonde used his fists to give him two powerful thrusts to the gut. The jailer doubled over and dropped to the floor, choking and spitting.

"He's a dangerous man!" the blonde shouted down to the jailer on his knees. "Make it now!"

The police walked up the stairs, the cellar door banging shut behind them.

Slava debated whether he should say something to his guard, still doubled over. Minutes later, the guard slowly rose to his feet.

"Are you okay?" Slava spoke through the bars. No reply. He thought better than to speak again.

The jailer stumbled back to his old rotting desk and found his long steel rod, leaning on it for support.

Had it been ten minutes, or thirty? Time moved so slowly. Slava had not moved, keenly watching the jailer. The old gorilla seemed to be in agony, whether from pain or humiliation Slava could not tell. Was he wrestling within himself, desiring to break out of this grimy rut? Was there even an ounce of goodness in him that made him think twice about just walking out of this forsaken job forever? Was he fed up with his life? Would he consider an offer of a new direction?

Simply pitiful, this picture of a wasted life hunched over his rod. He was a smelly, battered animal existing in an emotional wasteland. *Maybe I could speak to him about Jesus. Dare I?*

The only sound was the lone trickle from his cell's hose meandering down the waste drain. The pure water was immediately polluted before it had a chance to cleanse or refresh. *Would sharing the Gospel wind up trashed, as well?* Slava said a quick prayer and obeyed the inner voice within him.

"I can tell you're hurting," he shouted to the jailer. "Those men were very cruel to you."

Lord, I need some words from You.

"You must feel lousy, living like this. Have you ever wondered, I mean, don't you think there might be something more to life?"

The jailer turned slowly, facing Slava, his head still hanging low as he gripped his staff firmly.

"Can you imagine, even for an instant, that you might have been placed in this world for something much different? Can you believe that there is a God who created you for something much better than this?"

The jailer walked stiffly toward the cell, almost in slow motion.

Lord, is this going anywhere?

"Listen, we all search for our purpose in life. We all wonder if there really is a reason for living. Could I tell you why I think God has made us in this world? Would you let me tell you about it?"

The shuffling feet and clink of the steel rod with every step was the only response; the guard lumbered closer.

"You see, God made us, you and me. His desire was for us to live in this world and worship Him in glorious ways. He had a few simple rules for us to follow for our safety, but you can imagine what happened."

Now at the cell door, the jailer reached into his pants and pulled out a set of keys, fumbling for the right one. Slava took a couple steps back from the door.

What's this guy doing?

"Because man disobeyed God and tried to make it on his own, God let us receive the consequences, and the world became this mess of difficulties and hardship. Yet He still offered a way by which we could know Him and enjoy His good plan for our lives."

Slava felt his voice quivering as he continued to speak, the jailer now unlocking his cell. An urgency replaced the need for clarity.

"That way was through Jesus Christ, His Son," he shakily continued. "God sent His Son to die on the cross for our disobedience."

The jailer opened the door and entered the cell. He steadied himself on his feet and stood up straight for the first time, his height extending well over Slava.

"It is by believing in God's Son that you can know eternal life."

Slava took a close look at the man's eyes. One orbit still wandered off to the left, leaving a white socket. The other was red and swollen; it stared at him with a hazy, far-off look.

Something wasn't right. The guy wasn't getting it. He was no more interested in the gospel than swine nosing up to diamonds. He was in this cell for something else.

In less than a second, the guard had raised his rod directly over his head and with surprising speed, the steel bar was crashing straight down toward Slava.

Slava jumped just in time to feel the cool wind brush past his arm as the rod raced down along side him, just missing its target. It crashed into the ground, causing sparks to fly as it hit the concrete floor.

Only a grunt came from the jailer before a side swing brought the long rod around again. Slava leaped back, sucking his waist in to spare his torso from the blow. His right hand, held out for balance, caught the path of the bar with an excruciating whack.

"Aarrgg!" Slava cried out. He grabbed his limp hand, broken fragments of bone stabbing the thin skin. "What are you trying to do?"

The only answer was the bar swinging again from the opposite direction, this time a square blow to Slava's right side. He crumpled to the ground, a spike-like pain shooting through his rib cage. He held his breath, the pain unbearable. Starved for air, his lungs gasped and expanded. A writhing pang ripped through his chest. Bruised muscle and broken ribs rubbed harshly against each other. Shallow respirations took over, salvaging air while holding the cracked ribs steady.

With his good hand, he raised himself off the floor in time to see the guard once again hold the long rod overhead. With a painful scream, he rolled his body a full circle away as the concrete sparked again with the blow of steel.

The torment was overwhelming. Every move, each breath racked his body with spasms of agony. *Please God! Have mercy. I can't go on!*

He forced himself into a roll again, crying out with a heart-sickening wail. Again the bar missed its mark as points of light burned the cement.

Slava was helpless. His body spasmed with fine tremors from the pain. He looked up at his torturer, unable to control any other movement of his body. His head shook in anguish as he realized this was it. There was no escape. *Jesus! I'm ready.*

The jailer raised his rod a final time, recognizing the approach of the fatal blow even as Slava did. He reared back, the rod extending overhead, the tip reaching outside the cell door. The massive muscles of his arms flexed solidly as he brought the bar crashing down for the ultimate collision with its target.

The back swing, however, had caught hold of the electrical cord of the light hanging from the ceiling; the cord wrapped around the rod. With the speed of the forward thrust, the bulb cracked against the rod, crushing the glass. For a moment only, Slava could see the guard's arms begin jerking without coordination as he clumsily brought the bar down. The room went pitch black, except for a small electrical arc leaping from the open bulb socket to the bar wrapped within its grasp. The guard's feet convulsively slapped the wet metal grating over the waste drain.

Finally, the arc shorted out. Slava heard the thud of dead weight hit across the floor from him, the bar landing with a clang far to the side.

Mustering every unspent muscle, he dragged himself, an inch at a time, over to the body. His attacker made no noise, his frame motionless. In the darkness, Slava found an arm, limp and lifeless. Clasping hands with the guard, he began to pray.

"Father God, You know this soul."

He took a breath to speak again, crying out with the stabbing rib pain.

"God, may he have heard and understood something of You in his final moments. Did my words of Your love ever reach his heart?" Another shot of pain coursed through his chest. "God, I pray so."

Emotionally wrecked and critically injured, Slava eased himself to the side of his attacker.

The cellar door clanged open followed by the sound of footsteps, many of them, racing down the stairs. Slava had no strength to open his eyes, but he could see the shadowy rays of a flashlight shining in his face and around the room. Unable to respond, his mind absorbed the conversation of voices around him.

"Something went wrong!"

"Are they both dead?"

"Gdansk is breathing, but Leonid's had it."

"No! Did Gdansk kill him?"

"That's what Federov wanted. I didn't think he could fight like that."

"Call the mayor. Tell him Gdansk murdered his jailer."

"Got it. He's a murderer now."

"It's perfect! Grab him. We gotta move him to another cell."

Two hands slid under Slava's shoulders, wrenching his ribs with a piercing twist. His senses went black, his conscious threshold surpassed by raw pain.

Chapter 21

When the reddened sun sank in the Russian horizon it was nearly eleven o'clock, the lengthy twilight adding to the weariness of the Americans. The emotional frustration of existing in a world without words was taking its toll.

John and Paul had left the TV station after seeing the evening newscast. Galina Listyev again favorably presented the church to the Bolshoigorsk community. There was comfort in being around Galina, as she was the only bilingual Russian John knew. Yet, she was far too busy to serve as translator. The station's coverage of Gdansk's plight was critical, but she could not effectively do her job with some inept Americans bumbling around her.

Back at Gina's flat, John took inventory of the stamina of his team and found everyone wanting. The Hensleys, just back from their day at the Yakovlevs, were completely worn out. The tremendous activity and energy of that home, which had become a sort of command center for the church, left Joe and Alice spinning.

But the dreariest pair were Howard and Tony. When John returned to the flat, Howard met him with cried out eyes.

"He won't do anything, John. He just sits around on the floor, barely moving."

"Did he speak to you?"

"Finally, about an hour ago, he said his first words to me. Something like, 'I can't talk about it right now.' I said, 'C'mon Tony, tell us what happened to your eyes,' and he just stared away. I'm really worried about him, John. Do you think he's permanently blind?"

"I don't know, Howard. I just don't know."

John dismissed everyone to their host homes. The difficulty of facing Tony's blindness was too much to handle for the whole team. Better to let them rest, removed from as much tension as possible.

"In your host homes, let's all pray overnight for our situation here," John announced. "In the morning we'll need to consider every option the Lord may give us."

Everyone agreed and left, leaving John and Tony alone. Gina was still at the Yakovlevs. She had taken the Gdansk boys there to stay with Oksana for a couple nights. Any news from Slava would more likely surface at their flat via the television.

John was glad for this time, needing to, at last, give some prayer and thought to his team's future. First, however, he needed to see about Tony.

Walking into the living room, Tony was sitting on the floor with an unflinching downward gaze—no indication of recognition. John sat on the floor next to him and remained quiet for several minutes.

Finally, he nonchalantly broke the silence. "Galina asked about you today. She wondered why you didn't come see her."

No motion came from the young man's frame.

"I told her you weren't feeling well, and she said she was sorry to hear it."

John eyed Tony carefully. There was no indication of physical pain. He sat confined in an emotional prison, consumed by matters that no one understood.

"Tony," John spoke quietly. "Can you give me any idea of what is going on?"

Just as John gave up on a response, Tony spoke, his lips thinly moving. "I can't talk about it."

It was not an explanation or an apology. It was a fact.

"I really think tomorrow we should find a doctor," John offered.

Again, Tony went deadpan.

Minutes passed. John considered how he could contact a trustworthy doctor. With recent events, he felt any public exposure could endanger the team, just as it had the translators and Slava.

"John?"

His heart skipped a beat.

"Yes?"

John waited for more, but it took so long. Had he imagined his name being called?

"I think God has really tried to tell me something." Tony's face still stared at the floor as he spoke, his body motionless.

"I have really been stupid." Tony choked on the words. "I've really been a fool." Sobs came as he moved for the first time, kneeling low to the ground, bringing his face to the floor.

"Oh God!" he cried out. "Forgive me, Lord! I have been so selfish. Oh, God, forgive me!"

John remained silent. Was Tony going insane? Waiting out this private display of conviction, he felt like he was eavesdropping.

Tony continued deeply sobbing on his knees. Any attempt to console him would have been a feeble human interruption. Something eternal was happening.

* * * * *

"Father Federov, we've got to do something!" Mayor Babekov burst into his superior's office. "My councilmen are being hounded by people, asking if Listyev's reporting is true, demanding an explanation, wondering why the council cannot vote on the church. I have to tell them something!"

"Ah, Babekov, you worry far too much," the bishop balked, rocking back in his dark leather chair. "Everything is going just as planned."

It irritated the mayor to watch Federov gloat in his own power. He wanted out from under the bishop's thumb.

"I've got to call a council meeting, an open meeting." Babekov presented his plan, prepared to push his way around Federov if needed. "I have to meet with the citizens of Bolshoigorsk and deal with them up front. If we leave it to the television, Bolshoigorsk will become a little Moscow—the government, and yourself, Federov, will lose all control."

"Well, well, well. The king needs to meet with his subjects, eh?" Federov boomed with conceited laughter. "Afraid you're losing control of your people?" More ugly laughter.

"You're in this too deep, Federov. You're the one about to lose. Are you prepared to have the city discover who ordered the arrest of Slava Gdansk?" It was a wildcard Babekov played early.

Too early.

Federov jumped to his feet and leaned over his broad oak desk, grabbing the hand of his mayor. "Don't you threaten me, you conniving fool," the words were spit out in a dark whisper. "You have no idea what is going on, because you have no control. You have nothing, absolutely nothing, to bargain with."

Babekov's hand remained in the tight grasp, his wrist twisted just enough to make him lean the same direction to keep it from snapping. The vise grip turned his fingers white, but his pain was surpassed by riveting fear. All he wanted was out, but there was no escape.

Federov twisted his hand an inch more, causing Babekov to lose his balance. The bishop released his grasp, sharply pushing the hand away. Babekov flailed back two steps, tripping into a chair behind him. His spine hit the frame first and he crumpled into the seat, legs spreadeagled.

"Schedule your meeting, a city-wide meeting, for tomorrow night at seven o'clock." This was no longer Babekov's plan; it was Federov's order. "Tell your little newsy reporter all about it. Tell everyone about it! Just be sure to tell them that there will be a little news item announced about Gdansk. Tell them everything will make sense then." The bishop's voice quieted to the evil whisper Babekov hated.

"Tell them anything more, Babekov, and I will have your head."

Babekov ran from the room like a mouse released from a trap.

A blonde officer stepped from his hiding place behind a wooden screen. "He's no threat."

"That's my least concern," Federov fumed. "The babbling idiot has no clue. It's Gdansk and the Americans."

"What can they do now, Father? Gdansk is finished and the Americans have no translators."

Federov remained unsettled. "How long before the Americans leave?"

"They had planned to be here ten days, but we have word that their itinerary is being revised. They're running scared. Now they plan to leave in two days."

"Just like the cowards," Federov said. "First they woo Gdansk to their religion, then when there's trouble they drop him in their dust."

"It's not like our church at all," the officer joined in, seeking Federov's reassurance. "We held ourselves together all through the communist regime."

"That was our testing, indeed. But now we're able to reclaim our rightful place." Federov spoke with arrogant confidence. "The church has risen again as the supreme authority over the land."

"Never to fall again."

"Never. These Americans will not rip away what we have built. And Gdansk…well, he has shown us what he truly is."

The officer relaxed. Federov was controlled and leading.

* * * * *

"So that's it, John. Do you believe what I saw?" Tony sat at the kitchen table, eating his first food in a day's time.

"I believe you. And even if I didn't, how could I explain the loss of your sight? Something very serious—and very real—happened to you. I still don't understand, though. Why did the voice accuse you of persecuting the Lord?"

"You have to know my heart, John." It wasn't easy for him to talk. This was coming from deep down inside.

"I wasn't out there burning Christians at the stake, but I was doing it to Him inside. I don't think I had ever really trusted Christ—really believed Him to be who He said." Tony shook his head, ashamed.

"I have always looked for ways to protect myself. Like when Nadia was arrested, I blamed God for messing up. When we found out the church here was in trouble, I thought God had made a mistake. Even back when Sarah died, I was so angry at God. I knew He had blown it. Ever since I've been a Christian, I don't think I've ever really trusted Him. Oh, I knew He died for me, rose from the grave, all that, but to really trust Him for my life? I never did. I kept trying to make things work my way and accused God if they didn't turn out right."

"But, Tony," John offered, "I'm not that different from you. I mean, we all struggle with leaving everything in God's hands. Why do you think God made it so critical in your life?"

"I don't know. All I know is, for me, it comes down to this: do I truly believe He is God? If I believe it, then my life needs to reflect it. If I'm arguing with God, questioning His actions, second-guessing His plans, then I'm trying to remove His Godhead in my life. That's what I've been doing, John, and that's where I'm going to change."

John leaned back and sipped his tea. An hour ago, Tony had spent a lengthy time in remorseful prayer. Then, he surprised John by asking for food. Something had suddenly changed. He was still blind, yet, he was different.

John was fixing a slice of bread in the kitchen when Tony had carefully walked in, his hands guiding his way. He began to talk, telling about the bright light, the voice, the sudden blindness. John listened intently, but now was still bewildered.

"So what about your sight? Do you think it will return?"

"I have no idea. It's a constant reminder of what God has called me to. If my blindness leads me to depend on God for all things, I'll accept it."

"Tony, I can't believe how you're handling this."

"I don't know. But please, don't worry about my sight. I have to believe, now more than ever, that God knows what He's doing. With a little help getting around, I think we'll just have to wait and see." Tony gave a relieved smile, assuring John he was sincere.

It was the first smile John had seen on his friend for too long of a time, and it looked good.

"John, could you do one more thing with me?"

"Sure, Tony. I'm planning to be up a while yet. Have to do some serious praying about what the next few days will hold. Shoot."

"Well, I'd really like to hear a story from the Bible, you know, Paul's conversion? I remembered that he saw a bright light. The Lord said the same words to him as I heard before I went blind. Could you read that story to me?"

"My privilege." John got up and brought his Bible back to the kitchen, turning to the book of Acts and finding the chapter. He began reading, realizing that this would be Tony's sole source of Scripture from now on. He would not be able to read on his own again.

"'Then Ananias went to the house and entered it. Placing his hands on Saul, he said—'"

The reading was interrupted by a soft knock at the door.

Tony immediately tensed every muscle, grabbing the edge of the table, eyes staring senseless to the ceiling. Fear surrounded his countenance. John could only imagine his friend's flashback to yesterday when the police stormed the room.

Tony's voice quivered. "Who—who could it be?"

"I don't know, Tony. You wait right here, okay?" John got up, watching Tony for a response. He could hardly believe the conversion he saw.

Tony suddenly relaxed his grasp of the table and sat back in his chair. It was like a switch of fear was turned off inside.

"I'll be okay, John. God's peace is here, I can tell. I'll be okay. Go see who it is."

John walked to the door, still looking back at the kitchen. Tony sat calmly, transformed from the initial panic he showed. John wished he had as much confidence as he reached for the lock.

"Who is it?" John said softly through the door.

"I am Davron Egorova. I am a friend, here with Pastor Gregori Hatir."

John threw open the door and seeing Hatir, grabbed him in a bear hug welcome. "Man, are you a sight for sore eyes!"

The young, dark haired man named Davron looked at John and questioned him in English. "Sight for sore eyes?"

"You speak English!" John rewarded him with a similar bear hug.

"Come in, come in!" John excitedly ushered them both through the door. "Tony," he yelled. "You'll never believe it! Pastor Gregori is here, and he's brought a new translator!"

As they walked into the kitchen, Pastor Hatir suddenly stopped when he saw Tony. He exclaimed a phrase of Russian and Davron interpreted. "It is true! You are blind?"

Tony stood with his eyes glassy and unseeing, his head cocked to hear. "Yes, Pastor Gregori, the Lord has given me blindness."

A flurry of Russian flew out of Hatir, with Davron acknowledging that he had heard all this before. He began to translate, "Pastor Gregori has had a dream he would like me to relate to you. But please, let us sit."

Davron began with them around the table. "Two nights ago Pastor Gregori had a dream in which, Tony, you were blind. He saw himself coming to Bolshoigorsk to pray for you. And heal you. At the time he thought it to be preposterous. He gave it no further attention, but the next day he received word that Gdansk had been arrested and that you Americans might be in trouble. He made plans to immediately come to Bolshoigorsk."

"So God actually told you I would be blind?" Tony said in wonder.

"Definitely," Davron responded with Pastor Gregori's words.

"Have you heard about the local TV reports, too?" John asked.

"Yes," Davron translated after Hatir answered. "With guarded optimism, Pastor Gregori shares your excitement. We have just come from the Yakovlevs, and although there is no word on Slava, the city has announced a special council meeting tomorrow night. It sounds as if the church registration may be voted on then."

"Tomorrow night?" Tony exclaimed. "That's great!"

"Yes, we find it to be an answer to our prayers," Davron volunteered. "We only hope it has not come with too great of price."

"You mean Slava?" John asked.

Davron spoke briefly with Gregori and then responded. "Pastor Gregori and I have discussed Slava's circumstances a great deal. From the experiences of other Christian prisoners, we fear greatly for his safety. That is another reason for our coming to find you. Since there has been no word about Slava from the government, we are deeply concerned. We must also tell you that the entire American team is in grave danger."

"Surely the government would not risk an incident with us." John said.

"You will find our government's actions very unpredictable. The unexpected is often the case. Has that not been true for you?"

John put his hand on Tony's shoulder to gain some sense of comradery. "Then what do you suggest we do?" he asked.

"Pastor Gregori and I have made arrangements for you and the other Americans to leave Bolshoigorsk the day after tomorrow. With the help of your American consulate in Moscow, it was the earliest your flights could be adjusted. We must have you return to America as soon as possible."

"What?" John exclaimed. "You think it's that serious?"

"You do not understand. Your lives are at risk," Davron replied and then conversed with Hatir.

Tony leaned toward his friend. "I think he's right, John. Our usefulness here is about exhausted. They should know better than us about our security."

It was futile to argue. Even Tony agreed with the plan. It didn't seem right to leave the mission with so much undone. Yet, if the safety of the team was in the balance, John had little choice.

Davron spoke again. "We have a separate place for you to stay until you leave. We should go there now, as soon as you can get your belongings. Pastor Gregori has sent others to get the rest of your team and meet us there. It is not as comfortable, but it will be safe."

"You are serious," John said resignedly. "Well, I guess we'll get packing." He stood up to leave the table when Hatir interrupted.

"Pastor Gregori asks you to wait," Davron interpreted. "He asks if he could pray for Tony just now, for his eyesight to be restored."

"Certainly," John replied, with Tony nodding in agreement.

Hatir moved behind where Tony sat, placing his hands on the top of Tony's head. John watched closely, wondering what it must feel like for Tony to sense this godly touch without seeing. He grabbed Tony's hand to join in prayer.

It was almost musical, the prayer Hatir offered. His voice was different, as if he spoke now in a separate dialect. The sound was soft and reverent, nothing commanding or authoritative. As his prayer continued, the melodious words were more intense, as with an intimate conversation. Pausing frequently, he was listening, gaining the counsel of Another. Shy of pleading, Hatir continued in a respectful but fervent interchange. John could only say 'amen' in his own prayers.

Hatir slowly removed his hands from Tony's head and stepped back. John held no expectations and was ready to start packing when he saw Tony rub his eyes.

No, he wasn't rubbing his eyes. He was working something out of them.

In a moment something like a small contact lens fell from his left eye, another one followed from his right. They were shiny, like fish scales, and John saw them dissolve into the wood floor like tears as soon as they hit.

The silence of the moment posed the obvious question.

In slow motion, Tony raised his head, his eyelids closed. Real tears seeped out between the cracks as John peered into the chambers of his friend's sight.

"John?" Tony asked softly.

The portals opened a sliver's width.

"Oh, my Lord! Oh, my Lord! I can see! John, I see you!"

John grabbed Tony, unable to speak.

"I can see! Pastor Gregori, praise the Lord, I can see you!" Tony laughed and cried together as he gave Hatir a quick hug. Then he was back looking around the room again.

"Davron—you must be Davron! I can see you, too!" He darted into the next room, John following. Tony's eyes scanned the room, taking in every view from every corner. Then he dashed to the front door.

"I've got to go outside!"

He was out in the darkened street before John could reach the stairwell with Gregori and Davron. As they made their way out the doorway into the cool night, they heard the sound.

Neighboring Russians would never be able to explain the strangest cry heard in the middle of the night: a resounding howl, a sound of jubilation, a pealing whoop that echoed to the heavens.

Chapter 22

When Slava opened his eyes, there was no difference; the darkness was as black as when he was asleep.

There were other differences though.

Like the ice pick pain stabbing his ribs with each breath. And the swollen numbness of his right hand. Any movement of his wrist caused the numbness to explode with throbbing shock waves up his arm. Terrorized emotions flooded back with sickening nausea as he was forced to acknowledge that this was no dream.

If there was a way, he'd rather stay asleep.

That not being an option, he tried to make out his surroundings. Laying on the cool cement floor, he moved his left foot and found a heavy weight around his ankle. Shackles. He dragged his foot across the ground. The thick chain held tight after only a few inches. His right foot moved unbound, but reached cell bars three feet away.

Another jail cell. Probably the same cellar. Apparently the lights were out of order for a while.

He grimaced, not with pain, but in remembrance of his executioner's freak electrocution. Somehow he still pitied the man, holding compassion for a soul that never experienced God's love. Every breath reminded him of the pain the ogre caused, but he could not escape the fact that the last Christian the jailer saw before facing eternity was himself.

Lord, I hope I did enough, he prayed silently, another dart in his side stealing his breath. *I hope I said what You wanted. May I be Your servant in all things, God. My life is through here—let my last words count for Your sake.*

The constant pain, hunger, and thirst exhausted Slava's sense of comfort. With no physical relief in sight, his thoughts wandered in a spiritual delirium. As the hours passed blindly, he sought an intimacy with his Savior, hastening his passage to meet Him face to face. In his mind, it did not seem long to wait.

＊ ＊ ＊ ＊ ＊

"Just around the next bend and we'll be there," Davron announced to the three men in a line behind him. Each one was laden with a backpack or suitcase, vagabonds wandering a darkened road in the countryside of Bolshoigorsk. Though they had walked three miles, not a single car had traveled by at this midnight hour.

Davron led his company on to a rutted dirt path, holding tree branches back as the trail became awkward in the darkness. Soon they were in a clearing, a one-story dilapidated barn before them.

"Here we are," Pastor Gregori announced as Davron translated. "It is not as hospitable as we would like, but it will do."

As they approached the barn door, a small light flickered through cracks in the plank siding.

"Someone is already here?" John asked.

"Yes, perhaps the other Americans have come, or it may be some from the church," Davron answered. "They wanted to keep Nadia company."

"Nadia?" Tony exclaimed. "What do you mean?"

"Why, she is here with us, did I not tell you?" Davron answered. "She was the one who came to Pastor Gregori in Nizhnekamsk, telling us of Slava's arrest."

The rush Tony felt was abruptly restrained by the rusty-hinged barn door that could not open fast enough. Impatiently he watched Gregori unlock the old padlock. Thrusting open the door, Tony stepped in, his newly sighted eyes burning at first from the bright candle lighting the large open shack.

"Nadia, are you here?" he shouted, rubbing his eyes to hasten their adjustment.

He focused on a small huddle of Russians standing at one side, their faces yet blurred. In the center of the group was a tall, dark-haired woman.

Torn between wanting to run and wrap his arms around her and knowing not to offend the Russian mores, he stood frozen. Just resting his eyes on her seemed at least a soothing balm.

Cultural differences were cast aside as Nadia broke from her group and ran straight into Tony's arms, her grasp squeezing him tightly.

"Tony!" she whispered breathless in his ear. "I thought I'd never see you again!"

"I thought my eyes would never see you either!"

Breaking from the embrace, each stepped back to behold the other. Tony reached for Nadia's hand, and she gently offered it.

"There's a lot we need to talk about, Nadia," Tony said.

"Yes, there is."

He walked her off to the side of the barn away from the group. The distant flickering candle created sizable shadows, guarding their privacy.

"Uh, you go first," Tony awkwardly whispered, unsure of what to say. "What happened to you after the police took you away?"

"It all happened very quickly. The police gave us bus tickets to Nizhnekamsk. From there they told us we would board a plane back to Moscow. They tried to tell us that our services were not needed by the Americans any longer, that you would be leaving shortly, and that our school had requested our return."

"What do they take you for, idiots?"

"I don't know, Tony. I knew you and the rest of your team must have been in serious trouble. Then we overheard two of the police talking of Slava's arrest. On our way to Nizhnekamsk, Luda, Tonya and I knew we had to get help for you. Only one of us could take the risk of getting away, and I told the girls to cover for me as best they could. They were going to make up something about my visiting my mother in Kazan before returning to Moscow. Anyway, at Nizhnekamsk, I left them and found Pastor Hatir, who right away came back with me."

"That was risky, Nadia. You should have gone on home to Moscow." He said it without meaning a word of it.

"I just couldn't leave you and your team in danger here. And, I needed to find out something. Something I had to learn from you."

"What's that, Nadia?"

"You never told me how to believe." She hesitated. "How to believe in Jesus. I had to come back to ask you."

"You want me to tell you how to believe in Christ?"

"Yes, Tony," she answered quietly.

Her eyes looked directly at his, her globes immensely beautiful with a fresh and humble sincerity. "I know I am ready. I have considered it for a very long time. This is what He wants me to do. Please, will you help me?"

Tony trembled with joy. "Nothing could make me happier, Nadia."

* * * * *

Slava woke again. Or had he really ever slept? His senses were made freshly aware of his pain, jolting his eyes open.

At times the throes would gnaw him senseless. His mind wandered in a foggy arena of dreams and hallucinations.

The prison became his sanctum. Fighting to cling to consciousness helped avoid the ravaging delusions. While awake, he would quote Scripture over and over, pray out loud, recite hymns, anything that would keep his focus on the present and on His Lord. Facing the inevitable, he would soon begin to slip into a delirium again. More fervent prayer, louder speech, mightier concentration, would all succumb, sliding down a tunnel of haunting depravity.

One time it was a desert wasteland, collapsed in a sandy pit where his legs, buried to the hips, could not carry him to an oasis pond a short distance away.

Another time he shivered in a polar blizzard, his body bound only by a sheet frozen to his bare skin. As the snow enveloped him in loneliness and fear, he could barely see the outline of three figures walking past him; a woman it was, with two small children. If he could only—

"Oksana!"

His gasping scream caused the crushed ribs to knife him into reality, his only escape from the nightmares.

"God, no more nightmares! Clear my mind. May my eyes only see You." Complete exhaustion overcame him. "I can't stay awake. Lord, keep me awake—"

He began to slide again.

He was floating, weightless in a black vacuum. If it hadn't been for the chain wrapped around his leg, he knew he would have floated away like an untethered balloon.

He awaited the next tortuous vision.

It didn't come. Rather, an expanse of time passed, allowing him rest in lightless obscurity.

Then he felt a sudden jab at his side.

A bright light pierced the dark void, sharply waking his slumber. The poke to his side hit again, not painfully, but enough to disturb him.

"Quick, get up!"

The voice was behind him, coming from the direction of the light.

I'm afraid to look, Slava thought. *Afraid I'll be teased into a mirage of Oksana again.*

He stared straight ahead, trying to force reality. His dream continued.

Looking at his feet, the shackle at his ankle broke in two like a cracked egg. He jerked his leg up in surprise, the broken metal braces remaining in pieces.

"Go get your jacket," the voice came again.

Slava stood obediently, playing out the vision rather than fighting it. This delusion seemed almost a game, absent the horror of the others.

The beacon of light from behind shone around the jail, and Slava saw his cell door sitting ajar. Outside, his jacket hung on a hook and he grabbed it.

"Follow me."

The beam moved quickly, a spotlight following an invisible dancer. As the light moved across Slava, he unmistakably felt a current of wind, followed by a scent of mint. He raised his eyes to see the orator of his dream.

It was a spiritual being of some sort. A white radiancy veiled the ten-foot apparition. It wasn't a gown, but more of an aura that clothed the being. There might have been hair on its head, or light rays were filtering into the darkness, fluttering in a gentle breeze of their own creation.

Defining the image seemed of no particular concern just now. He was ready to do what the being said. Slipping on his jacket, he flinched much less at his hand's pain then he had thought, and followed the light to the cellar stairs.

Slava had never felt such freedom to move in prior delusions. Walking up the stairs was almost exhilarating, just being able to stretch his legs. He breathed easy, noticing only a little cramp in his chest now.

A grand dream! he thought. *Thank you, Lord.*

The starlit leader before him turned and bowed as if in receipt of the prayer.

A moment of panic halted Slava's steps. *Am I dead? Is this the end of my life?*

Though Slava's thoughts were not audible, the angel seemed to hear them well enough. "Follow me," the herald patiently repeated.

The door at the top of the stairs swung open by itself. The angel did not hesitate to go into the police chambers. Slava quickly caught up with it, trying to stay within its glow. The sight continued to amaze him.

It was the night shift, only three or four officers circulating around the desks. Not one raised an eye at Slava or his companion. Through the cigarette haze, Slava saw the blonde muscular policeman who had earlier pummeled the jailer. The guy looked directly at Slava, then shook his head and looked away.

They left the building without a soul noticing.

Stepping outside, Slava convinced himself this delusion could not represent death. There was no expectancy of heaven or eternity. He was simply following the angel down the streets of Bolshoigorsk. It had to be a divine vision based on his familiar longings. He gratefully accepted it as a break from the pain and agony of his cell. He only hoped the dream would last, that his ribs would not wake him from this—

"Aargghh!" Slava yelped. He suddenly staggered over to lean against a building. The figure of light disappeared quickly.

Slava reeled in the darkness, his hand throbbing. His chest panged again by sudden rhythmic thrusts of a blade in his side with each breath. He slid back to the ground, back to his cell, back to his shackles.

But no.

The ground was cold and gritty, not a smooth cement slab.

There were lights here. The old flickering neon sign of the beer parlor across the street strangely welcomed Slava's consciousness.

His legs remained unbound, no chains in sight.

Through shallow breaths, the air was cool and fresh in a misty rain. The pain in his side and hand made it real. There was no mistake.

This was no dungeon lockup. This was downtown Bolshoigorsk.

Forced to admit his pain, the return of his tormenting sensations confirmed what he was trying to believe was true. He took a deep breath, clenching his teeth to endure the blessed agonizing reminder that he was fully awake, fully aware of his pain. With his exhale, a hoarse cry embodied his excruciation, but more so his ecstasy.

"I'm free!"

Chapter 23

Shards of morning sunshine broke through the slits of the barn's plank siding to wake John the next morning. Counting heads, he noticed Davron and Gregori were gone, but the rest of the Americans, Nadia, and the few locals who spent the night with them on the dirty floor were still in their slumbers.

The barn door was just ajar. John dusted off his wrinkled clothes and quietly squeezed outside.

It was a beautiful morning. The grassy field surrounding the barn was tall and green with a forest of trees wrapping the borders of the clearing. Bees found their bounty in wild yellow and white daisies. A cool breeze blew John's hair slightly as he watched the distant treetops gently sway. There, a couple of hawks swooped in giant invisible swings back and forth over the tallest evergreens. The terrain could easily be mistaken for the foothills of the Pacific Northwest, and John caught himself imagining he was back in America.

That is, until he heard his name called with a sharp Slavic accent. He turned and saw Davron waving from behind the barn.

"Come over here, John. Gregori and I are over here."

John rounded the corner to behold a surprise kept as secret as the old barn itself. Gregori was twenty yards back, pole in hand, casting into a grand spring lake. The view was more than a portrait, bright reflections of the sun shimmering in the ripples. Gregori was a shadowed outline against the silver screen of water behind him.

"Hey, Gregori," John yelled. "What's the catch of the day?"

He and Davron quickly walked to the lakeside. John patted the pastor-turned-angler on the shoulder.

"How'd you ever find this place?"

Gregori dragged his line in while Davron answered the question himself.

"A handful of Christians from Bolshoigorsk have used this place for some time, actually before Slava's church began. When the church was underground, this was the common meeting place. In those days, they couldn't use it regularly for fear they would be discovered."

"You mean Bolshoigorsk had an underground church?" John asked.

"Oh, yes, a very strong one," Davron continued. "The Yakovlevs owned this barn and gave it and the land to the church. This lake is still used for the baptism of new believers. Last night when we were celebrating Nadia coming to believe in Christ as her Lord, it reminded us of the old days. Back then, persecution led people to do whatever it took to receive Christ. People were willing to suffer, willing to go to jail if need be, all to follow the Lord. In recent times, it has been a less common sight to see someone like Nadia, willing to risk her life—to find Christ." Davron looked wistfully across the lake.

Gregori seemed to understand Davron's expression, and spoke several sentences.

"Gregori says that the days of the underground church were very special. The church was vibrant, more alive. He said what we're dealing with now is reminiscent of those days—it makes him excited."

"Excited? How so?" John asked.

Davron received another lengthy response to translate from Gregori.

"The dream Gregori had before coming here—you remember—the one about healing Tony's blindness? Gregori said he had those dreams frequently back then. Healings occurred more often. Without explanation, they have all but disappeared. The church has become less of a reckoning force. Except for now. Something is happening among the people of Bolshoigorsk. The church is forced to risk much. Slava has been forced to risk perhaps his very life. Tonight's meeting may even mean the end of the church here. But the persecution we face is accompanied by a refining of our faith in God."

"I guess I'm surprised he's this elated," John replied. "I've been very discouraged, wondering if we Americans had contributed anything to your ministry at all. We caused more problems than we helped."

Davron translated John's words, and the expression on Gregori's face showed his disagreement. He laid his fishing pole down and stood in front of John, hands stretched to his shoulders. Gregori spoke directly to John this time, and though Davron offered the translation, John could not escape Gregori's stare as he listened.

"There could be nothing farther from the truth, John. You and the other Americans were the sparks that set our timber aflame. I have been told by others that you Americans worry too much about numbers. You want to reach many people, want to see grand responses to your preaching and ministry. That is not our prayer here in Russia.

"More than anything else, Bolshoigorsk needs believers who are willing to risk it all for Christ's sake. Our goal for evangelism is not to see many people say a prayer. We want people to count the cost of following Christ, willing to put everything aside to belong to Him. For our church to have an impact in Russia—that is the kind of believer we need."

Gregori dropped his stare and turned back to the glimmer of the lake, speaking now as if convincing the world.

"This adversity molds us, shapes us, forces us to depend on God alone. Then we see Him work." Gregori gestured with both hands at the beauty of the waters before them. "And He works in magnificent ways, yes?"

John nodded in agreement, though Gregori did not turn from the lake to notice.

"You know," John thought out loud, "When we first came here, I had a very tight agenda of what we wanted to accomplish. It seemed from the first day, when the police stopped our street witnessing, we met obstacles. I kept thinking this was the enemy trying to thwart God's plan. But you would say this was God using us in His own agenda."

Gregori turned to John and firmly nodded in agreement after Davron's interpretation.

"As I look back, I think you're right. Last night Tony tried to explain to me how, through his blindness, he felt God was calling him to a bold faith, a bold obedience. Meeting this kind of persecution can't help but make us depend on God, leaving no option but to trust Him. And He has been so faithful."

John was quiet, spent of words that could summarize all he had seen God do. He began to understand the challenge Tony had presented about completely believing in God for all things.

Gregori squarely faced John and spoke with a stern intonation. As John waited for the translation, he felt a shiver down his spine—these words were meant especially for him.

"My brother John, you have learned these things here, not for our ministry in Russia, but for your ministry in America. You have been the matchstick for our church in Bolshoigorsk. We were dry timber, ready to be ignited. Your American team has been the fiery torch that set our kindling ablaze. We will continue to burn with a white-hot flame because of the powerful conviction with which you brought the torch of Christ. But now it is time for you to return home. The light you have carried must be used again to ignite the Christians in America. Do not let your torch's flame go out. It is desperately needed in your home."

Gregori's words were like a prayer, but spoken to John. Lingering over the imperative message, John responded, "Amen."

* * * * *

"What do you mean, 'he's escaped?'" Father Federov roared, his voice echoing off the walls of his dark, empty sanctuary.

The blonde policeman's broad shoulders slumped as he braced himself for the wrath to come.

"We don't know how it happened, Father," the officer tried to explain. "He was beaten so badly he couldn't even walk. We left him shackled in a cell alone. When we checked on him this morning, his cell was unlocked, the shackles were broken, and he was gone. I was in the office all night, and I can tell you, no one came or went."

"Fools! You're all incompetent fools!" Federov boomed as he turned his back on the policeman.

The officer watched his superior carefully, wondering if his sentence would be immediate or delayed. His life was suspended by a thin thread dangling from the finger of the man before him. He had seen it happen to other underlings before—accidental drownings, unexplained car wrecks, mysterious disappearances.

Federov spoke again, his back yet turned away. His voice was solemn, quieter than the policeman expected.

"Find him. Do everything possible to find him."

"Yes, Father," the officer said. "Right away."

"If you do not find him before tonight's meeting," Federov continued in the low monotone. "Consider it your end."

This was no surprise to the policeman. He acknowledged it as a reprieve from immediate death.

"One more thing," Federov said. "Don't tell anyone about his escape. Especially Babekov. No one needs know. You will find him."

The officer made his exit without another word.

Federov walked into his office to his phone, dialing a number from memory. His words were curt and crisp.

"I may need your services tonight, you and your hardware."

He paused to hear an agreement.

"At the auditorium. If I remove my vestment, be prepared to terminate whoever is speaking. When I sit down, do it."

Another acknowledgment was received, and Federov hung up the phone.

* * * * *

To the bystander, he was just another bum; his clothes soiled, his face emaciated, his movement pained and clumsy. Another drunk, overfilled with vodka from the trash behind the saloons. Or had he begged this overdose from a bartender who had given in to get him out of his establishment? In any event, the morning traffic walking past his collapsed form on the bus stop bench ignored him.

Slava knew it would be impossible to identify his huddled body among the other drunkards littering this street. It would serve for his hiding until he could think through where he should go.

He couldn't go home. How much he wished to, but that would endanger Oksana and the boys far too much. It was not even safe to contact them. Not yet. Was there anyone else he could stay with? Not without risking his life and their safety. He had to think, there must be something.

His thoughts were repeatedly interrupted by passersby throwing trash in the receptacle near his head or carelessly bumping his body when scurrying around him. As the time approached for the bus to stop here, the crowd thickened.

He struggled to block out all the chatter so he could concentrate on his own concerns. He was hearing everything from weather reports to youthful exploits of the night before. But then the conversation turned to something of peculiar interest.

"So are you going to the city meeting tonight?" a man's voice spoke directly over him.

"I wouldn't miss it," a voice at his feet responded. "I want to see how Mayor Babekov squirms his way out of this one."

"He thinks he can tell us what church we should attend. Why is the city so afraid of this new church?"

A third voice joined in. "I talked with one of those Americans in the park their first day here. He was pleasant, and his thoughts on religion were interesting. I don't understand why the city had to muzzle them and arrest the church's pastor. For once I agree with the television news—the city needs to back off."

A bus breezed to a noisy halt as people crowded around Slava's bench to get on.

"Well, we'll find out tonight," the first voice said.

"What time is it going to be?"

Slava strained his hearing to catch the response.

"Seven o'clock. At the auditorium."

* * * * *

The people gathered at the barn. While it was a small crowd by American standards, the rich faith of these people made the gathering full to overflowing.

It was a midday meeting and hastily called at that. Yet, individuals continued to come. There were no curiosity seekers here; the attenders came at great risk. These people were willing to leave their jobs for an afternoon. Willing to wander out to a country barn in broad daylight. Willing to risk punishment and arrest—all to be counted among those sacrificially praying together for the future of their church and pastor.

This would be the last service the Americans would have with the Bolshoigorsk church before their early morning departure tomorrow. Their hearts were unified in desiring this time of severe worship and prayer with their Russian brothers and sisters.

Behind the barn, John had asked Tony to meet with him. Gregori wanted the Americans to share in the service, and John immediately knew Tony would have a fitting word for the group.

"Man, John," Tony responded. "My mind is whirling so fast, I don't know if I could put my thoughts together to share so soon."

"I understand, Tony. But God has laid His hands on you in such an incredible way. Your words could really encourage the church right now."

"Okay, boss," Tony replied with a confident smile. "Whatever you say."

"Before we go in, Tony," John added, "Tell me how Nadia's doing. How is all this affecting her commitment to the Lord?"

"She's an incredible woman, John. She's absorbing all this stuff like a dry sponge. Before believing in the Lord herself, she had a great understanding of what it meant to be a Christian. This isn't threatening to her at all. She knows God is in control."

"I still can't believe she would come all the way back here to ask you to lead her to the Lord," John said. "What a thrill that must have been for you."

"Not as much a thrill as it is terrifically humbling, John. That God would move in such a way to allow me the privilege—" Tony stopped, unable to say more without losing composure. It was all still very fresh, the awesome joy of leading Nadia into her relationship with Christ.

"You have very deep feelings for her, don't you?" John placed an arm of support around his friend.

"John, you can't imagine. I'm not sure what I will do when we leave tomorrow." Tony hesitated with a pleading look. "I've already had to say good-bye forever to Sarah this summer. I'm not sure I can do it again. I almost pray tomorrow never comes."

"I know, Tony. But it will come. I'm afraid it will come."

The two men walked into the barn again, more brothers now than flesh and blood could ever form. John could feel Tony's pain and would take all the agony if it would be easier on his friend. There was not a simple solution for dealing with this mourning.

Thankfully, as they entered the building the service was just beginning, distracting both of their attentions to the immediate moment.

All the activity in the barn kicked up a thin haze of dust, giving movement to the excitement in the air. The people were all standing, facing one end of the barn where Gregori was speaking. Davron was at his side, enthusiastically translating for the Americans standing together in the front row. Nadia was there as well, beaming an adoring smile as Tony moved to stand just behind her.

"So let us sing joyfully to the Lord as we ask Him to send His protection for tonight's meeting," Davron translated. "Let our weapons of warfare be the praise on our lips. Let us sing to the Lord, for He is good; His mercies endure forever!"

With that, the whole group broke out in a Russian song, Davron singing in English. "Let us sing to the Lord, for He is good; His mercies endure forever!"

It was sheer jubilation, the sounds raising the roof of the old barn. There were no instruments; the vocal strength of this group needed no organ or orchestra. The acapella singing was contagious to the Americans, and they quickly joined with the Russians.

After several repetitions of the chorus, John caught himself absorbed in the worship as never before. His hands were in the air, simply joining the rest of the crowd. He was able to release his concerns, letting go of every burden, knowing that God was here to take them. The only thing required was his praise.

It was an unusual service of worship for him. Stopping short of evaluating it, he wanted to capture this mood and take it with him. As he paused, he felt something oddly familiar about the freshness and joy he was experiencing.

The room was tremendously alive, the unpretentious zeal of these people giving their adoration to their Lord. It flooded the room with an ecstasy of sound and sight.

The dust in the air sparkled with the sun's rays, giving image to the strokes of light that broke through the crevices scattered across the roof. John admired the sunbeams as they shown across the walls and floor. The wood tones were enhanced by the light, bringing out the grain like a hand-rubbed oil.

Everywhere he looked he saw a polished sheen; the walls, the rafters, even the cane of an elderly man beside him reflected brightly.

Looking up, he saw movement in the air. A dainty whirlwind stirred the airborne particles as they glittered in the sunshine. Over Gregori's head, he saw a similar faint funnel of movement. Squinting to be sure his eyes were not blurred, he could not believe what transformed before him.

The small circulating air above Gregori began to thicken and lengthen into a dust cloud—no, more like gray smoke held confined in a column, encircling itself. It was a pillar, reaching to the roof and based just behind Gregori's head. If he moved left or right, the cloud would follow him gently, but exactly.

John took a quick glance to either side. No one else noticed it. Looking back at Gregori, the long pillar of smoke remained unchanged before him. He stayed with the strange sight until a movement in the corner of the barn's rafters distracted his gaze.

It was again a shiny fluff of fine dust, except there was no sun in this darkened shadow of the barn. A translucent mist wavered without shape, sparkling with an iridescence.

John stole his gaze away, just to garner his surroundings once more. The singing continued joyously; the worship found no cause for interruption.

In the front corner of the barn, another mist appeared, almost identical to the hues floating on the opposite side. John began to see several of these apparitions, now all over the rafters. It was as if they had always been there, not noticed until now.

As he took in the gentle movements of the glittering clouds across the ceiling, he felt less that this was something strange. There was a sense of belonging in the forms. Unconsciously his singing became more robust, as if exhorted by the images. Fueled by the praise, the shapeless colorings gained intensity as the worship continued.

The chorus had changed now, a slower, melodious song. Davron sang in Russian, but John barely noticed. His translator was worshiping. The precious intercession did not require an interpretation.

John swayed gently to the beautiful singing, watching the smooth ballet of starlit clouds above him.

His dream! That was it! He dreamed of this worship back in the states. The imagery was different, the setting, even the music changed. But this was the vision. He was peering into the heavens of worship. Though he saw dimly, he watched closely, delighted to see His Lord respond.

The singing was calm and serene, a quiet postlude to the joyous exclamations of God's goodness to man. People across the room were affected in differing ways. To John's right, a huddle of several were praying, heads bowed in a form of sincere community. Behind him individuals faced their Lord in various positions, from standing with hands raised, to flat out on the ground, all appealing to their God. Beside him, Tony stood with his hands over his chest, containing his breath in overwhelmed emotion.

John was awestruck by viewing the interaction of the souls of men with the heart of God. He fought within himself to join the ranks, but was too thrilled as a spectator to break away. This heavenly theater was on display uniquely for him, and he didn't want to miss a single act of God pouring Himself into these lives.

Gregori had stopped leading now and was himself on his knees in prayer, his back turned to the crowd. The smoky column above him was gone; John had not noticed when or questioned why it had disappeared. The glittering clouds above still confirmed the presence of God raining down on them all.

A low murmur of song came from individual souls, a blend of harmonies quietly humming, marked subtly with nuances of weeping or appeals. Though the language was unintelligible to John, he strained to hear every utterance, desiring to understand every interaction these people experienced.

That was when he heard it; he and several others at the same time. Heads bobbed up from their prayers as it occurred. A special sound, like a high timbre organ softly playing. At first it came from the back of the room, somewhere from above, but as it became more distinct it seemed to sweep around the room like wind whistling through pines.

It wasn't an instrument. It was voices, a chorale. The higher pitches were joined with a sonorous bass, reverberating faintly as it perfectly blended with the intonations. The barn was flooded with the music, the quality so vivid it touched the soul. John knew immediately what he was hearing and its Source.

He looked up again to see the gently rolling mists of twinkling lights. By his imagination he could pretend there were wings and bodies in their midst, but it was too grand a sight to see clearly. Every sensation of sight and sound was saturated in abundance.

The extreme joy of seeing these wonders of God gave way to a sense of his own undeservedness. He was overwhelmed with the mercies of His heavenly Father.

As the music swelled around him, John closed his eyes to cup the tears that overflowed.

Chapter 24

Slava watched the auditorium from the alley across the street. He had been there for over two hours, observing all the preliminary actions required for the town meeting. The custodians and extra hands were setting up chairs when he had arrived. Later, a couple of policemen had come and gone in a short visit. His friend Renat came with two others from the mayor's office. They had stayed the longest but left about a half hour ago.

And there was the brief visit by a lone man, looking a little out of place for Bolshoigorsk. Finely dressed in a black suit, his lengthy black hair was tied tightly in a tail that reached just below the back of his neck. His trenchcoat added to the strange appearance, especially on a sunny day on the warmer side of spring.

Maybe some out-of-town newsman scouting the scene, Slava thought.

Then people started to arrive. Just a few at first, but soon Slava could not keep track of the many faces entering the auditorium.

He was able to pick out Galina and her news team with lights and cameras. If the early activity had not confirmed that tonight's meeting was important, all the news gear was enough to assure Slava. Something big was going on.

Several people from his church arrived, always in pairs or larger groups. By his count, thirty or so of the congregation had entered.

Renat had returned, greeting the City Council members as they came; presumably to offer them a front row seat.

The strange man in the trenchcoat arrived again, still alone. He flowed into the crowd unobtrusively.

There was Gregori! How great to see him in Bolshoigorsk. With Gregori were the Americans. They all looked well. Nadia accompanied them, but he could see no other translators. What had happened to Tonya and Luda?

The doorways became more crowded as the seven o'clock toll approached. Slava needed to get inside, but he anxiously waited to see the one most important on his list. Had he missed her? Had she entered in one of the swarms of people and he hadn't recognized her? Though it had only been three days, it felt like years.

"God, please let me have one glimpse, to only sustain me through the night," he whispered in the evening air.

As if on command, a group of five women came down the street, four of them huddled around the center lady as they walked in mass. Though brief, he was able to see her face through the huddle as they approached the building.

Oksana. His lips tenderly formed the word.

She looked worried but strong. Seeing her presence strengthened Slava's own resolve. There was no way to get a message to her, but it was a comfort just seeing her safe and supported by friends..

He came out of the alley and made his way across the street, jacket collar flipped up against his neck with his head buried in the front. From the outside, security did not seem a concern, but he feared a checkpoint inside. Exaggerating a limp, he made every effort to look like someone else—anyone else.

People mingled in the breezeway, lined up to enter the auditorium in two single files at either side entrance. He wandered into a line with nothing but a prayer to offer to gain his risky admittance.

Approaching the hall, he saw two armed police at the entryway. One of them was the muscular blonde officer who had attacked his jailer.

They greeted each person who entered, but without a social intent; they were looking for someone.

With three people ahead of him, Slava thought of ducking out of the line to look for another entrance. This close to the police, however, would create a disturbance he needed to avoid. Sweat beading on his brow, he suddenly felt smothered, tightly bundled in his jacket.

The squawk of a microphone inside the auditorium made him jump. Renat's voice over the loud system instructed everyone to take their seats as quickly as possible. The meeting was about to begin.

Immediately, several bodies crammed him and those in front of him through the doorway. People pushed their way into the auditorium, not wanting to miss a moment of the meeting. The police were overwhelmed.

Slava grimaced as his ribs were crushed together by the herd, but he was safely past the police and in the auditorium. He made his way to the side to take in his surroundings as people flowed beside him in a steady stream to find open seats.

The chamber of the hall was a large two-story structure with seating for three thousand on the floor, now mostly occupied. A balcony surrounded three sides of the auditorium, and here the seats began to fill as well.

The stage at the front of the hall was surrounded by heavy red velvet curtains, their richness lost years ago. Now tears and stains served as a constant reminder that Bolshoigorsk was no longer what it used to be.

The charade continued with a show of political power on the platform. The seven members of the city council sat in wingback chairs of faded gold fabric around two long tables. They were joined by Renat sitting alongside Mayor Babekov. Beside the mayor, an end chair was conspicuously unoccupied.

Slava collapsed into an open aisle seat half-way down the left side. Beside him a heavy-set older woman took pains to show her disgust at his sloven appearance. At least his disguise was still intact.

Renat was at the center podium. "May we now welcome the honored presence of our special guest tonight, the Patriarch of the Bolshoigorsk City Church, the most holy Bishop Federov."

Immediately the floor of the hall rumbled with the movement of chairs. Everyone rose to their feet and stood quietly. After an inordinate amount of time, one side of the stage curtain ruffled and unfurled, revealing the bishop in full regalia.

A white silk knee-length brocaded robe fluttered around his tall frame as he walked to the front of the stage. The vestment glittered from the pearls and crystals embroidered throughout the raiment. On his chest, a large golden cross jeweled with emeralds, rubies and diamonds served as the vestment's clasp. A long black underskirt hid his feet, so that he appeared to almost glide across the floor. His head was adorned with a black velvet miter, woven with gold threads and adorned in front with a golden cameo.

Raising his hand to the audience, he received the awe they offered, then made a rehearsed turn to the empty chair at the table, his robes flowing smoothly behind him.

On his turn the people obediently took their seats again. Slava was amazed at the plebeian response of this people in the face of such mock piety. He could not take his eyes off the bishop, who curiously walked behind his chair at the table and remained standing.

Federov looked directly to the left side of the auditorium, to the balcony, and nodded his head before turning back to the podium.

Slava followed the bishop's gaze. Standing in the third row of the balcony was the trenchcoated gentleman with the bobbed hair.

Federov knows that man?

At the microphone again, Renat gained everyone's attention. "Mayor Dmitri Babekov will now provide us with the evening's agenda."

As the mayor approached the podium, Slava looked to his right where he had spotted Oksana. She sat with Gregori and the Americans, as well as several of his congregation, perhaps twenty rows over on the main floor.

He wished he could join them. Not a chance. Not yet.

"Ladies and gentlemen," the mayor began. "We are here to address a concern that has quickly become misinterpreted by the media. We desire to set the record straight with you. It has always been the city's policy to honestly present every issue before you, the citizens of Bolshoigorsk, and we shall do the same with this concern tonight."

Slava settled back in his seat, hopeful that the mayor's words were true. He could not help but watch John, Tony, and Nadia busily bent toward each other in close conversation as the mayor began. Nadia must have been translating for them.

The mayor was now reading from a script. "Many of you have heard of a small sect in our community which we have tolerated in the name of religious freedom for a little over one year. This group of thirty or so call themselves a 'church', and have recently been a focus of the news media. They are led by a man they call their pastor, Slava Gdansk.

"Indeed, the group has struggled in keeping their fold together, as very few citizens of Bolshoigorsk expressed an interest in participating in their services. However, the group became so desperate in their desire for growth that they invited six Americans of their same faith to visit our community. The sect took these Americans to the streets of our city and distributed propaganda to innocent bystanders, whether they expressed an interest or not. The city was completely unaware of this activity, and we were greatly concerned when citizens of Bolshoigorsk brought this to our attention."

Slava fidgeted in his chair, realizing where this was heading.

The mayor would hesitate, even stumble over occasional words. It was not a forceful address in the least, and obviously not the mayor's own words. The message still sounded out clearly.

"This was when we felt that the safety of our citizens was jeopardized," the mayor continued. "We ordered the Americans to no longer solicit the people of Bolshoigorsk until they met with the city to gain permission for their activities.

"I personally met with representatives from the American delegation. Though I would compliment their polite sincerity, we still found their material to be merely religious propaganda. We instructed them to keep their activities confined to the small group led by Slava Gdansk."

Slava saw John lean forward to Nadia who passed word to Gregori. At least he would hear a less biased appraisal of these events. But how could the whole city hear the truth?

The mayor continued to read. "The next day, we learned at the same time as many of you that despite our request, Mr. Gdansk and the Americans had contacted local news reporters to exploit the media with more of their misguided religious beliefs. It became expedient on the part of the city to speak with Mr. Gdansk personally and ask him to refrain from his attempts to brainwash the good people of Bolshoigorsk. When I requested that our officers contact Mr. Gdansk, I only then learned that this man had recently been terminated from his job at the Bolshoigorsk Refinery because he had repeatedly given false information on his time card. This actually led to his arrest about one week ago, as he had tried to defame Igor Chulstarisk, manager of the refinery.

"When our officers contacted Mr. Gdansk to arrange a visit, he responded abusively and attempted to evade the officers. They were forced to physically subdue him, just to protect themselves. The officers brought Gdansk to the city offices to meet with me. At this point, he was certainly not under arrest, as the media has loudly proclaimed."

Slava was simmering in his seat, ready to jump to his feet with objections. His character was being publicly ridiculed. He controlled his anger enough to pray. His time was coming.

"Mr. Gdansk continued to exhibit violent and irrational behavior. Until I was able to meet with him, our officers felt that, for his own safety, he should wait in one of our prison cells. Although Mr. Gdansk was not under arrest, I must believe the police acted in the best interests of the city. I had not realized just how dangerous Mr. Gdansk was until too late."

Babekov's hands trembled as he held the script. Taking a deep breath, he continued. Slava slouched in his chair, recognizing the final assault.

I regret to have to tell you that, in what could only be described as a fanatical rage, Mr. Gdansk violently and in cold blood attacked one of our jailers while trying to escape from the city offices. Mr. Leonid Bryl, employed by the city of Bolshoigorsk for the past forty years, died from injuries he received at the hands of this deadly and despicable man, Slava Gdansk."

Gasps rippled across the auditorium. Slava looked at his wife. No emotion. He knew that look. She knew it was a lie, thank God.

Nadia was completing the translation for the hunched over Americans. Slava watched them all lean back, questioning looks on their faces.

Glancing up at the trenchcoat in the balcony, Slava was surprised that the man took no notes. He sat back casually as if watching a dull soap opera. His gaze seemed to be left of the podium, where Father Federov continued in his stance behind his chair. The curled lips of a smile formed on the bishop's face.

The mayor tried to regain the attention of his audience. "Therefore, I am tonight issuing an order that the sect led by Slava Gdansk be summarily and immediately disbanded. I would fear that the mentality of this group may rise up again to endanger the people of our city. Such a violent and deadly organization, whatever their so-called claims, must not be allowed within the confines of our country.

"I also wish to publicly announce that the American visitors are being placed under house arrest, where their activities will be constantly monitored. Even they have apparently realized the less than fortunate circumstances of their visit here, as they have arranged for an early departure back to the United States tomorrow morning."

The mayor puffed himself up, seeing the people hang on every word he spoke.

"Citizens of Bolshoigorsk, you have trusted me as your mayor with protecting your welfare in our city. I hope you have found our actions sufficient, despite the tremendous regret we have over the death of Mr. Bryl. Slava Gdansk will be punished to the fullest extent of the law for his deadly actions."

Babekov folded his papers and walked quickly from the podium amidst chatter and whispering scattered throughout the auditorium. Slava could hear only bits and pieces of conversation around him, but they held incredulity and disgust. He felt like trash, stomped on and tossed out to the fire. How could he express his innocence? Identified by this crowd, he would be mercilessly attacked.

Police officers had moved to either side of where the Americans were seated. Any move on their part would risk their own safety against an all-out riot.

Electrified with anger, the audience was posed to respond. They were convinced that they had been betrayed by the small group of believers who offered an apparently perverted message of peace and forgiveness. The mayor's address was meant to be powerfully convincing. Though weakly presented, it carried the theme adequately enough.

Father Federov approached the podium, ushering an immediate hush to the crowd. Another calculated move, Slava was sure.

"Good people of Bolshoigorsk," Federov boomed his bass voice mightily. The man was self-assured, acting as if he held this mob in his hand. It seemed true.

"You are not a people of lies, but a people who seek the truth. You did not stray from the teaching of our holy fathers, and I commend you— I commend each of you—for standing against this attack on our church and our community. You have shown your wisdom and faith as you have resisted the influence of false religions, particularly this, bred by the capitalists in America.

"I stand with you in support of Mayor Babekov's quick response to this devastating assault to our faith. I remind you once again that there is but one God, and there is but one church," his voice rose to a thunder. "The Bolshoigorsk City Church will remain true to our one God, and we will remain true to you."

The bishop turned with a flurry of white silk flowing behind him like a peacock's tail. The council members immediately, almost on cue, began to clap. The auditorium en masse broke out with applause.

Federov made his way back to his chair, but again came behind his seat and remained standing.

Slava felt sick. Nauseated by the city's conniving manipulation of this crowd, he realized his sentence of death was inevitable.

Renat came to the microphone as the applause died down. He was the only one on the platform not clapping. Slava remembered their last conversation back at Gina's flat when they discussed more about real truth than anything Federov could have conjured up.

Slava knew his friend. He knew Renat was close to believing that night. Now, as Renat took the podium, Slava saw him vulnerable, insecure.

"We will now open the platform for any questions from the audience," Renat began. "You are invited to come to the microphone on the floor and provide your comments to the mayor and city council." Renat waited, then spoke again. "Please do not be afraid to speak on this important issue, as the council desires to have insight from you as citizens of this city."

There was an uncomfortable silence across the auditorium. Slava could feel the weight of distraught emotions combined with the fear of questioning the authority of the city, or worse yet, Father Federov. Would anyone dare oppose the decision the government rendered?

"I have a question," the female voice spoke firmly into the microphone.

"Yes, Galina Listyev." Renat recognized the news reporter. "Please ask as you wish."

"Mayor Babekov, I wish to address my question to you."

Slava sat upright in his chair, straining to see the brave woman willing to take on City Hall.

"I, too, as many of you know, have met with the Americans during their visit here," Galina began. "I found no indication whatsoever that they were threatening or violent. As those of you who saw our program might recall, I was able to report on a very precarious situation involving one of their translators. Two Americans bravely protected her and actually saved her from serious harm. Can you provide any evidence of how you deem the Americans' visit a threat?"

Mayor Babekov rose from his chair slowly. He eyed Father Federov, but got no response. Moving to the microphone, he nervously pushed his hair across his bald scalp.

"Miss Listyev, I am thankful you were able to come this evening."

He was stalling.

"We always wish to welcome the press and are happy to have your questions. Uh, please do not mistake my earlier comments as any criticism of your careful news reporting. I believe you were misled into believing the claims of this sect as much as we all were." Babekov cleared his throat several times, though he had no need.

"Uh, Miss Listyev, I have met with the Americans also, and, uh, I cannot state that we have certain evidence of any plans for further violence or disruption. However, I suppose one would wonder if, after, uh, what had happened in the jail with Gdansk, if—"

Suddenly Mayor Babekov turned to see Father Federov towering over him. A curt word was whispered to him, and Babekov moved away from the microphone, cowered by the power exuding from the bishop.

"Perhaps, Miss Listyev, I could shed some light on your question," Federov spoke calmly and controlled. "I know something of the evidence you may be seeking." His words were polite, but their tone had a distinct edge.

"I did happen to watch your news program featuring our American visitors." He paused to gain some commonality with his audience, linking arms with the people of Bolshoigorsk in saying, 'I watch the news just like the rest of you.'

"If I recall correctly, the Americans you spoke with were involved in some type of brawl just prior to your interview, is that correct?"

"Well, Father Federov, I would hardly call it a 'brawl'. They were merely protecting themselves and their translator."

"I see. But I do recall a rather nasty cut on one of the Americans' faces, am I right?" The question was leading, but Galina could not help but honestly respond.

"Yes, that was Tony. He was hit broadside by one of the men in the bar and responded only in self-defense."

"And yet," Federov leaned across the podium, now speaking to the audience more than to the lady at the floor mic. "And yet, did you not all hear Miss Listyev remark on that program about the incredible force used by one of the Americans? Did he not severely injure the man he attacked?"

"I am not aware of any serious injuries, Father Federov." Galina tried to respond calmly, but felt less assured that she was able to defend her own line of reasoning.

"Miss Listyev, I am surprised that even in your own reporting, which you suggest is fair and balanced, that you did not seek to provide both sides to your story."

"But Father Federov, I was there! I saw the whole thing myself!" Galina's impatience was glaring.

"May I introduce to you the man who was attacked by the Americans that night? Adolf Zlotnikov, parishioner and custodian for our fine church for the last eight years, would you please come out?"

Federov gestured to the left side of the stage. Out hobbled the big man from that night at the bar. A woman, presumably his wife, was on one side of him, with a police officer on his other. He limped with one leg, his back bent painfully over as he moved.

"Mr. Zlotnikov would tell you the episode that night was much more than just a shoving match, Miss Listyev. Our city's church is now faced with the loss of its best caretaker."

Galina was taken back by the slackened shape of the man before her. It was him, but he certainly seemed more crippled then she had ever realized on the night of the interview. At a loss for words, Federov was happy to fill in for her.

"So you see, citizens of Bolshoigorsk, the Americans are well-prepared for violence if need be. Perhaps they even provoked the rage we witnessed in Slava Gdansk. In any event, I think the mayor has seen a dangerous situation quickly evolve, and his actions to defuse it immediately must be upheld."

Slava watched as Federov ended Galina's question with another sharp turn, his silk vestment flying behind him. There was no response possible, even though Slava himself doubted the integrity of the custodian and his injury. Who would dare accuse the man of malingering in front of his wife and his priest?

Renat returned to the podium and looked across the crowd before he asked, with much less confidence this time. "Are there any other questions?"

Slava could see Renat sweating, his skin pale.

"No more questions, anyone? Please, this is the time." Renat reached a finger into his collar to loosen it. "We are here for you, so please ask."

Silence was all Renat received. The heavy heat bore down across the auditorium. People began to move uncomfortably. Minds were made up. These citizens were ready to adjourn. There was no reason to linger.

Renat looked feverish standing at the podium, his forehead glistening. His white hands grasped the lectern for support as he looked over every corner of the hall for a single response. Seeing none, he spoke again, his voice trembling.

"Well," he cleared his throat. "If no one else has anything to say—I think I better."

His face was chalky white as he mopped his brow with his bare hand, adding more sweat than relief.

"There is something I must tell you all. I'm not sure how to do this. But someone must tell you all."

Slava prayed earnestly for his old friend. He saw Babekov wiping his forehead, afflicted with the same ailment as Renat.

Even Father Federov was getting warm. He removed his outer vestment and laid it over the back of his chair. Slava watched him glance up to the left balcony again. The trenchcoat was still there. The man suddenly sat straight up, reaching deeply into his coat. Slava looked back to the platform. All eyes were still on Renat.

"You see," his voice trembled, "I have known Slava Gdansk for several years. Just a few nights ago, I went to his home. I even visited his church." He cleared his throat nervously again. "As long as I have known Slava, I have to tell you—"

Slava was glued to every word, but couldn't help notice Father Federov. For the first time, he took his seat on the platform. As he did so, the dark stare went up to the balcony again. Slava followed it to see the trenchcoat open with a hand on a metallic object. The man in the balcony leveled his arm straight out, the glint of steel in his hand clearly a revolver.

"NNNOOO!" Slava screamed, leaping from his seat. "NNNOOO!"

At the same instant, a short blast came from the gun; a spark of light seen only by Slava and Federov.

All other eyes were on Renat—now crumpling to the floor, a spot of red at his throat quickly swelling.

Chapter 25

"NNNOOO!" Slava continued to cry, hobbling to the front of the platform, fighting through layers of people to reach his fallen friend.

Tony jumped to his feet at the crack of the gun shot. Unfamiliar with the sound, he was puzzled by the collapse of the deputy mayor. The man screaming and clawing his way through the crowd around the stage added more confusion.

Slava appeared as a derelict, a drunk one at that. He held one arm close to his side, clutching his chest as he awkwardly tore through the crowd. Tony could only see the left side of his face which was mostly black and blue, his eye swollen half shut.

Despite the appearance, something looked familiar. Tony leaned over to John. "That's Slava!"

He looked behind him where Oksana sat. He could see it on her face: a look of anticipation, undaunted by the wounds.

"Oksana, it's Slava!" he cried to her in English. She understood enough and shook her head, moving into the aisle. Tony could see her brink of tears about to burst.

"Nadia," he yelled to his side. "Let's help Oksana get up there." The crowd around him was standing and gawking, with frequent outbursts in Russian.

They reached Oksana, but then had to cut through the crowd, pushing and shoving against a whirlpool current. Throngs approached the platform while just as many were trying to escape the opposite direction.

The heat of the room hung like a cloud over the highly charged emotions. With the crushing pressure of bodies around him, Tony feared for the safety of Nadia and Oksana as anxieties mounted higher and higher. A storm of fear and anger was about to strike if some control was not quickly achieved.

"People! People!" The deep commanding voice roared over the loud speakers.

Immediately, the crowd's movement lessened as heads turned again to the front of the stage. Father Federov was at the podium, his arms outstretched as he called everyone to attention.

"We must respond without panic. Listen to me—the situation is under control!"

Tony could not understand the voice, but he was amazed as the people hypnotically calmed down across the hall. He grabbed Nadia's hand to guide her and Oksana closer to the front. Moving more easily through the crowd, they reached the stage as Federov continued speaking.

"This is, sadly, another example of the violent nature of Gdansk's sect, but we have the situation contained. There will be no further harm." How Federov should know, no one questioned. It brought a unanimous relief to the crowd just to hear his controlling reassurance.

A panicked voice yelled from the floor next to Federov, "Someone call a doctor! We need an ambulance right away!" It was Mayor Babekov, kneeling out of view at his deputy's side.

As Federov realized the microphone had picked up the call for help, he responded to the nearly mesmerized audience, "Yes, Mayor Babekov, help is on the way."

A flurry of activity remained around Renat's fallen body while Federov stood calmly, soothing the anxious crowd. "Everything is under control—the situation is contained—this is just an example of what can happen when religious sects get out of hand."

Tony saw Babekov frantically trying to move Renat's body from the podium with the help of a couple city council members. Blood had stained the mayor's white shirt, and a large red pool glistened wet on Renat's chest. As they lifted his unconscious frame, Renat moaned.

Leaving Nadia and Oksana, Tony jumped onto the platform to help the mayor. Moving Renat behind the side curtains, Tony could see a deep graze across his neck. They laid him down, and a council member held a cloth against the wound. Tony's elementary medical schooling took hold as he felt a strong pulse at Renat's wrist.

Babekov stood beside Renat, murmuring to himself in a craze. Tony put a hand on his shoulder. Knowing the mayor could not understand, he tried to use his most soothing tone.

"He'll be alright. It looks like it's superficial. He'll be okay."

It did no good. Babekov ranted back at him in Russian, almost pleading. Tony could not make out a word of it and shrugged his shoulders. He looked to see where Oksana and Nadia were, finding them with Slava just behind him.

Oksana's eyes were glowing with tears, her arms locked firmly around her husband. To a stranger it was an odd sight to see a woman wrapped around such an unfit beggar.

"Slava!" He gave a gentle hug to the wounded warrior. After a slight grin, Slava's eyes fell on Renat. He and Oksana kneeled at his side.

Nadia came up behind them and Tony caught her arm. "Tell them I think Renat just has a flesh wound. If they can keep pressure on it, he should be okay. Be sure someone called an ambulance for him."

Renat was yet unconscious but looked comfortable, Oksana cradling his head. The bleeding appeared controlled with the pressure dressing still held by a councilman at his side.

Slava stood behind his wife. Tony saw a distant look in his eyes. Staring toward the podium where Federov continued to reassure the crowd, Slava acted as if he was hearing a different message. His head was cocked, listening to something in the air. He bent over to squeeze his wife's shoulders. After whispering something in her ear, he walked toward Federov.

* * * * *

"Here you go, Slava!" Brael encouraged. "You have absolutely nothing to lose! God is with you—go in His strength! Let His words be your words, Slava! This is it!"

* * * * *

The words could not be heard as such by Slava. He had no sense of anyone speaking to him, angelic or otherwise. Yet, he could not refuse what he was drawn to do. He felt a tingle at his spine, his whole body pulsating with a driving need to act.

* * * * *

"It's got to be now, Slava. There is no one else who can do it like you," Brael urged. "You can do it, all with the might of the Lord. Go, now!"

* * * * *

Slava walked slowly across the platform, his belittled appearance starkly contrasted against the rich attire of Federov. Without any hint of intimidation, he walked right to the side of the bishop.

* * * * *

In heaven's eyes, Slava's clothing shined golden with a divine shroud around him. Angels fluttered on every side. Brael was behind him whispering words of encouragement. "Yes, Slava, yes! The words will be given you. You've got to go forth. Do not fear, Slava. God is on your side!"

* * * * *

He had not felt the protection of the Lord as strongly as now.
"Father Federov, I would like to address the crowd, please."
Slava's words were considerate, though he had to interrupt the bishop to gain his attention away from the microphone.

Federov turned to look briefly at the battered face beside him. "Please, sir," Federov barked. "Not now." The words were polite but the dark tone sarcastic. "We're in the middle of a crisis. I must control this crowd."

"Father Federov," Slava patiently responded, "I think I can help settle the audience."

With blatant animosity, Federov scowled. The two dark caverns that held his eyes bared their emotional power of supremacy. "And just why do you think you'd have anything to say?" he snarled, immediately returning to his microphone and his audience.

Before Federov could speak, Slava interrupted once more.

"My name is Slava Gdansk."

The sound was a whisper, but it was like a thunder crack to Federov. Facing Slava, his towering frame swelled as he took a deep breath.

The next instant, Federov's hand moved so quickly Slava could not even think to dodge it. The huge backhand slapped his face, Slava's head whipping back like a yo-yo. Yet, he was able to stand his ground.

It didn't hurt! Slava thought.

Even Federov was surprised. The blow should have leveled Slava to the ground. He turned to his microphone, at the same time grabbing Slava's upper arm tightly.

* * * * *

Brael restrained Federov's grip, preventing the intended crushing pain. He had easily taken the hand slap, allowing its force to smack his angelic face harmlessly.

Angels whispered to Federov with confusing directions.

"Talk to the crowd—ignore this little man!"

"Better get away, make a run for it!"

"Where's your hired gun? Can he still get a shot off at Gdansk?"

"You're done for! It's all over!"

The thoughts whirled around him in a matter of seconds, causing the bishop to swim in indecision. Then a louder voice more clearly pronounced a thought. Other angels softened their tones as a single voice became more distinct.

"Just let Slava speak. He'll dig his own grave. Let him try to address the crowd. You can always blast him away with your sharp tongue."

* * * * *

Federov addressed the waiting crowd. "Ladies and gentlemen, I need your attention." His large voice sounded, and, in obedience, the people looked to the stage.

"We have a surprise visitor, dear citizens of Bolshoigorsk." The bishop's voice was deep and condescending. "You may all be interested in hearing this man beside me, as he thinks he has something to say to you. I give you…" he paused in his sarcasm to cackle the name, "Slava Gdansk!"

As Federov stepped away, Slava looked across the hall, oblivious to the spiteful looks of anger thrown back at him. Gazing up to the left where the trenchcoat's gun came from, he saw the man was gone.

His thoughts were sure. He was prepared to speak with confidence. These words came from beyond him.

"People of Bolshoigorsk," his speech was gravelly. He reached up to adjust the microphone, at the same time working a drop of moisture around his dry, swollen tongue. He tried again.

"People of Bolshoigorsk," he found his voice. "My name is Slava Gdansk. Please give me a moment."

The angry looks remained, but the silence of the crowd bid him to continue.

"You have heard tonight that I am a liar, that I am a lunatic and that I am a murderer. I stand before you accused, but I seek your decision.

"I meet with a group of people who have found that the Lord God is alive. He seeks men and women to follow Him. We have never sought to harm anyone, and we have made a practice of obeying the government. These Americans visiting our church believe as we, and have showed us, even more, how loving and powerful our Lord is. They are a kind and peaceful people, bringing to Bolshoigorsk only a desire to share the message of the living Lord to you all."

Slava looked over at the American team standing with Pastor Gregori. He smiled warmly at them, conveying publicly a deep appreciation for the entire group who had carried his church the past week.

He turned back to the audience. "I desire for each of you to understand and believe in the Lord. We serve a God who longs to have a relationship with us that is purposeful and brings meaning to our personal lives. Despite my desire, however, there are those who have sought to prevent our church from sharing with you the truths we know about God."

Slava spoke without harshness, but with a sincere fervor. He raised his bruised and swollen wrist with an obvious fractured deformity.

"I bear these marks humbly, and do not ask for your sympathy." He stepped beside the podium and, controlling a grimace, raised his shirt briefly, revealing a wide black and blue swollen band across his right lower chest.

"I ask for your understanding, however, that there is One who bore a more severe torture than this. He is our Lord, in the name of Jesus Christ. His suffering, to the point of His death, was for our own evilness. He took the pain that we deserved, so that we could be forgiven by God. This is the message I bring you tonight." Slava turned his head upward, pushing back tears that were beginning to roll.

"To those of you responsible for my marks, I seek no harm to come to you." He looked sideways, acknowledging the eyes of Mayor Babekov and the city officials. "I forgive you. I only hope that you will find it in your soul to see the deeper pain you have brought upon the Lord Christ, and experience His forgiveness."

There was a lengthy silence. Slava was biting back his emotions while individuals across the crowd dealt with their own. Unusual sounds of quiet sobbing were heard from various points.

A weighty cloud of remorse rolled across the room, like ocean fog smothering a beach front. Though there were scoffers, they were silent, either by their own conviction or by divine gag.

"My words are nothing polished," he stammered, his words choking on tears. "But before you and before my God, I am not a liar, a lunatic, or a murderer. I am only Slava Gdansk, pastor of the Bolshoigorsk Christian Church."

Slava stepped back from the podium and Oksana moved to his side, their arms locking. Her eyes were moist as together they gazed heavenward across the auditorium.

Suddenly, her fingers dug into his side. He saw it, too.

Hundreds upon hundreds of angels gradually waxed into focus, dotting the room, lighting just above the heads of the people. Each one was still, except for the gentle movement of soft golden wings. Their bodies shined so brightly the detail was indistinct. Slava looked at Oksana and saw the ecstatic joy in her eyes. It was no dream. Together they took in the heavenly sights with high pleasure.

The angels moved lazily in the silence, slowly floating in a drift. Then the angels' motion became more deliberate. Before Slava and Oksana, they took flight in a blur of light, sparklers dashing in ovals and lines. Their actions were synchronous, a dazzling display of organized dance. One could follow a small group of angels choreographing a beautiful three-dimensional geometric shape, or view the entire room in the wonderful complexities of symmetric form, more grand than any imagination.

The effort was not for any man's enjoyment. Slava realized this was a performance fit only for their Lord. He was seeing what was not to be seen: the worship of angels before their King. Hugging Oksana tightly, he watched the sights of praise continue.

Riveted by the angelic ballet, the Gdansk's were unaware of what was occurring on the floor of the auditorium.

* * * * *

John did not behold the heavenlies at this moment; he was overwhelmed by the work of God around him. First it was the wail of a man up in the balcony that pierced the air of the hall. The sound remarkably resembled the cry Tony made two nights before in his remorse before the Lord.

Someone was struck with a repentant heart.

While John was craning his neck to see from where the cry had come, he felt a tug at his shirt. Looking around, there stood before him a young man, in his early twenties at most. His eyes were fervent and penetrating, wide with fear. He stammered in seldom-used broken English, "Pl—Pleese! Tell m—me. Aboot, aboot G—God!"

Just then, other Russian faces came up beside the young man, the same pleading look in their eyes. "Pleese!" the man begged, waving his hand to include his friends.

"Of course," John replied, bewildered by the young man's awkward urgency in the midst of this chaos. Looking for Davron to translate, he was surprised at what he saw to his left.

There was Davron, but he was already translating for the Hensleys, grouped with six men and women. Mr. Hensley had his pocket New Testament out, going over some Scripture.

Just behind them, Paul Jonas had a group of four people around him going through the basic Gospel tract he had received in his mission training. The booklet was in Russian, with Paul's copy bilingual, so that he could communicate each page.

Another wailing cry interrupted John's thoughts, over to his right several rows back. It was the same quality but a woman's voice this time. Another heart pierced.

Scanning the crowd, John recognized individuals from Slava's church scattered behind him, similarly surrounded by other Russians. One group was strikingly in prayer, all on their knees with the metal chairs pushed aside.

A tug at his shirt brought John back to the young man. "Pleese!" the man begged with urgency.

John dug in his pants pocket for his own copies of the bilingual tract, his adrenaline pumped. *A revival! This has got to be a revival!*

* * * * *

Up on the platform, Tony and Nadia remained with Renat, still unconscious. No medical help had yet arrived, but Tony saw no evidence of Renat's condition worsening.

Nadia related to Tony the words Slava had shared from the podium. Though she had risked much in her young life as a new believer, she witnessed the greater stake Slava had laid down for his Lord. She was overcome. Slava had spoken from a pained heart with words filled with grace. She fought with her own tears in translating the testimony.

"Oh, Tony, he has suffered so horribly for the church here, and yet he offers forgiveness to his persecutors." She looked up for a moment, controlling her tears. "That is what Christ does in a person, isn't it? That is the love of Jesus Christ."

"It is a love that no man or woman can express on their own," Tony replied with comfort. "It is a love only found in God. I am so glad you have that same love in your heart now, too."

The councilman sitting at Renat's head interrupted them. He pointed to Renat, who was now moving his head side to side.

"He's arousing," Nadia said, taking the cloth from the man. She held pressure at Renat's neck, gently wiping his forehead with her other hand.

The councilman kneeled back, relieved of caring for Renat's injury. Yet, he still looked anxious. Tony saw pearls of sweat across his brow. The man whispered urgently to Nadia.

She beamed back at him with a knowing smile, then looked towards Tony.

"He wants to know, too! This man just asked us to tell him about the God Slava follows!"

Over a few minutes Tony described the Gospel to the councilman, named Leo. Nadia translated, then shared her own story of coming to believe on the Lord. Moments later, Tony and Nadia kneeled with Leo in prayer to Christ their Lord.

* * * * *

Angelic pirouettes shot out from the small corner behind the east curtain where the heavenlies celebrated another lost sheep returned to the fold. With a blinding brilliance that would make men's eyes squint, they joined the extravagant explosions of eternity's rejoicing across the great hall.

Salvation had come to Bolshoigorsk.

Souls across the auditorium were saved by the handfuls. Some were led by Americans, some guided by Slava's church people, and many individually dealt with the conviction of their hearts denying for too long the existence of their Creator and Savior. A fresh awakening, sounded solely by the Holy Spirit, swept across the town meeting for hours into the night, until every last person who was called met the Master at the perfect moment.

This moment, determined ages ago, planned before time was born, guided by prophets and judges, apostles and disciples, missionaries and ministers, now was appointed through the work of a humble, battered pastor and a handful of followers.

Salvation had come to Bolshoigorsk. Not one soul saved regretted seeing it occur any other way. No one, seeing their Lord for the first time, suggested it should be done differently, or considered for a moment that a mistake had been made. Every believer knew that this was the centerpiece of God's plan. A grand and glorious order was in place, consummated in this moment.

Salvation had come to Bolshoigorsk.

Chapter 26

"Did anyone see where Federov went?"

The great hall was almost empty now at nearly four in the morning. A small circle of friends had gathered at the front of the auditorium, enjoying the afterglow of a most tremendous evening.

Each one had a story. They excitedly took turns telling of the wonders of the past several hours. More than once the circle turned to prayer, praising God for his protection and providence.

Slava held the group in astonishment with his stories of prison brutalities and heavenly rescues.

Tony and John related the frustration of Tony's blindness, and spoke in hallowed awe of Pastor Gregori's healing touch. Gregori quickly denied any responsibility, the glory falling solely to God.

And everyone related story after story of testimonies from those who had this night committed their lives to Christ. Similar accounts of people overwhelmed by the awesome love and forgiveness of God threaded through each story, weaving a splendorous pattern of revival.

The tapestry was almost complete when Tony offered the question that had been forgotten in all the excitement: Where was Federov?

Of the group, only Nadia responded. She had seen him behind the curtain when the ambulance came for Renat.

"He was plainly confounded by what was happening in the auditorium," she related. "I was so excited myself, I didn't give him any attention."

"How about Mayor Babekov?" John asked the group. "Did anyone see him?"

Gregori spoke and sought Davron's translation. "Gregori says he was running around backstage ranting and raving. He was a crazy man, shouting, 'I'm next! I'm next! I know I'm next!' A couple of councilmen tried to help him, but he ran away from them. Gregori says he'd finally lost his mind."

"That's much the way he was with me when I tried to tell him Renat would be okay," Tony recalled. "He didn't seem in touch with reality. He was really scared."

"Frankly, I'm more concerned about Father Federov," Paul Jonas spoke up. "Do you think he would still be a threat to us?"

"Davron, ask Gregori and Slava about that," John said. "Is there any way we can find out what happened to him?"

Davron offered the question. They spoke between themselves before Davron replied.

"I will go and see what I can find out. Gregori says you Americans will be needing to get your bus in about three hours. He expects no problems in your departure. We both share your concern for Slava's safety—although after this night, we're convinced that protection is at hand."

Slava smiled, giving credence to his surety. Although he was famished, injured, and exhausted, he had all the enthusiasm of a child on his first day of school.

John marveled at what this pastor had to look forward to. Slava was at the threshold of a whole new ministry for his church. There would be hundreds of follow-up calls to make, the need of a larger meeting facility, and immediate organizational demands that Slava and this church could never dream of.

Slava was certain to become an overnight sensation in Bolshoigorsk. With Galina and her news team covering the town meeting, the morning television would communicate the headline story with fireworks. The church would become a household word, and Father Federov would be critically damaged, even in the most objective reporting. The false religiosity of the community would be sent into a tailspin.

And Slava would be back at the helm of his church, guiding his congregation through the unchartered course. He could at least hope the path would be in less choppy waters.

As John looked at the young pastor, he took comfort. The shy leader he met a short week ago now sat before him, bruised and battered, but with a spirit that burned brightly. Whatever Gregori thought was the 'torch of Christ' from the Americans, something had certainly ignited this young pastor.

John dreamed of the challenges and victories Slava was about to face; he stared at him in admiration. Then Slava turned towards him. True to form, Slava smiled and blushed, embarrassed that John had been watching him. He pulled his jacket around himself in modesty, grimacing from the shot of pain caused by the move. Beside him, Oksana brushed his hair gently, ready to do anything to relieve his discomfort.

"Hey, everyone!" John called out. "I just realized what heels we've been, making Slava and Oksana stay with us all this time. We need to let them go home."

"That's true," Mr. Hensley responded. "There's no reason for them to stay around here. If Gregori doesn't mind helping us, let's send the Gdansk's home."

"Agreed," Paul said. Tony nodded his head as well.

"Davron, ask Gregori to stay with us, and let Slava and Oksana go home," John returned.

A short discussion later, Slava and his wife reluctantly began the difficult task of saying good-bye. Nadia followed them to each American to translate words of gratitude exchanged both ways. It quickly became an emotional farewell.

After speaking with every other member of the team, Slava finally approached John.

"John, I know it is you I will miss the most," Slava hesitantly spoke through Nadia. She barely reached the end of the sentence before she broke into tears. Tony came over and put his arm around her. She was unable to translate.

John reached for Slava's good hand and took it in both of his. The skin was crusty and rough as he grabbed the fingers tightly. A warm rush swept across him. Looking deeply into Slava's eyes, his face expressed every bit of compassion and love possible.

"I know you can't understand me, my brother," John spoke quietly. "But I must tell you that you have changed my life forever. From now on I will strive to attain the faith you have shown me."

Slava blinked humbly and smiled, unable to acknowledge the words. John was saddened. He couldn't communicate how much their time together had meant. He feigned a smile back to Slava and loosened his grasp.

A small tear formed at Slava's eyes. He slipped his hands out of John's and brought his arm tight around his friend's neck. Despite the pain he must have felt, he hugged John long and hard. A bond forged between them needing no words.

They had fought at separate posts in the same battle and had found victory together. As two reluctant leaders, they both shared the experience of finding the strength of God in their own inadequacies. Unable to express such emotions in words, their embrace communicated it all.

Suddenly, Davron came running down the aisle, out of breath. He spoke rapidly in Russian to Gregori, stopping frequently to catch his breath. Nadia offered the short phrases in translation as she listened intently.

"Federov disappeared—police are looking for him in connection with Renat's shooting—he vacated his flat hours ago," Nadia translated. She then gasped in surprise.

Davron turned to repeat the news himself to the Americans.

"The police found Mayor Babekov dead in his office about an hour ago. A single gun shot wound in the head. They found a suicide note."

"No—it can't be," John uttered in disbelief.

"Suicide?" Tony questioned. "No wonder he was running around so scared and crazy."

"Are they sure it was suicide?" Paul asked.

"They're investigating," Davron responded. "Apparently the note implicated Federov with the hit man at the meeting. That's why the police are looking for him."

"And that's why Federov may be long gone," Mr. Hensley added.

"You know what this means," Nadia spoke, a gleam in her eyes. "This means Renat will be mayor until the next election."

"That would be great for you, Slava," Tony said. "He would be very willing to work with your church. He's obviously not afraid to stand up and offer his support."

"I'm still surprised Mayor Babekov would commit suicide," John said. "He must have been more troubled than I had ever realized."

Thoughtful for a moment, everyone was silent, contemplating the mayor's eternal choice.

John turned. "Slava, we'll be praying for you and Oksana these next days. There will be many changes facing you. But for now you must get some rest."

The couple, arm-in-arm, smiled appreciatively to the Americans and began to make their way down the aisle to the front entrance.

"Have a safe trip home to your families," Oksana offered in Russian as Davron translated.

"We wish to see you all very soon," Slava added.

The farewells continued from the Americans as they waved good-bye. The excitement of their own departure took away some of their sorrow. In a couple hours they would be leaving Bolshoigorsk for American soil. The anticipation of going home kept the mood upbeat in the empty auditorium. Conversations excitedly broke out about Federov's disappearance and Babekov's death.

Except for a young couple slowly walking hand in hand to the other side of the great hall. John couldn't help but imagine their sadness. He whispered a prayer for God to bring them comfort. It would be a most difficult parting.

"That's tough," Paul said, coming up behind John.

"It sure is. I just hope Tony can handle all this. He took it so hard when Sarah died. Now he has to say good-bye again."

"If I didn't know better," Paul added, "I would wonder about Nadia and him. They seem just right for each other, you know? He's a bit reckless in his fun-loving nature, and she's a

determined, sound-minded girl. They would balance each other."

"Yeah. I guess God only knows."

Across the room, Tony yelled for Gregori. "Come over here for a minute, would you?" He motioned with his hands, a big smile on his face, and Gregori walked across the hall to the couple.

"What do you suppose is going on?" Paul asked John.

* * * * *

"Gregori, I need your advice," Tony said out of earshot from the others. "What would you say if I wanted to stay here in Russia, maybe for another month or even two. Would it be possible to be of service to you and your church in Nizhnekamsk, or to stay here in Bolshoigorsk and help Slava?" Tony spoke excitedly, but gave Nadia a chance to interpret before he went on.

"I know it sounds crazy, but Nadia and I would both like to work with one of the churches. Of course, we want the chance to be with each other, but we also want to be used by God. Do you think we could live and work for an extended time around here?

Tony watched eagerly for any expression from Gregori. The pastor acted less surprised than expected, and his response was calm. Gregori spoke in even tones, but Nadia bubbled out the words.

"He said it might be possible!" she exclaimed. "He said he can see God working in our lives together, and he's willing to help us try."

Tony gave a big sigh. "You really think so?" He could hardly believe Gregori's ready acceptance. "I mean, we'd need places to live, a job to make some money, extend my visa. You really think it might work?" Tony seemed ready to talk Gregori out of the idea, just to be sure it was real.

After Nadia translated, Gregori gave Tony a confident smile.

"He says the housing would be no problem, in Bolshoigorsk especially," Nadia said, almost breathless herself. "The new mayor would have a lot of pull with the visa. He says, 'if God is behind this, he knows it will work.'"

Gregori grabbed Tony's hand and made a statement seriously. Nadia slowed her speech in translation.

"But he says you must have John's approval. That will be God's sign that it is from Him."

Tony looked at Gregori, then at Nadia.

"Yes, that's true," Tony said more to himself than anyone else. "John knows me well. He's our leader. I need his blessing."

He went to where John stood with the Hensleys, Paul and Davron. It seemed an eternity walking across the hall.

"John, I need to talk to you."

"Sure, Tony. What's up?" Tony could already hear a hesitancy, a sense of reluctance.

The Hensleys started to get up and move away, but Tony caught Mrs. Hensley's arm.

"No, please stay, Alice," Tony said. "I'd like you all to hear this."

Looking at John, Tony could see a 'no' already written in his eyes. He had to ask.

"You all know Nadia is very special to me. I mean, she's touched my heart in a way like no one else ever has." Tony hesitated, wanting to bear his soul honestly.

"This time in Russia has affected me deeply. With all that has happened to me here, I just don't have a peace about leaving. You know me—I have no family, no ties back in the States. I was planning to return to school in the fall, but even that seems much less important just now. I say all that to ask you: what would you think of my staying behind in Russia?" Tony kept talking to cover his friends' shock.

"You might think I'm nuts, but I really feel God leading me. Besides the chance to get to know Nadia—she's a very special reason for me to stay—I also feel like I could help the ministry here. Gregori says he thinks it's possible. He would help me find a place to live, get a job—but primarily I would stay here to help Slava with the church."

Tony watched the surprised expressions across the group. No one said a word. He couldn't blame them.

"I know it's a bombshell to drop on you all, but so was my joining the team in the first place. Remember how crazy it seemed for me to even come to Russia? God opened the door then, and I think He's telling me to stay."

Tony added the clincher. "John, I respect your opinion greatly, and I can only do this with your approval. Gregori insists on it, and I think he's right."

Tony's eyes were set on John. He saw his leader wrestle inside. The circle was silent.

Nadia stepped alongside Tony, making the sudden decision all the more difficult.

"Goodness, Tony," John began. "That's a tall request. I mean, what about visas? How would you travel home in the future?" The questions flooded out of John's overwhelmed thoughts. "What about money for you? How will Slava use you? He doesn't even know about this, does he? There's so many things that you have no answer for right now."

"I know, John," Tony pleaded. "I don't have answers. I guess I'm willing to trust God to work those things out."

"Well, you have an awfully strong trust," John returned. "Tony, I can't let you do it. You're my responsibility on this trip, and it isn't wise to leave you here on your own. I know how much you care for Nadia, but I think your feelings have shaded your judgement. I'm sorry, but I really think you must come home with us. That has got to be my decision."

Tony's face went white. He dropped his head in defeat. John had actually said no. He turned and walked away from the group, embarrassed and disappointed.

"Maybe you can make arrangements to come back later," John shouted weakly. Nadia turned away to follow Tony, her eyes full with tears. The two walked across the hall as John stood flustered, feeling alone despite the small group around him.

"Don't you agree, Paul? Can you imagine leaving Tony here?" John asked.

"I don't know," Paul responded. "I'm going to trust you on this one. It seems preposterous, yes. But God has done remarkable things on this trip. I can't say I would be surprised with one more. Don't worry about Tony, though. He'll respect your decision. I would just be mighty sure that you said what God wanted you to say. Don't regret your decision."

Eyeing Paul, John struggled with his counsel. His answer to Tony was the only one possible. The problem was, he felt miserable about it.

The hall was silent. Suddenly the great anticipation of the Americans' departure turned into frustration. Fatigue overwhelmed everyone; emotions were at a breaking point. With less than two hours before the bus would come, it was an endless wait for John.

For the couple across the hall, however, the time was far too short. The young pair held each other quietly, cementing every memory possible as their time elapsed.

Minutes passed without anyone saying a word. John glanced towards the Hensleys, seeking a nod of approval. Instead he felt the stare of their questioning eyes. Joe shrugged his shoulders while his wife looked on with sympathy. Neither of them wanted to offer an opinion. From their expressions, a visit with them would cast more doubt.

Gregori and Davron stood over in the corner of the auditorium, going over details about the Americans' departure. John questioned seeking Gregori's counsel, but convinced himself he had to stand by his decision.

It was done. Final. Over with. He had to stop second-guessing. Tony will get over it, probably even on the bus ride. He'll forget about it. Time to get on with getting home. There.

Then why do I feel so lousy?

He needed some air and told Paul he was going outside. Walking down the long aisle distanced himself from Tony and Nadia, only increasing the pain he felt in tearing them apart. His thoughts were thankfully distracted as he stepped into the cool Russian air.

John welcomed the brisk morning in the streets of downtown Bolshoigorsk. A couple of elderly women walked the narrow street, gently interrupting an otherwise silent morning. It was only six o'clock, but the sun was already advanced to an American mid-morning sky.

Breathing in the crisp air was refreshing, reminding John of all God had provided on this trip.

Why did it have to be so difficult now, Lord? We have overcome so much. Why is this so hard?

John's prayer was interrupted by a young lady's quiet voice behind him.

"John, may I speak with you?"

It was Nadia, alone.

"Sure," he replied, trying not to act surprised. Turning away from her, he didn't want her to read the frustration he felt. "It has been a tremendous experience working with you as our translator."

"Thank you," she replied meekly.

"You have an incredible talent in communication, Nadia. I hope God will open doors for you to be able to use your skills."

"Thank you, John," she repeated, sounding a little bewildered by the compliments. "But that's not why I came out here."

"Yes, of course not," John sighed. He knew he had to face her—face himself—with this dilemma.

"I just wanted you to know," Nadia began hesitantly. "Tony is accepting your decision. He—we both—respect you greatly, John. If this is what you feel is best, we will accept that as God's will for us. I just wanted you to know that."

John turned to Nadia, seeing her sincerity.

"Thank you," he replied. "It means a lot for you to tell me."

"Yes. Well, I think I will go back inside. It's a little too cheelly—is that the right word, cheelly?—out here for me."

"Yes, chilly. That's right, Nadia." John smiled at her continued effort to master English. "Thanks. Thanks for coming out to tell me."

Nadia turned to go back inside; John felt the cool air much less refreshing now.

He had to do something.

"Nadia," he called out. "Come back here a minute, would you?"

She returned, and John looked at her intently. She was no longer a young college kid working as a translator to pay her room and board. She was a mature young woman, serious in her purpose and determined to make the best of her life.

"Can you really imagine Tony staying here in Russia? Do you really think it would work?"

"I do not know." She paused thoughtfully. "Honestly, all of life is very new to me these days. I am seeing everything differently. It is trying to see God's perspective, right?"

She asked, more to be assured that her grammar was correct. John nodded, affirming her intent as well.

"It is exciting to respond to life knowing God is guiding it," she continued. "It makes me willing to accept difficult challenges and consider the impossible. I suppose that is why I can accept Tony leaving. It means that God has something else in His plan. I—Tony and I—can both look forward to that."

Her thoughts were honestly shared. It was not an emotional appeal at all. She was matter-of-fact in her theology, and John was astounded by the truth of her words.

She offered one more pearl. "Tony has taught me to believe that God knows the absolute best for me, and that He never makes a mistake. Knowing this brings me comfort."

She turned and left. For the brief moment, John was the pupil, and this young, newly Christian girl was his teacher. Staring at her as she walked back inside, he was amazed at his own lack of faith compared to this days-old believer.

After no more than a minute, he followed her inside. His spirit was confident in what he needed to do.

Tony was with the others now, Nadia just approaching his side.

"Tony, Nadia," John called out. "I've got something to say to both of you. Really to all of you." He stood before his team.

"Tony, you asked me a difficult question, and you trusted me to give you God's answer. I'm humbled that you would be so assured that I would speak for God. But I must tell you that you're wrong." John spoke sternly, like a father correcting a child.

"I answered you in knee-jerk fashion. My own human wisdom was woefully inadequate. For that I apologize."

His tone softened now; he spoke to Tony as a friend. "I respect you, Tony, and I hold high your faith in Christ. If you feel God is leading you to stay in Bolshoigorsk, I will not prevent it, no more than I would want to stay the hand of God in His desire for your life. You are free to stay if you feel led to. I will do everything I can to make it work out smoothly for you."

John knew the words were right, and he looked at Tony, confident his response would be God's. Davron whispered a translation to Gregori while the rest of the group looked to Tony for his answer.

"Well," he began, "I guess I'm pretty convinced. John, you continue to amaze me with the heart you have after God's own. Thanks for giving me the chance."

He stopped short, causing the silence to stab everyone's hearts.

"So, Tony," Alice spoke first. "What are you going to do?"

"Well, Mrs. Hensley," Tony looked her straight in the eyes, drawing out the suspense for a few more seconds. "I'm staying!"

The air was immediately pierced by a high pitched whoop, barely human, but now well-known. Tony held his head back and let go of the deafening sound. It ricocheted across the auditorium in celebration, bouncing across the hall in repeated echoes. A chorus of joyful laughter and cheers arose as the rest of the team joined in the clamor.

This time the angels were silent. The human rejoicing below the heavens radiated up exclusively separate, bringing a glory that did not require any angelic assistance. It was a beautiful and sweet aroma, freely expressed and excitedly delivered to the Throne.

It was the angels' turn to be amazed. They watched the humans' praise-filled celebration give God unique honor. In wonder, they reveled in seeing God's plan continue to unfold, perfect and ageless.